First Published in 2024 by Little Acorn Publishing

ISBN-13: 9780995653467

Little Acorn Publishing

This book is dedicated to my mother and father for the great childhood memories of times spent in Whitstable.

To mum for her love of books and Whitstable.

To dad for the service he gave in the 8th Army in Africa during the Second World War.

A THANK YOU TO H FRASER FOR THE
WONDERFUL BOOK COVER ARTWORK

1

1971

This was the day life changed.

No Blacks, No Dogs, No Irish was what welcomed Michael. Every bed and breakfast window offered rejection. Brought up on a council estate in Belfast to parents with little time for him, he moved to Kent on the southeast coast of England at age fifteen. Some say it was the luck of the Irish, but Michael knew there was no such thing; determined to fit in and make a success of his life, he kept his head down and worked hard. Became part of society and worked his way through the ranks, and learnt on the job. Each day he picked up new skills in the trade, and the prejudices spat his way helped him master the art of how to deal with people, the biggest part of being the boss. Early on, he learnt that those who worked for you had to respect you. You had to be able to read people. And, most of the time, he got it correct.

A Jaguar E Type, a car he could only have dreamt about when he was younger. During the day, it shined like a diamond on display in a jeweller's window, but it took on a darker shade in the current light. Its British Racing Green factory colour could be mistaken for black. He fumbled inside his pocket to find the key; after several attempts revealing his success to the man stood next to him with the raincoat on and hood over his head, protecting him from the rain and at the same time obscuring his face, took the key from Michael and opened the door. With arms outstretched, hands rested on Michael's shoulders; the man helped guide him into the luxury tanned leather seat.

A slow deep voice, many octaves below regular pitch, spoke, 'Drive carefully,' Michael tried to make sense of this unfamiliar world, but too confused to take everything in, he focused on the steering in front of him, 'drive fast and don't let the fuzz catch you'. Fuzz. Catch You. Drive Fast - the words echoed in the non-existent canyons of the Kent countryside. Michael turned the key in the ignition, and the engine roared into life.

First gear found with a crunch and then out of the shingled driveway, narrowly avoiding the wrought iron gates by inches pulled onto the main road leading from Canterbury to Whitstable. Michael had driven the road many times before, aware of the smooth undulating surface offering a gentle wave-like relaxing motion to the drive. But the climb seemed steeper tonight. The car struggled to make the climb. He pressed hard down on the accelerator to give the car more power, but then the road melted into a level, even surface.

Tonight's game had gone well. He palmed the outside of his jacket pocket to check he had remembered his winnings. Thursday nights had been poker night for the last year. Tonight, made up of the usual crowd, business associates from the building trade and one or two extras each week to keep the interest and excitement rolling. There had been more extras this week than usual. He was pleased with that, evidenced by the bulge of banknotes he had confirmed, with his hand caressing the outside of his jacket's breast pocket. It had been so good that he folded on his last hand with a pair of aces, a pair of eights and the queen of hearts. A guaranteed win, but why take chances? Those days were behind him.

Leaning over to turn the radio on he jumped back when a voice came from the behind him.

'Hello,' a soft, gentle voice. Michael looked in his rearview mirror but saw no one. Again, the soft, gentle voice spoke, this time distinctly childlike, 'Hello, hello, Michael.' This time he twisted himself around but still saw nothing. As he turned back to face forward, he jumped in shock, losing control as his hands fell from the steering wheel. Regaining control, he looked at the young girl with blonde hair sitting beside him in the passenger seat.

'What the hell, where the hell did you come from?'

'I am from your mind, Michael. I am inside you, of course.'

'What?' he wanted to scream, wondering if and hoping it would make her and the nightmare disappear. Always a rational thinker, solving problems, he continued the conversation of madness. 'Who are you?'

'I'm Alice,' he looked at her dressed in a puffed sleeve blue dress and white pinafore. Was this some elaborate joke played by the guys at the card game? But how had she got into the car? It was impossible for there was nowhere to hide in a two-seater sports car.

He laughed to hide his fear and confusion, 'What, Alice in Wonderland?'

'Of course, do you know the story?' The colour of her dress faded from blue to green. 'See, am I still Alice in Wonderland?'

'I don't know what the fuck you are, but I am going to stop, and you are going to get out of this car.' Pressing his foot on the brake the car sped up. He looked down to check he had connected with the correct pedal. He had. Returning his view to Alice, or whoever this girl was, her dress had now changed colour to yellow. 'You see, Michael, sometimes they will lie to you.' She smiled as if it was some game she was playing before continuing, 'And do you know what the moral of the story is?'

'What? No, I don't; please tell?' He questioned now in

anger from the confusion.

'Sometimes, they don't have morals.' The car veered off to the wrong side of the road. He clicked the stick on the side of the steering column to activate the wipers to clear the windscreen. Ready to confront Alice, find out who had set her up, he looked at her and was about to speak but froze when her face, with its pinkish youthful complexion, started to become pale and her red lips faded grey and bloodless; her face began forming wrinkles, ageing at an unnatural speed. Again he checked the road ahead, and when he returned his eyes to where she had been sat, there was nothing but an empty seat; she was gone.

With only a little over two miles from home, he pressed down further on the accelerator as he took a sharp left bend, again almost losing control of the car. He didn't care; he just wanted to get home. Trying to concentrate on the road ahead but struggling, confused by what had happened. Losing control of his senses frightened him. He knew it had nothing to do with what he had drunk. One whisky was all he had throughout the whole evening. Drinking had never been his thing.

The rain, now heavier, made it even harder to see. He clicked the wipers to rapid speed in the hope of clearer vision. With each swipe of the blades, they removed the torrent of water falling from the heavens. Each time for a matter of seconds, the view of the road would become clear and then obscured again by further gushes of water thrown at the windscreen. Sweat trickled down his forehead and into his eyes. He slid the heater peg to blue, trying to cool the car; now, in the middle of the night, in winter, he was burning up. A car six months old, surely the thermostat could not be malfunctioning.

Still, the heat increased; it didn't matter, he told himself, with fewer than two miles from home. Increasing his grip on the steering wheel, he focused with fixed eyes glued on the road ahead. In his hands, the wood-rimmed steering wheel became softer. Melting in his hands, he turned the wheel, but it was mush. He smashed his hand against the side-window willing control back into his life and for the madness to disappear. And it did; the steering wheel returned itself to its normal state. The temperature in the car dropped while the wipers continued their job wading away the water.

Ahead the water attacked the road as another voice came from his side, 'Dad,' a gentle voice, as soft and as innocent as Alice's had been earlier. But this voice he recognised. Terrified, hearing his son's voice, he turned quickly to look. But the seat remained empty as he forced down a desire to scream. In an attempt to avoid distraction, he focused on the road ahead. Rain blocked his view until the wipers did their job to provide desperate seconds of clear vision. Unforgiving, the rain came again, the wipers helplessly fought against the bombardment. Another swipe of the blades cleared his view, and in the direct path, his car hurtled, stood his son. He pulled hard and fast on the wheel trying to avoid his nine-year old boy. A sigh of relief expelled with the belief he had avoided killing his son. He relaxed, thinking he would be home soon, but his eyes opened wide, for in front of him stood a red telephone box on the bend. Too close to avoid. The force of the impact smashed Michael's ribs against the steering wheel. The sound of the crack, as a twig snapped under foot in the woods, followed by immeasurable pain scraping through him. His neck flopped forward like a rag doll hitting the windscreen before throwing him back again into the seat with force. He sat still, breathing pure rawness. The salty taste of blood touched his tongue after its journey from rolling down his forehead. Life drained, his existence limited to seconds. He looked at the rear-view mirror with a lightning bolt crack split through it, doubling up the image of the road behind, his son looking on towards the Jaguar E-type mangled against the red telephone box; their eyes met, the boy turned his back to the scene and walked away in the opposite direction.

Two police cars and an ambulance arrived within

fifteen minutes. They had already been alerted by reports of a vehicle driving recklessly out of control down Radfall Hill, Whitstable. Michael McNabs' death certificate recorded it as an accident. Tests showed the alcohol in his body was within the legal limit.

His nine-year old son did not attend the funeral.

2

Callum sat on his black plastic cushioned silver framed chair at his white Formica-topped desk and stared at the yellow concentric circles trapping themselves on the red wallpaper in front of him. Or perhaps it was a castle's fortress offering protection; he wanted to lose himself within those confines of safety.

His mind wandered, and outside, the gentle hum of a petrol lawn mower played a ominous melody as he tried to study. With fewer than twenty-four hours to go, time exponentially increased its pace as every day passed since the requirement to read aloud and present their written homework to the class was announced. It approached, now racing towards him like a juggernaut, out of control, ready to smash its victim to pulp. At that moment, he felt like mush. Legs weak, arms all pins and needles, and nausea erupting from within. To stop time now was a gift Callum wanted more than anything. Tomorrow, he would stand up in front of the class and read his essay on Richard the Lionheart. The king of England showed no fear when he led the Christian Crusaders into battle against one of the most formidable leaders and warriors the world had known, Saladin of the Muslims. The night before the Battle of Arsuf was Richard shaking? Was he struggling to find his words?

Callum doubted it very much. Wishing he could be like King Richard, brave, strong, and admired. He would have had to have done something of noteworthiness to deserve such accolade. That was where he fell short; he had no doubt. He had been told and reminded of his inadequacies on many occasions, the imprint now carved deeply and etched within, impossible to forget.

History was a favourite lesson of Callum's. Along with Maths, English, Geography and Physics, Physics not quite so much, but he still expected a high grade. This put him in the top group at school. Being in the top group was easy when you worked as hard as he did. There was little else for him to do. He had no friends. No real friends he could call upon if needed. There was, of course, Stephen Watts. Was he a friend?

Stephen held the record for the thickest lensed glasses in the whole school. They often sat together by default in Physics and Maths because nobody else wanted to sit next to them. Stephen didn't do the other subjects Callum did. In those classes, he sat by himself. They didn't speak much, apart from on the topic areas they studied that week. After class, they would walk out into the playground together. Stand there for five minutes without saying much and then Callum would take out his magazine and read until the bell rang for the next lesson. It wasn't that Callum didn't try to make conversation; he did; he would say things like.

'Did you watch Happy Days, Saturday?'

Or,

'How about Starsky and Hutch?'

The answer would always be, 'No.' Friends - perhaps not the correct word, Callum thought on reflection. It used to be different, but now he struggled to know where he belonged, accepting his shyness and insecurities and keeping himself to himself as much as possible.

Outside there was the clanking of metal. Callum got up from his desk, sat sideways to the window, unable to concentrate, and looked to the houses opposite. Across the road, he saw an old man with wild, wired silver hair tending to Mrs Wickes' garden as he did each week. The clanking noise was his spade, followed by the fork thrown in the back of his rusty, worn jeep that had seen better days. Callum watched as he pushed the palms of his hands into his back and stretched and contorted his face to release the aching of his muscles. After stretching and twisting, he recoiled to his normal stooped posture. The old man stomped back to Mrs Wickes' front garden from the jeep with his head hung low. His stoop hid his height, which Callum estimated to be nearly six and a half feet. He was tall and strong, like a boxer with muscles bursting from his arms. Callum wished he had arms like that; he looked at his own stick-like puny body. The man slapped off the motorised lawn mower with his gloved right hand, killing the music to make way to the familiar shouts of misery and anger from the floor below - again. Callum wished the old man would start it up again to drown it out.

He was there every Wednesday when Callum returned home from school, and at this time, every Wednesday at six o'clock, he would pack up. Callum had taken little notice of the old man before but welcomed the distraction diverting his mind from tomorrow. He watched him kneel before the flowerbeds as if in prayer.

Mrs Wickes' garden outshone all others on the road, full of colour, yellow and pink chrysanthemums three feet high, and red, white and pink roses stood valiantly guarding the front lawn and warning off predators. The cul-de-sac had fifteen houses, all detached and all with pleasant and cared-for gardens, except number twelve. He looked down and compared the long grass that had not seen a blade for two months. And that was when Jim, his step-father, in his typical Sunday afternoon inebriated state, decided Callum was a lazy git, who did nothing, should cut the grass.

A brand new, blue 'S' registration Cortina Mark IV Ghia, glistened with pride, pulled into number six next door to Mrs Wickes' house. The back door flung open, and Darren

Vaughan climbed out with a satchel slung over his shoulder. Back from St Nicholas, private school education, brand new car and a holiday in Majorca last year. The unfairness of it vexed Callum. He envied his life and wished he too could also have some of it. Callum and Darren used to be friends when he was younger and went to the same primary school. After school, they'd cycle up and down the road and race, playing football or tennis. Darren would win every time. In the summer, they would swim in Darren's back garden. He had an outdoor swimming pool, with water cold as ice, but that didn't stop the excitement. Nobody else had a swimming pool in their back garden that Callum knew. Indoors they would play board games like Monopoly, Cluedo and Football Subbuteo. But Darren was never allowed around Callum's house.

'My mum says I'm not allowed around other people's houses,' that's what he would say. But Callum knew the word *'other'* meant specifically his house. Word spread since Jim moved in. It was the looks at first and then the whispers. And then words spoken aloud, spoken without care. At first, when Callum was younger, he didn't pick up on the signals but now, at the age of fifteen, he saw all.

That's the drug dealers' boy …

Old tart, 'er ole man was hardly cold when he moved in …

You wanna keep away from them sort …

None of them true, or so Callum chose to believe, but it made him stoop as he walked. Head to the ground keeping himself to himself, hoping no one would notice him. He wondered if the old man, who he looked back towards, was also hoping nobody noticed him.

Callum focused on the old man who loaded his lawn mower onto the back of the jeep. Removed his gloves, looked up to the sky and wiped the sweat from his brow with his forearm. The bright sun forced the old man to squint and look up towards the window where Callum stood. A feeling of guilt, as if he had been caught doing something he should not, forced him to quickly hide to the side of the window out of sight. Slowly he leaned his head back to view out of the window. A puff of smoke blasted out of the exhaust, hung in the air as if it had arrived in a place it liked and did not want to leave but then disappeared as quickly as the jeep drove off.

'I'm goin' out if ya' can't be bothered to cook like a proper woman.'

'Clear off then, see if I care.' With the windows open, the sound carried from downstairs to his bedroom and down the street. The old man had diverted Callum's attention. The hum of the lawn mower had masked the argument between Jim, and Rachel, his mum. It was a technique he had developed over the years to block it out. No need to put his hands over his ears, instead, he pulled his shoulders in tight, tensed all the muscles in his body and squeezed his eyelids closed, and his eardrums would automatically close. Shutting out the sound and sight of the world he did not want to hear.

***

Rachel stood, arms crossed with her back to the television. She eyed the porcelain figurine of a mother holding a baby on the mantelpiece to her side. The thought of throwing it at him tempted her, but she controlled herself, knowing she would later feel regret from losing a memory of better times. Standing in the doorway of the lounge, Jim glared back at her. In the midst of rage and argument, Rachel tried to remain calm and process the situation through her head to find an answer, but she found none. A strong element of disbelief repeatedly reminded her she had fallen into the hamster wheel again.

'Go on then, clear off, just wish you'd never come back.' Any excuse for a game of cards or to get out of the house, and he would take it. In truth, Jim didn't need a reason. A moment's silence filled the lounge, occupied only by the background noise of the television with Sue Lawley speaking of some impending disaster in Central Africa. Rachel's eyes, loaded with daggers, penetrated Jim's. He spat out a choked laugh, left the lounge for the hall where the upright coat stand offered his brown leather jacket that he swiped without thanks and threw over his shoulder.

A quick, sharp shock jolted through her body. Unsure if it was from the noise of the door slamming or the fear the frosted glass panels that covered the mass of the area would shatter into a quintillion pieces. She moved into the hall to watch through the frosted glass his kaleidoscopic body move up the path and climb into his white van. Engine started, revved with fury, and he was gone. Sue Lawley continued to depress.

Rothmans of Pall Mall offered instant relief, dropping the new packet of twenty, less one, onto the kitchen countertop. Her latest New Year's resolution had been to cut back to no more than ten a day. September, and she was on her second pack already today, and it was just past six. No chance - always next year.

Frantically she drew on the cigarette, and with each puff, she slowed and eased her juddering hand. Stabbed it and grinded it into the ashtray, like letting out the final bit of air from a tyre before all her anger was released. She took another. Now she could enjoy it, perching herself up onto the kitchen stool. Clawing through the back of her dark black, unkempt hair, aged thirty-eight, grateful for no grey, although she did not know how. Smoke hung in the kitchen and dining area. Rachel sat and looked at the table, chairs, and drinks cabinet, all six years old or more. When they first moved into Gratton Drive, it was all new.

The house and furniture gleamed with hope, as did her dreams for the future. Now it all looked old and tatty. Living together for one year and married for four. Apart from the early days and since they married, they had argued through most of it. And, more and more as each day passed, the intensity of the arguments increased. It was different when she was with Michael; they had money. But it wasn't the money alone that caused the problems. Maybe it had been too soon to remarry, but Jim was kind. And, at the time, she desperately needed comforting—someone to talk to, who would hold her and listen. Callum was too young to understand, and she had to be there for him, and having a father-like figure around, she thought, was the right thing to do.

Jim had been a regular at The Pearson's Arms, where Rachel worked. The pub at the end of the High Street perched on the seafront breathed in cool salty air from the waves that brought in only hope and happiness at the time. It had been a part-time job. Something to get her out of the house as Michael worked so hard building up his business. They didn't need the money. It was the social side she liked. Jim would come in and have a couple of pints of Guinness on the nights Rachel worked, Tuesday and Wednesday, and they would chat between her serving other customers. They had met before. Jim had done a lot of work for Michael on the houses they were building. He had a good reputation for being one of the best plasterers in the area, and Michael only wanted to work with quality tradesmen.

Michael held a party and hired out the function rooms at The Royal on the seafront in Tankerton. It proved a double celebration, Michael's thirtieth birthday and England, Michael's adopted country, winning the world cup final the Saturday before, which gave the party an extra special edge. Life could not have been better. They hired a band, and beer and wine flowed heavily; she couldn't remember how but ended up dancing with Jim. Michael, not usually a big drinker, was drunk and oblivious to everything around him for one of the few times in his life. But she liked the attention sucking it up in vats. After that, they always spoke when he came into the pub. Rachel was unsure if she imagined it but thought he had become a more frequent customer since the party, that she still held a little guilt.

They got to know each other better after Michael's car crash. Jim would drive Callum to places. Clubs and sometimes school when he was going to be late, Jim would pick him up. It was just what Rachel needed, time to do nothing. The world had fallen in on her. From having everything, she had nothing. With Michael, she had so much, business was thriving, and that was how they bought the house in Gratton Drive. Chestfield, they had dreamed of living there but never thought, in reality, they could afford a place in one of the most affluent areas of Whitstable. Michael raised a colossal deposit to secure the mortgage, and even with the repayments, they had a comfortable cash sum left over each month. Michael was good with money and an excellent businessman. They were going places, *'Ten years, fifteen max, Rach,'* and they would have the mortgage paid off, he told her often, with that big smile, that smile Callum inherited and reminded her of Michael every time. It was paid off in five years, with the life insurance.

Life alone, living with only ghosts, she couldn't handle. People could talk and look down on her; let them, it was her life. What had it to do with them? What right had they to judge? And, of course, there was Callum. Surely it was better to have a man around the house. A mentor, someone to look up to, would be better for his upbringing. It all made sense. It felt natural, almost destined, so Jim moved in. It was a year since Michael's accident, or eleven months to be exact, which in her mind was as good as a year. At first, life smiled. To make love again, or was it just sex, she could never be sure, but it was good; occasional twinges of guilt quivered knowing it was better than with Michael. Michael focused on work, and the bedroom was where he slept. Being held by Jim in his arms, gifted security and sex was the confirmation. During the night, she would wrap her arms around Jim's stomach as he slept, watching him breathe gently.

Wedding vows were the switch turning him into another man. Before the confetti touched the ground, things changed.

She sucked on the Rothmans to the filter and slowly extinguished the embers in the ashtray.

Jim had convinced Rachel to give up working at The Pearson's. It would be good for her. Give her time to recover and take life easy. But as the months passed, they spent less time together. Jim out with friends, and Rachel stuck at home. Recession hit hard in seventy-three, work dried up, Jim's income dropped, and it was now their only income, which brought on financial pressures and arguments grew more venomous each time. Vodka became her friend. Each year it got worse, from knight to monster. Everything had changed.

***

Callum paced his bedroom. His palms sweated. He had to focus, or tomorrow would be a disaster. A disaster, it was inevitable, and he already secretly knew and wondered why he was trying to kid himself. Holding his open exercise book, he closed his eyes. The harder he tried, the harder it was to recall the words. If only he could learn it by heart. But his mind went blank, shutting off in a panic.

He sneaked a glimpse at the words, 'Richard I, King of England reigned from 1189,' closed the book and tried to remember how long he reigned. It had gone. It was not that he did not know, but a door slammed shut and locked itself tight, blocking the information. Influenza was what he wanted, to be hit by a car or, best of all, struck down by lightning— anything to get him out of school tomorrow.

3

Golden Wonder Smokey Bacon Crisps were probably not the best of breakfasts, but Rachel had overslept, Jim had not returned home last night, and with no milk in the fridge, it was the best option available. Instead of taking his regular, direct route to school, he cycled down Herne Bay Road to Cookes Stores on the seafront. Callum leant, back arched and leg cocked against the white pebble-dashed wall of the shop looking out to the sea. Across the road on the grass bank opposite, the model boating lake stood reminiscent of better times. His model yacht with a main sail and jib, oiled grooves lined the deck and a cockpit he would place his toy soldier in, capsized and sank. The plastic soldier drowning, screaming to be saved, and his dad, his real dad, waded in to save yacht and man. And his seven-year-old boy who would never forget. The powdered flavour of bacon for breakfast comforted his infrequent repose.

The plangent sound of a sixteen-ton delivery truck broke his reverie and obscured the view. Diesel kicked out as the driver killed the engine and the rancid fumes filled the air. Not wanting to waste the time of a condemned man, he picked up his rusty blue framed bike, crossed the road and sat on the bench looking out to sea. Life-sized yachts sailed the calm sea with a blue-skied picture postcard background; men and women on board relaxed without a care in the world. He inhaled the air, fresh and calming, engulfing the short moment trying to capture an impossible peace in some meditational ritual. A banshee's scream of rubber against metal crushed the moment. He swung his neck to see Nigel

Ferring on his Chopper bike. Not a new Chopper, but still something Callum would have loved to have had. The purple paint was intact, and the chrome wheels shone from what Callum assumed Nigel Ferring had polished religiously and regularly. Callum pictured himself sitting on the bike, cool and Hell's Angel like, the little latent rebel inside him called.

Although Callum didn't like to think it, there was a kinship between them. Both were odd fits, and neither with any friends, the only difference Callum saw was Ferret, as he was known at school, was short, skinny and suffered from a body odour that kept the flies away. Callum was none of those; he certainly had no body odours, bathing every night without fail; hygiene was one thing his mum was most fastidious about. And Callum was tall for his age, although skinny, there were plenty of other kids skinnier, and his black hair inherited from his mum fell, Hollywood-like, below his collar.

'Hi, Callum,' Ferret's tinnitus shrilled voice flew across the road, recoiling Callum into the bench where he had stretched out.

'Hi, Nigel,' cringing the returned greeting across the road, embarrassed to be associated with Ferret.

'Have you done your History project?' The shrill ruptured Callum's short state of calm, firing reality with fury back at him. Blue skies seemed to fall, and black clouds of hell gathered to suffocate him. They hadn't, but it seemed that way. Callum did not reply but scraped a smile and was relieved to see Ferret not wait for a response but turn and enter the shop leaving his Chopper upright on its stand, leaning to its left, to taunt Callum of another thing in life he did not have.

A Jeep pulled up next to the delivery lorry where the driver was now unloading several crates onto the pavement. It was the gardener's jeep, Callum recognised before the old man climbed out and followed Ferret into the shop.

Callum's mind was now starting to panic. He had been able to hide somehow and control his panic, but in less than three hours, he would have to read his history project to the whole class. Second lesson of the day, he loved History. He loved to research the Kings and Queens of England. Plantagenets, Tudors and Stuarts, he could not get enough, losing himself in some real but fantastical world. And writing pages upon pages and submitting for marks, which he received an 'A' grade, was easy. It was no surprise considering the time he spent researching, hours down the library and reading book after book. But reading out in class filled him with dread. As each hour drew closer, his mouth dried, his stomach churned to a point where nausea took hold. He looked at the sixteen-ton truck and thought about lying underneath its wheels as the driver climbed into his cab. The driver would not see him, he was sure, and he would drive away, ending him. He may not even notice insignificant Callum crushed as easily as a melon. It would be painful, but it would be quick; he pondered the idea as a possible answer to avoid the long, suffering five-minute monologue where each word leaving his lips would increase in pain.

'Bastard,' the shout came at the same time a tin of Coca-Cola hit the ground and fizzed its half full content up in the air. Ray Blackman, whose orbit everybody avoided, was with Neal Tennant and Simon Clegg. It was Neal's Coke Ray had thought it hilarious to grab out of his hand as he was taking a glug and throw it to the ground with such force it exploded like Mount Vesuvius on steroids. 'Christ's sake, Ray, I was drinkin' that,' Neal protested, looking the figure of hate, in his brown Doc Marten boots and yellow laces, cropped hair to grade one and short sleeved grey school shirt that showed off his overdeveloped biceps for someone of fifteen years of age. He was bigger than Ray, but Ray had the added strength of insanity about him. Everybody knew that and gave reason and explanation as to why most kept out of his way if they possibly could. He was a legend in the area, and there had been boys who had travelled from Canterbury and as far afield as Margate to prove themselves and take him on. All returned home, bruised and bloody nosed. Callum had never witnessed any of the fights, but the stories circulated the school faster than the BBC's daily headlines.

Callum didn't like Ray. Not because he was a bully and made Callum's life a misery. Ray and his two cronies did that to all the kids who were smaller or weaker than them, which were all the kids in the school. Callum had an additional bitterness and anger towards him that he had told no one. Ray Blackman was going out with Lucy Curtis, the girl Callum had had a crush on since primary school.

On Lucy's seventh birthday, she invited him to her house for her party. It wasn't just him; around twenty other kids, all from the same class, were there to celebrate her birthday. Something happened that day he had not been able to shake off or could ever forget. Lucy laughed, it was not the first time she had laughed, but it was the first time he had really heard her. So sweet and happy, it made Callum smile. They became friends, always saying hello and exchanging smiles whenever they saw each other. At the time, Callum was more into sports and spent most of his time with the other boys on the field chasing after a football. In their final year of primary school, Lucy invited Callum around for tea. Her mum had sent a note for him to take to his mum and arranged to drop him back home afterwards. Tea was excellent, but what was nice was the way Lucy kept touching Callum throughout. He hadn't thought about girls and wasn't thinking he wanted a girlfriend. At that age, it was not the thing boys did. They would laugh at him, which was the last thing he wanted. Secretly, he couldn't help but admit that he was enjoying it, maybe more than running after a ball on the school field with fifty other boys. They finished tea, and Lucy's mum cleared the plates away and went into the kitchen, leaving the two of them to play Ludo at the table.

'I've never lost a game of Ludo,' Lucy teased.

'Me neither,' Callum responded, concealing the fact he had never played Ludo before.

'You think you can beat me?'

'Easy,' Callum joked, not wanting to lose but at the same time not so worried if he did over a silly board game.

'Okay, let's have a dare for the one that loses.'

'A what?'

'Getting scared,' she teased again, and then it was agreed the loser would have to carry out a dare the other chose. Callum's red counters made their way around the board, and Lucy slouched behind, with Callum gaining the lead on each turn. What had not been decided was what the dare would be. He tried to think of a good dare that would be funny. Not too bad that he would have happily played on the other boys at school. Eat ten marshmallows in a minute and try to whistle at the same time. Two red counters home and only two to go, with Lucy, still having none home looking cute but annoyed, Callum thought. Balance a spoon on your nose for a minute. No, he preferred the marshmallow one. Lucy got one yellow counter home and then another, and then a third. From being in the lead, he had now fallen behind. Opposite she sat, the biggest smile developed on her face; although Callum was now worried he might lose, he loved looking at her cute face. She looked Callum in the eyes and mysteriously seemed to know she was about to throw a six and get her final counter home and win the game.

Six.

'Don't believe it; I was miles ahead.'

'I told you, I never lose,' she said and jumped up from her chair on the opposite side of the table and moved with speed and sat down next to him. Her smile, which fascinated Callum, appeared again on her face. 'Okay, so I win, and my dare for you is,' she paused and then pointed and pressed her index finger to her temple and screwed up her face as if in some deep thought over what the dare could be. 'I know,' she sparked up as if the light bulb had just come on, 'kiss me.'

'What!' Panic, fear, embarrassment, Callum could not count the number of emotions rattling with confusion from those words. 'No, that's not fair.' He liked her and secretly thought, revealing to no one, she was pretty- but kiss her. That was something he was not ready for, and it never crossed his mind when accepting the dare. He had been tricked.

'What's not fair? A dare is a dare. Kiss me,' she repeated, 'on the lips.' She moved closer to him, and Callum tried to back away. 'I won't tell anyone.'

'Okay,' he conceded. She pursed her lips and leaned in towards Callum. Both with eyes wide open, Lucy's for not wanting to miss the experience of kissing a boy for the first time and Callum's for being absolutely terrified. He followed her lead, pursed his lips, moved closer and approached as if they both would burst into flames when their lips connected. Contact was made, and in trepidation, Callum tried to pull away, but Lucy put her hands around Callum's head and held him there. Within seconds he started to enjoy her lips, and his body relaxed before Lucy released her hold and pulled away. You never forget your first kiss, he had heard someone say.

'Are you gonna buy me another one, you tosser?' Neal continued his rant, not letting it go.

The Coke lay on the pavement dribbling its last dregs over the lip of the tin. 'Oh, for fuck's sake – here,' Ray flicked a ten-pence piece at Neal for him to replenish the drained can. Neal caught the money, said nothing, turned and headed towards the shop when Ferret exited.

'Hey, Ray, look who it is?' Neal called out to Ray and Simon.

'Oh yeah, it's little Ferret,' Ray manoeuvred like a fired up marine and stood in his way. Callum sunk down into the bench sneaking a view through the gaps in the wooded struts.

'Where do you think you're going, Ferret?'

Ferret looked confused by the question. He realised Ray Blackman and his Band of Sorry Men were not the brightest kids at school, but even for them, he thought the question was plain dumb, 'To school, of course.'

'No, you're not. Not until ya' pay the toll,' Ray said, his face now showing no form of jest or humour.

'I have no money.'

'Is this your bike?' Simon Clegg joined in and was now sitting on Ferret's Chopper.

'Yes, leave it alone.'

'Or what Ferret features? What ya gonna do about it?' Ray pushed him in the chest; Ferret stayed on his feet but staggered back with fear inscribed across his face. Simon had now got off the Chopper, knelt down, and started letting the air out of the front tyre. The other two laughed, taking their eyes off Ferret as he sneaked around Ray. Quickly Ray turned and grabbed the bag hung over his shoulder. 'Oi, not so fast; what you got in here?' He said, unzipping the bag, pulling out the school books inside, and throwing them in different directions. The three of them laughed as they did so.

'Stop, or I'll report you at school.' Ray's face changed from a smile to a look that could kill and pushed Ferret hard, forcing him to fall to the floor. Neal dived on top of him and held him to the floor as Ray approached and glued his forehead against Ferret's.

'Tell any living being, Ferret, and you're dead meat. Get it, and I ain't kidding.' Callum wanted to leave but did not want to move and bring attention to himself. He was unsure if they had spotted him as it had all kicked off so quickly. Through the wooded struts of the bench, Callum saw the old man appear from the shop. Ray still had Ferret on the ground, and Callum wondered if the old man, tall, strong and imposing that even Ray would dare not mess with, would break it up. Instead, he went back to the jeep, head down, climbed in and drove off.

'Hey, you lot, get off him,' shouted the lorry driver who had finished his delivery to the shop. The three of them walked away without saying a word. The lorry driver and Ferret collected his books scattered around the pedestrian area at the front of the shop.

Callum mounted his bike and rode off, hoping to remain invisible.

4

'Richard the first, also known as Richard the Lion...,' his breath became heavy, only a few words into his presentation. Breathe, he told himself, just halfway through the first sentence. He must finish the sentence, but had forgotten how to breathe. Gasping for breath, how he wished he had rolled himself snuggly against the back tire of that lorry. There would be no pain now. With panic thrashing through his head, he had now forgotten what he had said. Start again, calm down and relax, he tried telling himself, but there was no time for that. He had to speak now – in front of the whole class. Shit – he wanted to cry, but that would make matters worse. Others had spoken and completed their two-minute talk about famous people in history. In the class, he probably knew more about history than anybody else. Why was he having so much trouble?

'Lion – arsss,' from the desk behind him came a hushed, verberated whisper taunting him. Of all people he wanted to be sat behind him least was Ray Blackman and next to him, grinning away like a Cheshire Cat willing him to mess up, was Simon Clegg.

He had arrived late for class, trying to find his bag that had mysteriously gone missing. After searching for five minutes, he eventually found it at the end of the corridor outside their form classroom. No prizes for guessing who had hidden it there. On arriving at his History class, he looked around for an empty desk. The room went quiet as he entered, and thirty-something faces stared back at him. Already the lesson was in progress with Helen Simpson reading aloud her essay.

'Callum, come in quickly and sit down,' Mrs Jacobs ordered, with a look of disappointment and toned voice of annoyance at the inconvenience of the interruption, 'Carry on, Helen.' It was not a good start, making him even more panicky as if he could be any more than he was already. Callum looked around the classroom. At the front, all the desks were taken; by the window, he saw Lucy sitting next to Jane Cole, always together, best of friends. Lucy's blonde hair reflected the sun that shone through the window. He wanted her to turn and look at him. Give him one of those smiles that made him always feel so good inside. But she didn't. Why would she? Callum was nothing to her; that ship had sailed. Scanning the rest of the class, he saw two desks free, both next to each other, one row from the back of the classroom where Ray Blackman sat directly behind. It got worse, the last place he wanted to be seated, but there was no choice. In his indecision, the class had started a murmur of whispers and sniggers. 'Callum, hurry up, please. The seat over there, quick, come on, boy,' Mrs Jacobs, with more frustration in her voice, pointed to the execution chair he had already spotted. 'QUIET,' Mrs Jacobs fumed and smacked the bamboo stick she always had to hand on a pile of books on the desk in front of her bringing an instant silence, like a plug pulled out the TV, leaving a sudden eerie hush over the classroom.

The pounding of his heart was now pumping the blood around his body at a hundred miles an hour. Nerves tingled in his arms which were shaking as he took his seat. Around the class, everywhere, they stared. Faces ready to crucify him when he messed up. Helen Simpson continued her essay about Emmeline Pankhurst and the Suffragette movement. Behind Callum, he heard Ray's whispers to Simon and Neal, 'Should put 'em back in the kitchen where they can be some use.' Mrs Jacobs heard the whispers and eyed them to shut up.

'In nineteen-o-three, she with her daughters, Sylvia

and ...,' Helen spoke with clarity and clearness in her voice. Confidence exhumed, although Callum heard not a word she said. He sat there, tense with his leg playing to the rhythm of a thousand beats, double quick-time, under the desk. All he heard were the voices in his head telling him he was going to mess up and forget what he was talking about, convinced everybody would laugh. The talk of the class, he predicted. The target of ridicule on how useless and pathetic Callum McNab was and provider for that day's entertainment. Callum never understood the joy how most of the class' entertainment was found in someone else's suffering.

A sudden crescendo of noise erupted with a round of applause led by Mrs Jacobs. Callum would not have realised Helen had finished if it was not for that. Not me next, please, he silently prayed.

'Thank you, Helen, that was excellent,' Mrs Jacobs congratulated. Callum kept his eyes focused on his exercise book open on the page, trying to avoid eye contact with Mrs Jacobs, although he could not help but raise his head. And what most he wanted to avoid, he had fallen right into the trap, the accidental meeting of eyes. His eyes open wide, staring back at Mrs Jacobs, sucked into a hypnotic trance, fearing they were going to pop out. Mrs Jacobs' eyes pierced his, deep inside where she could see the fear he held. Licking her lips in pleasure, along with the others in the class, she saw her opportunity to inflict pain at his expense.

In her grey dress, she stood there authoritarian, making her look Victorian. Dickensian sadism, relishing the pain she inflicted. Mrs Jacobs had not moved with the times or the fashions. On alternate days she would switch between a grey dress and then a black dress for the three years Callum had attended her class. He guessed she wore the same attire at the weekend, fitting with the sequence. A smile crossed her face, and Callum waited for those dreaded words.

'Neal, can we hear your essay?' Callum worried it was audible the sigh of relief that left his body.

'Sorry, Miss, I didn't do it,' Neal replied, in an, *I couldn't give a damn* voice.

'You have had all week to prepare, Neal. Please do it for next week. You will be first on the list.'

'Yes, Miss.'

'Ray, how about you? Have you prepared anything?' She was working her way around the desks, and Callum was expecting the same answer from Ray as Neal had given. Closing his eyes made no difference; he couldn't see anybody, but he knew he was still visible to them, and there was nowhere to hide.

'Yes, Miss, I 'ave. Worked really 'ard on this, Miss,' he said. The shock almost made Mrs Jacobs fall back. There was a gasp of amazement around the classroom.

'Marvellous, Ray, please stand up and read out your person from history but first tell us who you have chosen.'

'Yeah, of course, Miss. It's Adolf Hitler.' A muffled giggle waved throughout the classroom, and this time Callum was convinced he saw Mrs Jacobs topple backwards.

'Quiet everyone, Ray, please begin.'

'Alrigh'.' He leaned down, opened his bag at the side of his desk, and ruffled for the exercise book he had forgotten to get out in preparation. Forgotten or purposely left in his bag to create further disruption. Mrs Jacobs looked on, clearly agitated but trying to remain composed. 'Righ', I got it,' he said, fumbling through the pages. Simon and Neal openly found the whole performance funny as they snorted with laughter. 'The war started in nineteen-forty, and Hitler was the boss of the krauts,' the classroom roared into an uncontrollable laugher. Mrs Jacobs slapped the bamboo with extra force to silence the class.

'Ray, please. When giving an account of history, I would prefer you use the correct terms. They were not Krauts. They were the German soldiers, and the start of the war was in nineteen-thirty-nine.'

'Sorry, Miss – I carried out research and interviewed some ex-soldiers that were in the war, and they said they used to call them Krauts. Gotta admit the year bit, they were a bit vague about that part, so you could be right.'

'Thank you, carry on, please,' Mrs Jacobs prompted, looking like she lied with her encouragement and wanted it to end quickly. Very quickly. Callum didn't; he hoped Ray had a thirty-minute script there that would take them to the end of class and get him out of reading. Lightning was the more likely event that would happen to get him out of the situation.

'Nobody liked him, the Krau... I mean, the Germans might 'ave, but in the end, we won the war, and he killed himself in the bunker with his missus Eva Braun who he bonked just before.' Again, the classroom erupted; again, Mrs Jacobs cracked the bamboo.

'Quiet, I will not have this behaviour in my class. Everybody, not one more sound from any of you. Or you will all be staying behind tonight for double detention.' A pin drop could be heard, and Callum saw Lucy's face as she turned towards the back of the class, brushing her hair backwards with her hand. There was that smile that he still loved to see. The smile was, of course, for Ray's shenanigans. What was it she saw in that moron?

For close on a minute, Mrs Jacobs stood at the head of the classroom, her back to the blackboard, looking at each pupil, in turn, daring them to make a sound. Then her face deflated in exhausted defeat of the battle as Neal Tarrant's hand went up in a slow periscope movement. 'Yes, Neal, what do you want to ask?'

'Yes, Miss, I have a question,' The whole class waited, knowing a question from Neal Tennant was going to be something ludicrous and could end with the entire class in detention if anybody cracked, and judging by the strained expressions on the faces there were a few that were close. He did not disappoint, 'If we have to read our essays out, and we have to remain silent, how do we do that?'

'Out,' Neal knew it was coming before he had asked the question, 'wait outside until the end of the lesson. Keep quiet, and after school, report to me for thirty minutes detention.' Neal left and closed the door behind him, and again Mrs Jacobs stood silent. This time there were no questions, just silence. The only sound was the clock on the wall that ticked its seconds away. Knowing chances were he was next to read, Callum looked at the clock hoping the lesson was nearing an end and there would be no time for his essay. Fifteen minutes to twelve, panic set in. There was no way they would sit there for another fifteen minutes, convinced they would fit at least another three essays before the end of class, condemning his life to misery. Calm in the classroom spread, as did the fear in Callum's stomach.

'Callum, can you start us off again please with your essay.' The burning sensation hurt from the bullet that entered his body Mrs Jacobs had fired. His heart, nearing cardiac arrest. With immense effort trying to ignore the pain, he focused hard on the words in front of him. They were clear but made no sense. The letters jumped and moved on the page, celebrating entropy while dancing the Danse Macabre leading Callum to his death. This was why he had tried to remember it verbatim, but the door in his brain slammed shut again. As the cell door closes to lock the prisoner in, the door shuts in his head to lock him out.

'Richard the first, also known as Richard the Lion...,' he had to say something. He could not just stand there. Struggling to breathe, he felt he was going to pass out. *Lion-arsss* the voice of his tormentor jested. 'He was king of England in ...' the dates hidden somewhere in the depths of his mind. Punishing him for everything he had done. He fumbled for his notes, distracted by the comments only he could hear.

'Come on, we're getting borr-ed,' it was Ray's hissing

voice. Ray continued his torment, thumping on the desk. A slow plangent sound, loud enough for only Callum to hear, penetrated his mind adding chaos to confusion.

Forget the dates; carry on, he told himself. 'He was king of England and led the crusades. It was the third crusade.' Callum had somehow unlocked the knowledge and information he had stored away. 'The year was eleven-eighty-nine, and he joined Phillip the second of ...' and then, for some reason, Callum felt drawn to look to his left. The desk occupied by Simon Clegg, picking his nose and indicating to Callum he would be sending it his way once he had emptied the contents. At that moment, he felt something wet hit the back of his neck and roll down the back of his shirt. Whilst Callum had been talking, Ray had built an arsenal of spitballs he now had lined up on his desk and was firing through the empty Biro pen casing. He felt another hit that followed the earlier one's route, sliding down the back of his shirt.

Concentration had gone. Desperately Callum tried to remember where he was in the essay but another spitball was followed by another in quick succession. Tension grew inside, and he heard a hidden laugh from someone on the other side of the classroom who had spotted what Ray was doing, encouraging him only more. For an eternity, Callum stood there, frozen to the spot. He wanted to run but was stuck by an invisible but powerful glue. A war was exploding inside his head. SCREAM, RUN, do something, but he could think of nothing but panic. Then his chair behind him came sliding into the backs of his legs where Ray had kicked it. Cry, he had to, and then run. Keep on running so never to be seen again. He could no longer talk; stress triggered throughout his body, and he felt a warm flow running down his leg. Immediately he knew what it was, but the question was, had anybody else realised. Without hesitation, he picked up his bag by the side of his desk and ran towards the door, knocking over his chair as he went. He looked back, and on the desk was his exercise book, but it was too late to go back and get it. Slamming the classroom door behind him, he was past caring; he knew he was already in trouble and figured slamming the door would make little difference. Outside in the corridor, he paused, dropped his bag on the floor and looked down to check his trousers to see how bad the damage was. There was a dark patch around his crotch, but thankfully not as bad as he had first thought. Maybe they didn't see. Maybe he had got away with it. What he did know was he could not return to the class. For now, at least, he would just run. He looked up, and as he did, he remembered Neal, who had been sent out of the classroom earlier and told to wait in the corridor. There he stood, looking directly at where Callum had been looking seconds earlier. Neal's face widened, and a roar of laughter escaped with a cry of, 'He's pissed himself, oh for fuck's sake, can't wait to tell everybody 'bout this.' Callum picked up his bag, turned, and ran as fast as possible. He didn't know where he would run; just as far away as possible was all he could think.

5

The sight of Jim's coat on the stand next to where Callum hung his made his lip curl with exacerbated bitterness. The familiar sound of the television from the lounge chatting away to no one as Callum entered the lounge and witnessed Jim flat out on the settee. Mouth open, breathing out with a vibrating snort on every in-breath, the results Callum assumed from a lunchtime session down The Wheatsheaf with the rest of his losers mates.

'You're home late?' He didn't want to answer questions about where he had been. He didn't want to lie to his mum, but he could not tell her the truth. After leaving school, he knew he could not come home, or Rachel would have asked why he was home so early. Instead, he went to the sea front and lay on the beach, hidden from the world, tucked up against the wooden breakwater. Sitting there looking out to the sea, he pictured Reginal Perrin stripping off and diving into the sea, faking his suicide. He thought it was an option for a brief moment, but the plan had too many holes. Instead, he read his school books. Concentration had been a problem with the constant return of the horror of earlier tormenting him.

The spam fritters smelt good which Rachel was frying up as she spoke. It was one of Callum's favourites, spam fritters with lashing of baked beans, but even with the inviting aroma he absorbed, nothing could cheer him up today. 'Where have you been?'

'I went for a ride after school down to the seafront.' It was not a lie, he thought, just an incomplete truth.

'How was school?' His mum asked in a voice that sensed there was something wrong.

'Not good,' Callum replied, trying to bring the subject to a close.

'I had a visitor earlier.' Callum's heart stopped; maybe one of the teachers had called around to see if he had come home. He could take no more; today's stress levels had already passed their recommended pressure point for any normal person. 'Lucy Curtis dropped by after school,' his mum continued; what the hell did she come round for, his breathing again started to struggle, 'and dropped your history exercise book off.' What did Lucy tell his mum? Please, no, he told himself. Jim, who had been asleep on the settee in the front room, and Callum wished he had remained that way, appeared at the kitchen door.

'Dinner ready yet?' Jim stretched in the archway to the dining room, exposing his hairy stomach under his vest. Callum wanted to throw something at him. Not because his day had been exceptionally stressful, it was simply because he always wanted to throw something at him. Was food the only thing that stirred this guy away from lounging on the settee watching television? Trapped between the two of them, his mum, in one corner by the oven, and Jim, in the other, standing by the doorway blocking Callum's exit, should he need to escape, he considered a high possibility if the questioning continued. He didn't want to talk about today, and least of all, he did not want to talk about it with Jim there. 'Who's Lucy?' Callum looked around for a heavy object to throw at Jim. Although he knew he wouldn't, the repercussion would be too great.

He remembered what happened the last time he lost his temper with Jim, pathetically slapping his arms towards him. Jim stood, laughed and slapped back hard, throwing him to the floor. Leaving him in one corner, screwed up in a ball, crying with his mum screaming in the other. Jim threw a half drunk bottle of vodka at the wall shattering the glass and both their nerves too, before leaving in one of his moods that they feared his return.

'Is that your girlfriend?' He teased.

'No, she's an old friend of Callum's,' his mum interjected, 'she said you got upset and ran out the classroom when you did your presentation.'

'I don't want to talk about it,' he said sheepishly, needing to bury himself somewhere, feeling sick deep inside.

'You weren't crying at school, were you,' Jim returned to his teasing tone, 'what's wrong with you, you big girl.'

'I wasn't crying.' That much was true. He wasn't, he almost was, but he wasn't crying. It was worse than that, and he hoped to God that word had not spread, and there stood a slim chance of that, and Lucy had not told them the rest. Even the thought of it made him want to shrivel up and disappear.

'Leave him alone,' his mum tried to calm the situation, 'it's not his fault.'

'The boy's got something wrong with him,' Jim continued, not leaving it alone.

'Jim, pack it up. You're not helping.' Jim found this strangely amusing and fell into a fit of laughter. 'Dinner's ready. Go sit down at the table, and I'll dish it up.' Callum could not face sitting at the dinner table with the two of them trying to explain what had happened. He didn't know what had happened. It had never happened before; it was just that everything had got on top of him, and he had lost control of his body. Everything had shut down. How could he explain that? It was bad enough trying to speak to his mum about it. With Jim, he could forget it. Callum looked at Jim, still in fits of drunken laughter. There was not a sensitive cell in his body and he was completely devoid of experiencing any empathy for another person. A normal person, that is, Callum thought, but maybe there was something wrong with him, and he wasn't normal. Maybe everybody was right. Everybody else in the class had given their presentation and read out their essay without a problem. Even Ray Blackman was able to without a problem. Why was he so screwed up?

'Okay, come on, son,' Jim hooked Callum's neck in the crook of his arm, trapping him like a wrestler, 'tell me what made you cry today at school.' Callum wriggled clear of Jim's grip and pushed past him.

'I'll eat later. I'm not hungry at the moment,' Callum said and left the room and made his way upstairs to his bedroom.

'That's all right; I'll have the cry-babies portion.' It didn't need to be a fist for Jim to throw to make the last punch. Upstairs, Callum laid face down, sinking deep into the pillow on his bed to find darkness.

Rachel pounded the spam fritters and slapped the beans on the plate. A plate for one – she too was no longer hungry. With Jim sat at the dining room table, Rachel pushed the plate in front of him. He looked at her and said nothing. The open-plan kitchen - dining room area was a regret, as she stood, arms crossed, cigarette lit, facing the man who at one time she thought as her rescuer but had now become her jailer. Each bite he took, she hated him, more for what he had done to Callum and what he had done to her. Callum had been such a happy and confident boy before Michael's accident. But the monster who sat there had been chipping away at them both. The chisel's pointed edge cut piece by piece, shaping them both into pawns he could manipulate at will. It was at times like this, her thoughts scared her, believing she was capable of murder. On the draining board lay a carving knife Jim would use on Sundays. His favourite meal of the week, a Sunday roast, the only thing he ever did in or around the house was carve the meat. The early evening sun shone through the kitchen window, striking the blade; glinting its reflection. Rachel followed the juddering reflection from the blade. Its path took a direct line that reflected on Jim's neck. It shook teasingly, back and forth, up and down, across his throat. It would be so easy.

The glass on the counter beside the hob from where she had her first drink of the day was empty. In need, she unscrewed the red cap of the vodka and poured herself another. Took a glug, and the thought returned, telling her it would be possible. When he was asleep, he slept heavy, especially if he had been to the pub at lunchtime; nothing would awaken him. Creep up whilst he was sprawled out on the settee and run the blade across his throat. Then finally, she would be released. Free from his claws that dug into her so deep. If only she had the strength to do it; knowing she did not, a tear rolled down her cheek. She was trapped, with no way out.

**

Callum got off the bed and went to his desk. The history textbook Lucy had returned sat there as a big question mark. He had not seen Lucy's reaction in class. It all happened too fast; his body's auto-drive had taken control. Run was all he could remember, run and get the hell out of there, with laughter from his tormentors piercing his ears. Did she see? Did anybody see? Or was it just Neal Tennant? If that were the case, it would be his word against Callum's. The kids at school loved scandal, and if there was something to latch on to, they would take it. The only thing Callum had on his side was that Neal Tennant was well known for making stories stretch to great heights, so he hoped that no one would believe him and think it was another one of his exaggerations. But that did not answer the question, why would Lucy return his book? It was out of her way from home, and she would then have had to walk all the way back. It would have taken her an hour extra to get home. It made no sense. Maybe it was some kind of a joke; maybe she and Ray had thought it funny to rub his nose in it. After all, it was Ray who had been the instigator with his comments and spitballs he had fired at Callum. Surely Ray would have something to say if Lucy had come by herself. If only he could roll back the clock.

Since his father's accident, he and Lucy had not spoken much, but neither had she been cruel to him. It was just the Ray business Callum could not get his head around. What was she doing with him? Lucy was bright and intelligent; it made no sense. In all other ways, she was the same, the fun and friendly girl she was when he had first known her. Lucy and Callum had not fallen out. No big argument. They just drifted apart and found new friends, like many of the other kids at that age. The difference was that Callum hadn't made any new friends. He was alone, and he felt it bad at times. Maybe, in some crazy universe he knew did not exist, he and Lucy would be friends. Girlfriend – boyfriend sort of friends. Somewhere he needed to find the nerve to talk to her; it was as simple as that in this universe he imagined. But in reality, all the words were in his head he wanted to say, but when he came to tell them, a barrier came up that blocked them out. Just as they had today with his presentation. And he knew the notion was ludicrous. Lucy had grown up and become one of the most attractive girls in their year. And he had become a dork that nobody wanted anything to do with. Incapable of holding a conversation with anyone and the one everybody avoided at break time. He was the one who sat by himself and read a book because that was the only option available to him. Stop thinking about Lucy, he told himself. What's the point? Chances of them getting together was as high as Ray Blackman getting straight 'A' grades in his exams. The sooner he put her out of his mind, the better. It would only lead to upset. Forget it - Over and over again, he told himself, but no matter how hard he tried, he could not get her image out of his head.

The pillow on his bed was damp from his tears. The chain of thought took him to his dad's accident. Only bad things happened to Callum. Three months away from school was a long time, and it changed him. He was an alien, a stranger in a new land on his return. The other boys didn't know what to say, and Callum didn't want to talk about it. So the perpetual cycle began, and with each week that passed, the situation got worse. With no one to talk to and no friends, he replaced football with books and lost himself in his studies.

Tomorrow was Friday, the last day of school before the weekend. He could go and thank Lucy for bringing his book back. Then he would find out if it was some kind of a joke or not. Whatever the outcome, he saw no good from it, and he didn't think he could face school at all. Tomorrow he would be hot news. Everywhere he went, there would be the whispers, the looks and those who would take fun in laughing outright. Maybe he could change schools. What would his mum say? He knew what Jim would say, and it wouldn't change tomorrow.

Maybe he could skive off. Overcome with relief with the light-bulb moment, why hadn't he thought about that before? Loads of kids did it. The teachers knew but never said anything. The fewer kids to teach, the easier life was for them. He decided that if he skived off Friday, things might have calmed a little by the time Monday came around. It had to be better than facing it tomorrow. Still nervous for Monday's reaction but feeling more relaxed by the idea, at least the delay gave him time to think; he lay back down on his bed, closed his eyes and tried to shut out the world.

Spam fritters were consumed after the news finished at nine-twenty-five whilst watching some detective program in the lounge with his mum. Hearing the front door close was Callum's cue; Jim had gone out for the evening, it was now safe to venture downstairs free of ridicule. The mascara smudged beneath his mum's eyes, wedged itself in the creases of the curvature of her nose, giving clear evidence she had been crying again. But Callum said nothing. It was rare she went a day without tears. They didn't talk much; his mum tried to calm Callum, 'Try not to worry about it,' she would say; Callum shrugged the words off, and his mum did not press. It was good to get out of his bedroom and stop his mind rolling round and round. The spam fritters were good, the dumb detective on television not so, but he solved the crime eventually. After the bad guys had been arrested and locked up, Callum said goodnight to his mum. She rose from the armchair she had been sitting in and hugged Callum. It was unusual for her to show emotion like that, and at first, Callum thought it was to comfort him from the trauma of the day he had experienced. But the length of the hug led him to believe it was his mum in need of assurance as much as him.

6

Tankerton was the place to avoid; he didn't want to be seen by anyone from school and draw even more attention to himself, so he headed in the opposite direction. He pedalled north up Chestfield Road, passed the golf club where the posh old men unloaded from the boots of their cars heavy bags full of drivers and irons, laughing and chatting to friends they intended to spend the morning with, attempting to get a ball in a hole for a reason Callum could not fathom. It was a pleasant route, and he would take it a few times a year. It was his secret. It was something he had to do. It was a feeling he would not be able to explain to anybody, bringing a sense of comfort in a macabre way. It was a two-mile cycle ride from home to Radfall Hill, and on his way, he thought about the other kids who would be arriving at school. He was sure by now they would already be laughing with each other at his expense. Get them out of your mind, he told himself. Today he was determined, or he would try his best not to worry about school. The bullying, the remarks – sticks and stones and all that – but he knew it was impossible and not true.

The sun-kissed wheat in the field to his right shone golden on a warm morning, delivering a welcomed respite from his stressed thoughts. A trickle of sweat ran down his forehead. He came to a halt, dismounted and rested his bike against the red telephone box on the sharp bend of Radfall Hill. Slowly he ran his hand across the outside of the telephone box's metal frame. The red paint flaked; the glass panels aged and weathered. A glass pane at eye level had a curved crack deep through the glass. He thought of his dad and wondered if this was the last thing he saw. The red telephone box flashed through his mind's eye, coming towards him at eighty miles an hour. It made no sense how a moment in one person's life could change so many. He wanted so much to turn back time; he would offer anything but knew it was impossible. Standing there looking out onto the fields and the woodland area to the North, he let himself feel the calmness of the silence around him. The difference between now, a soft breeze and a gentle whistle and nothing else and then, with confusion and chaos of that night when ambulances and police cars had their sirens blaring out, shouting to the world about the tragedy that had occurred. The incongruous difference between the two seemed unfathomable. A Ford Cortina drove past and backfired, breaking the clean country air with the brume of exhaust fumes, reminding Callum that school would have started and he needed to get out of sight to avoid being seen. A few yards up the hill in Canterbury direction was a turning into Radfall Ride on the right hand side.

A dirt track that Callum had never been up before but could see it went in the direction of the woodland area to the north. It looked like an excellent place to hide, a place to get lost for the day. With a whole school day to waste, he climbed back onto his bike and juddered his way along the dusty, earthen bumpy track that was just wide enough for probably one vehicle. To his right, a stream had dried up to a muddy mush from the lack of rain over the last few months. Further up the track on his right, he cycled past a couple of old cottages hidden from view by trees and wild gardens with hedges splayed out with wiry strands. He cycled for about a mile before coming to the last of the cottages. There was not a soul around. He had ventured in far enough to mute the sound of the traffic driving up and down Radfall Hill on their daily commutes and shopping trips. The track became even harder to navigate, so he got off his bike and pushed. The trees grew denser, and the only sound to be heard were the birds talking, and the odd howl and crack of twigs as the wildlife went about their day. In the beauty of the Kent countryside that Churchill had called the Garden of England, Callum thought how right he was. He walked deep into the woods, lifting his bike over tree trunks that had silently fallen across the rarely trodden path. He walked for about an hour before the path opened and reached the grass bare crest of a hill. In a clearing, there was a vista looking out for miles across forest, fields and farmland. The landscape looked so peaceful it was hard to believe there were any problems in Callum's world. Pushing his bike through the rugged terrain and from the sun's heat, he took off his coat, laid it on the ground and sat down. He took the plastic bottle from his bag he had filled with orange squash and quenched the thirst built up from cycling and walking.

Clearing his mind, he screwed up his coat and laid his head on it as he looked at the cerulean sky above. If only he could stay there forever, but no matter how peaceful and relaxing the moment was, his mind drifted back to school. There was no doubt the other kids would have missed him. Unlike other days they would have wanted him to be in today, especially Ray Blackman. The mystery of Lucy returned. He wondered what she was doing and if he had crossed her thoughts today. The sun was intense, and when he closed his eyes, it was still light, but he refused to open them. It was an opportunity to catch up on a sleepless night. The stress of yesterday had crept up on him, and not long after closing his eyes, Callum accepted with gratitude the welcomed feeling of drifting away into a deep sleep.

***

It was the prodding to the arm that woke him. His eyes opened in shock, blinded by the sun, shading the rays with his arm, before adjusting his focus to see a long stick tapping against his arm. Above him was an old man.

Callum recognised him immediately as the gardener from Mrs Wickes' house. For a moment, Callum, confused by the sudden intrusion into his restful sleep, tried to remember where he was. What was the gardener doing there, and why was he prodding him with a stick?

'Need to check your boots before you put them on in the jungle,' said the old man.

'What?' Callum replied, more confused than ever. The old man pointed with his stick to Callum's trousers. Callum jumped from horizontal to upright like an Olympic gymnast and started thrashing away with both arms at his trousers and shirt that was swarming with ants.

'I guess they thought you wanted some company,' said the old man, his stick pointed at the most enormous anthill Callum had ever seen, a metropolis of the ant world, not more than three feet from where he had fallen asleep. The sight of the ants busying themselves in their millions made Callum squirm even more. In panic, unable to brush the ants off him, Callum frantically started to unbutton his shirt and threw it wildly that would have hit the old man square straight on in the face if his reactions had not been quick to catch it. The old man continued to brush the shirt, trying to help get rid of the ants that had taken a liking to Callum's grey school shirt. The ants now decided to crawl from his trousers to his shirtless body. They were spreading fast, and the only thing Callum could think of to avoid them was to remove his trousers. He unbuttoned, unzipped and pulled them off over his shoes, leaving him jumping around in nothing but his red Y-front underpants, white sports socks and black shoes, doing some kind of anti-ant dance that produced little reward. The old man let out a gruff laugh at the image.

'It's not funny,' Callum complained.

'It is from where I'm standing,' the old man said, now finding the situation even funnier. Callum continued to dance about brushing his legs, arms and hair, repeating the process over again. 'You need to wash them off, or you'll be dancing around like a randy hyena that arrived late at the singles ball for the rest of the day.'

'Thanks, Einstein; where am I going to do that?' The confident, quick retort was unusual for Callum, but it had shot out with the panic.

'You need a lake that you can jump in,' the man helpfully added.

'Where's the nearest lake?' Callum quickly replied, desperate to clear his body of the accommodating ants.

'Faversham, I think,' the old man replied after some thought. 'Yeah, Faversham, there's a very pretty one there.'

'What! That's bloody miles. Have you not got any water? You gotta help me. I've got to get rid of these damn things,' Callum screamed, continuously brushing the ants away, but it made no difference.

'Hmm,' the old man hesitated with frustrated thought before he continued, 'I have a shower you could use, five minutes walk.' Callum looked up, unsure of what to do. He had never met this man before, he knew him only as the gardener for Mrs Wickes' house, but he was crawling in ants. The old man looked distracted and was looking up the path. 'But before you decide, I would recommend you go and hide behind that bush. Don't want to give these ladies a heart attack, do you now?' Callum looked in the direction of the old man and saw three women; they must have been in their seventies, grey hair flapping in the breeze, walking in their direction.

'Shit,' could things get any more embarrassing, he thought. And, he remembered, of course, they could. He went behind the bush and hid.

'Good morning, ladies, lovely day for it,' said the old man, 'picking blackberries, I see, had much success?' And continued into some long story about how they had been plentiful this year. Callum thought the old man was taking pleasure with the thought of Callum stuck behind the bush, in his underpants, crawling with ants whilst he exchanged pleasantries and chatted away as if he was at a Friday morning mothers' meeting. Eventually, they moved on.

Callum reappeared from behind the bush. 'Did you really have to drag out the conversation so long?'

'Never a wrong moment for politeness,' the old man said, but Callum thought he was wrong. And the time to be abrupt and rude was precisely now.

'You have a shower I can use, you say.'

'Five minutes, but here,' the old man passed Callum his khaki jacket he had slung over his shoulder, 'better put this on. Can't have you scaring the good ladies of Whitstable with those sparrow legs of yours.'

'Thanks.' Callum took the jacket, which was far too big for him, but put it on anyway. They put Callum's shirt and trousers into a carrier bag the old man had brought with him for blackberry picking and walked off. The old man led the way; he was a towering figure of a man that Callum had to look upwards when they spoke.

'What's your name?'

'Callum, and yours?'

'Potts, nice to meet you.'

Potts was right; it was only five minutes, if that, but what amazed Callum was that he recognised the path from the one he had walked earlier. His hour-long walk had taken him in a complete circle. Potts pushed open the gate in the middle of a line of wooden panels that spread across fifty yards that guarded his property against the outside world. Inside it was wild. Potts, the gardener, had taken no busman's holiday, Callum thought. The only part not overgrown in the front area was where the Jeep that Callum recognised as Potts' was parked between two trees, and next to that was a boat on a trailer with a green underbelly from the seaweed glued to it. Across from there was a wooden table with a couple of crooked chairs. Directly in front of where they had entered, a distance of twenty yards stood a hut. A hotchpotch shack of mismatched timbers constructed what Callum thought had a loved and charming look to it. Two windows, with red curtains drawn, looked out to the front. They walked around the back of the hut, and there was three further outbuildings of similar craftsmanship.

'It ain't much, but it's mine.' At the rear of the hut were a door and a hand-made wooden plaque with the words - *Potts' Place*. 'What you need is the shower.' Potts, with his stick, pointed to one of the outbuildings, 'Shower or bath? We have all mod cons here?'

Callum was unsure if he was meant to laugh, so he didn't and simply replied, 'Shower if that's okay.'

'Of course, luckily, I refilled the shower yesterday.' Potts took Callum to the largest of the outbuildings and showed him inside. There was a cast-iron bath with no taps, and next to that was a wooden structure which at the top had a large tank with four ropes hanging down. 'It's straightforward enough, pull a rope, and that opens the water to shower down on you, four ropes; if you're not clean by then - tough luck.' Potts started to make his way to the door, 'almost forgot, clean towels over there. Five star accommodation.' Potts closed the door behind him, leaving Callum slightly dazed in disbelief.

Callum removed Potts' jacket and put it on a chair beside the thread-worn towels. He ran his hand over one of the four ropes and followed the rope with his eye up to a wheel attached to a tank. Each rope was attached to its own tank. Still itching and still with ants visibly crawling on him, he removed his underpants and threw them on the chair with Potts' coat. Pulled the first rope and screamed, 'SHIT,' as ten gallons of freezing water came thrashing down on him.

Outside he heard the gruff laugh of Potts, who had been waiting and knowing, 'Sorry, forgot to turn the heating on earlier.'

'BASTARD.'

'Manners, Callum, that's no way to speak to someone who has helped you out.'

The smell of bacon greeted Callum when he left the shower. His clothes were waiting for him, hung on a chair outside. Ant free, Potts, he guessed, had somehow cleared them off. He dressed, followed his nose to the front of the hut and found Potts sitting at the wooden table with a plate of rolls with bacon. 'Thought you could do with something to eat,' Potts was right; Callum was famished. He remembered the jam sandwiches in his bag he made that morning, which Potts had left by the chair where Callum was sitting now.

'I brought some sandwiches with me,' Callum said as he opened his bag and saw that they too had been attacked by the ants. He emptied the contents of his bag onto the floor, 'Sorry.'

'I think the bacon will be more appetizing.' Potts smiled.

'I think you're probably right,' Callum replied, now able to see the funny side and laughed about the ant incident. Bacon was good, with the fat crisped up just as his mum made it. It had been the strangest of days, but Callum felt rejuvenated. The ant incident had taken his mind off his home and school troubles.

'So, tell me,' Potts spoke, looking up at the branches of one of the many trees that towered above them in the area they sat, 'what you doing sleeping in the middle of the woods? In an anthill.'

'I was tired.'

'I could think of better places to sleep. How come you're not at school?'

'I had a day off.' Callum followed Potts' line of vision and focused on what he believed to be the same branch. It was more comfortable to answer the question without looking him directly in the eye.

'And, you wear your school uniform on days off,' Potts said, as a statement rather than a question. Callum knew he had been caught out. It wasn't the most thought out of lies, and at the same time, he didn't feel pressurised by what Potts had said. Potts' tone sounded more out of interest than an accusation, and he brushed it off without pursuing it further.

'I know you,' Callum worried his tone may have come across as rude. 'Sorry, I mean, I've seen you cutting the grass at our neighbours', Mrs Wickes.'

'Ah yeah, Mrs Wickes, has been working there for many years now, lovely lady, Mrs Wickes.'

'It's strange, but over the last couple of days, I've seen you a few times. Yesterday at Cookes' stores, on the seafront.' Potts said he went there a lot and enjoyed a walk along the seafront when the weather was good. 'Did you see those boys, Ray Blackman and his mates picking on Nigel Ferret?'

Potts responded abruptly, 'No, I didn't see them.'

'You walked straight past them,' Callum said in disbelief.

'I said I didn't see them,' Potts said with palpable anger. 'Besides, they're just kids. You always get kids picking on other kids.' A tension blotted the air; Callum regretted raising the question. Potts had been kind to him, and he did not want to do anything that upset him but was confused about why the question bothered him. 'Anyway, let's not worry about that,' Potts' tone returned to its relaxed manner as it were earlier, 'do you want some more tea?' Callum was pleased with the change in subject and accepted with thanks. Potts went around the back to get more tea.

Potts returned with tea and cakes, which they drank,

ate, and continued chatting. They spoke about school and how one of Callum's favourite subjects was history. Potts revealed he was in North Africa in World War II but changed the subject when Callum asked what he did there. 'That's for another day. Do you like blackberry pie?' Potts asked.

'I think so; not sure I've ever had it.'

'That's what I was doing when I found you. Picking blackberries, that is,' Potts explained. 'I was gonna bake a pie with them tomorrow.' He hesitated before asking, 'If you wanted to call round tomorrow, I don't get many visitors. It would be nice to have some company.'

'Sure, that would be fun.' Callum was pleased to have made a friend. Albeit a friend older than his mum, he found Potts exciting and intriguing, and he was comfortable in his company. 'How long have you lived here?'

'Oh, 'bout thirty years it'll be now.' Potts got up from his seat and continued, 'Come, let me introduce you to Marilyn and her friends.' They walked out to the back and passed the outbuildings.

'How much land you got here, it goes on forever.'

'Yeah, as far as the eye can see, Callum. In all, there's about two acres, all woodland.'

'Amazing,' Callum replied, fascinated by how someone not that many miles from him could live in such isolation and peaceful surroundings. Directly behind the outbuildings was a cleared area where he had grown vegetables, herbs and fruit. And then there was Marilyn with her friends. Marilyn, the chicken, and her three friends, Lizzie, Doris and Sophia, clucked in excitement when they saw Potts, who gave them some food which he shared with Callum to hand out. 'Marilyn is the boss, as you can see.' Callum watched Potts making sure she got her feed before the others. 'Blondes have more fun.' Marilyn and Doris had white feathers, whilst Lizzie had brown and Sophia black.

For the rest of the day, Callum helped Potts dig up an area where they planted some lettuce and radishes. Potts explained that it would be the last crop of the season, and Callum was keen to see them grow, so he was glad to think he was coming back tomorrow. Shortly after four o'clock, Callum headed off home. On the ride home, he thought about Potts and the life he led. It seemed perfect to Callum. Tranquil and away from the traumas that people in this world created.

7

Callum woke early for a Saturday, and despite the worries festering in his head, brightness shone about the day he welcomed with unfamiliar optimism.

Midday, they had agreed to meet at Potts'. It was still too early, but he needed to get out and go somewhere, so he decided to cycle to the seafront after breakfast and pass the time there. A regular Saturday would have started with breakfast, followed by him going to his room and spending most of the day checking through his schoolwork, but today was to be different.

His mum brought toast and a pot of tea to the dining room table and joined him. Callum wanted to tell her about Potts but realised he would then have to say how they met, raising the question of why he was not at school.

'I thought I'd cycle down to the seafront today,' he said as he took a bite of the toast he had loaded with strawberry jam. 'I'm meeting some friends from school, so will be gone most of the day.'

'That's nice, you should get out more,' his mum encouraged, 'it's good that you are doing so well at school, but you need to get out with friends as well.' Although Callum had kept his eyes focused on the toast, he glanced up to see joy or relief; he was not sure which exactly, on his mum's face. Callum enjoyed the times he and his mum spent alone together. The atmosphere was different. The door to the lounge opened, and they stopped talking; silence and coldness shivered through Callum. Jim entered, hair wet and slicked back, his white vest wet from where he had just washed, and newspaper rolled up, he had pulled from the letterbox, under his arm wedged high up to his armpit.

'Orright,' he said to nobody in particular.

Callum grunted, 'Yeah,' and sped up, eating his toast so he could escape from the dining room, which Jim had loaded up with Old Spice filling the room with a vile tang. Out of the house, anywhere, where the air was cleaner.

His mum rose and left the table. 'I'll get you a cup,' she said with a smile and returned to fill his cup with tea from the pot. 'Shall I do your toast?'

'Thanks,' Jim said in surprise. They usually were at loggerheads; Callum kept his head down as the civil tone continued. 'Callum's off to the seafront to meet some friends today. That'll be nice, won't it?'

'Guess,' Jim agreed without interest, offering little more. 'Yeah, probably going out later me-self.'

'That's fine. I'll get dinner ready for when you get back.'

Jim looked at her with suspicion, 'Orright,' he said, slurping his tea, wondering over the pleasantries.

'Okay, I'm off now,' Callum said, and took his plate and mug to the kitchen before leaving.

For September, it was a fine day, the skies a clear blue as Callum cycled along Herne Bay Road toward the seafront. Taking in deep breaths of fresh air into his lungs as he pedalled, extra doses, intoxicating him with renewed faith, now life had reached a turning point. No longer was he going to be stressed by the kids at school. His mum at breakfast and the pleasant manner she had spoken to Jim he hoped would last. He doubted it, but whatever happened, he was determined not to let it get to him. It was never his mum who caused the arguments. It was always Jim. Maybe, he thought, they had come to some understanding and agreed the fights were pointless. Nobody gained, and logic prevailed. Up Tankerton Road, he smiled as he passed a mum and dad with a little boy of four or five years of age laughing hysterically, flying back and forth, held between the two of them as they swung him by the arms. At the roundabout, a little further on, he circled it twice, as was his custom, before passing the ice cream parlour to his left and tennis courts reaching the seafront immediately after. He dismounted from his bike and sat on the grass verge. There, he looked out to sea. Still several hours before he had planned to meet Potts, but content to sit and watch the waves roll in over and over again in their perpetual motion carried out every day.

***

With a chirp in her voice, Rachel asked, 'Where you going today?' as she took the plates from the dining room table into the kitchen.

'Meeting Steve and a couple of the boys. Thinking we'd go for a beer at the Pearson's,' he said disinterestedly, without looking up from his newspaper, The Sun, with page three his main focus after the sports pages.

'I'll get dinner for when you get back. Shall I do that fish I bought yesterday?' Rachel sat back down at the table.

'Yeah, sure,' suspicion increased in his voice as he eyed cautiously.

'I was thinking,' Jim looked up and waited, knowing and expecting, 'I was thinking, maybe, I could buy a car.'

Jim laughed, 'I knew you were after somethin'. How you gonna buy a car? You got some money hidden away?'

A nervousness attached itself to her voice, 'I thought, maybe, you could lend me the money, and I could pay you back. I could get my old job back at the Pearson's.' By the end of the sentence, her tone had moved from nervous to begging.

'Don't I give you enough; you don't need a job,' Jim threw his paper down on the table with force, 'after everything I've done for you.'

'It would be good for me to get out and see more people.' Although Rachel did not know who those people were. There had never been many female friends, even when Michael was alive. Women from Callum's primary school she had occasionally spoken to, but there were no close friends. Kathy, her sister, she hadn't seen since her mum's funeral, the year Jim had moved in. Kathy had never been very keen on Michael, and it was clearly evident from her reaction she thought even less of Jim. The only family she had left now lived in Walton on Thames, the other side of London, two and a half hours' drive from her when traffic was good. On a few occasions, they had spoken on the phone, but Jim always complained about the cost of the bill, which then always ended in arguments. After a time, she cut back on the calls from a few to eventually none.

'You're unreal, you are – I go out and work all day, and all you have to do is cook a meal. Look at the state of the house, always needs a clean. If you wanna get out more, why don't you go and cut the grass.' Jim got up, swiped his paper from the table and brushed past Rachel; she flinched as he did so. 'I'm going out. Sort yourself out, and don't give me all this crap when I get back.

***

The smell of the blackberry pie absorbed Callum as soon as he closed the gate behind him. He walked around the back to the outbuilding, where he found Potts at the oiled-filled stove, 'Ah, Callum, perfect timing,' Potts said with a smile and placed the blackberry pie on the top of the oven, with the fruits, dark and deliciously inviting juices bubbling and breaking their way through the pastry topping. They sat down at the table at the front outside of the hut as they

54

had yesterday, and the conversation came as easy as it had yesterday. Potts had made scrambled eggs, beans and toast for lunch.

'Courtesy of Doris,' Potts said.

'I shall thank her later.'

'She will appreciate that,' Potts joked. They finished lunch, and Potts brought out the blackberry pie with a jug of custard. It tasted good, and Callum savoured every spoonful. They spoke more about Potts and how he lived. He kept himself to himself; he said, 'that's the way I like it.' Throughout the summer months, he didn't need that much. For most of the food, such as vegetables and fruits he grew, he would hunt rabbit, catch fish from the shores, and occasionally take his boat out to sea. Crabs were easily found at low tide on the beach, giving him the meat he needed. Out the back, he had created a pool with a crab farm that meant whenever he had a taste for crab, it was there to hand. Gardening jobs gave him enough money to pay the bills needed and top up his food throughout winter. He liked it that way. The tranquillity, the remoteness and the music of the leaves as they rustled with the breeze, living in the woods with no one to bother him, gave him all he had needed over the years.

'Don't you miss people?' Callum quizzed.

'No,' Potts replied without hesitation.

'But you invited me around.'

'Yeah, but it wasn't planned,' Potts said and then paused, seemingly giving his response to the question more thought. Maybe something occurred to him, and Callum wondered whether Potts was craving some company and, over time, had simply forgotten.

'So, what was that all about yesterday? Why were you not at school?' Callum felt a bit shaken by the question but felt the truth was best.

'I needed to get away from school.' Potts said nothing, and in the long silence, Callum felt an obligation to explain. 'That boy who was outside the shop, his name's Ray Blackman; he bullies everyone at school.'

'I lied yesterday. I did see him – I thought it was best not to get involved,' Potts said, lowering his head, 'I thought it was best you kids sort out your own problems. I think I was wrong.'

'Yeah, well, he seems to be sorting everybody out at the moment,' Callum explained. 'I was reading out my homework, doing a presentation in class, and he kept on making stupid remarks and kicking my chair, and I ended up getting upset. So I just couldn't face another day there.'

'Are you going back Monday?'

'Yeah, guess so.'

'Good,' Potts said with a sense of relief in his voice, 'education is the most important thing that you can get yourself. And, unfortunately, you have to learn to face up to bullies. They are everywhere in this world.'

Potts' tone was pensive, and Callum thought he might be holding something back, 'Have you ever had any similar experience?'

'I doubt there's a person alive who has not faced some kind of bullying.'

Nineteen-Thirty-four

Potts' chin jolted to the right along with the rest of his body from the impact of Briggs' glove. There were two sets of gloves stored in the gym room. It was a race to see who could get there first. One pair had lost half its padding, and the other had not. An unfair advantage inescapably gained by the one who got the ones with half the padding, and now he felt the full force of the unfair advantage planted on his cheek. Briggs was a big boy, carrying excess weight over muscle, but at fourteen years of age, that counted for a lot. The kids surrounding the school boxing ring cheered, baying in eager anticipation for blood.

During break earlier in the day an argument broke out between Potts and Briggs. It had been on the cards for a time. It was inevitable; the question of who was the toughest kid in school would have to be sorted out sooner or later. And that time had now arrived. Potts was ready to settle it there and then, and he would have if Mr Thomas had not intervened. Grabbing Briggs by the scruff of the neck and Potts by a clump of his blonde hair, Mr Thomas authoritatively spoke.

'Boys, if you are going to fight, you will do it as gentlemen, not like some riffraff slogging it out at the local boozer.' Potts disagreed with this philosophy and thought the riffraff – slogging – pub scenario would serve most of the boys better for when they left school. Which was the end of school term – and Potts couldn't wait to get out and away from school life. As soon as he could get out in the world and start earning some money, the better. He had seen the benefits school had given the older kids on the estate where he lived. The answer – None. A complete waste of time. 'Three P.M. in the gym.' It was the school's mantra; when two boys wanted to sort their differences out physically, they would do it in the school boxing ring at the end of school and not in the playground. Not good for the school's reputation, so they claimed. Contrary to the school's wishes and knowledge, most were sorted out in St David's park, away from the school, out of sight of the teachers. But the Potts and Briggs altercation flared up quickly, and Mr Thomas' eagle eye spotted them before a punch had a chance to be thrown.

Before Potts could react, Briggs laid another on him;

with three rounds at three minutes, the way this was going, Potts would not last three more seconds. Briggs was tough, the toughest kid in the school, so he claimed which was recognised by most, if not all, as fact. Potts had been in fights before at school - many. And with his natural height and strength in the boxing ring and at St David's park, he had won them all. And, he had known before each fight he would. Every fight had always been against lesser opponents. Someone smaller, weaker than him, an unfair contest and the gloves worn then were never a concern. This time it was different; he could feel Briggs' strained knuckles from his fists through the leather and thin or non-existent padding. Potts needed to escape Briggs' fists pounding at his head like a Fokker Eindecker World War One machine gun. If he could get a few seconds to regroup, Potts was confident he could get a few punches in that could turn the fight. The initial shock had worked from Briggs' full-on attack, and Potts knew or hoped he had to tire soon. That was when he would make his move. For now, he would have to take the punishment. It was nothing new; he was used to taking punches. From the age of five, he had felt the back of his father's hand's rage at home. From the age of ten, that turned into full fists; as Briggs laid the punches, he saw nothing but his father, allowing the anger to build up inside as on many occasions before the pressure valve exploded. He knew he could take it; with that in mind, he started taunting Briggs.

'Come on, Briggs, is that all you got, you fat pig?' The wide grin across Potts' face made Briggs see red. It was then he lost his cool, letting down his guard, giving Potts the opportunity he wanted to open up. A quick left jab to the nose brought the natural reflex for Briggs to close his eyes. Potts knew now was the time to take advantage. A few further left jabs, followed by a right hook, brought Briggs to the floor. Potts was about to carry on punching Briggs whilst he was on the floor, but Mr Thomas, fast as a panther, got in first to pull him away and started his count to ten as Briggs lay dazed. One, Two, Three, Four, Five, Six and Briggs dragged himself off the deck. Potts couldn't believe it; he thought he had laid him out for the count. Potts' anger increased from the audacity of it, and he flew in again, this time to finish the job. Mr Thomas blew the whistle. 'No,' Potts could not help himself from expressing his disappointment that the first round had ended and he could not finish him off.

'Gentlemanly conduct, please, Mr Potts, or you will be disqualified,' Mr Thomas scoured at Potts. A minute break between rounds, Mr Thomas checked with them both if they wanted to carry on, a pointless question as they both confirmed. Second round, no mistakes, Potts kept telling himself over and over in his head. *Kill him. Kill him.*

Potts' ears welcomed the shrill of the whistle and raced back towards Briggs, making sure he got in first this round. A mind fuelled with aggression and hate. The boy in front of him had to go down. Potts laid punch after punch; each one he landed like a skilled, experienced, professional boxer. It was the only thing he knew how to do, with gallons of hate inside him. With each punch he landed, he no longer saw Briggs in front of him but his father. The man who had bullied him all his life was now getting his comeuppance. Again Briggs went to the floor. Mr Thomas again started the count. This time Potts knew Briggs was not getting up.

The two boys showered together, with Mr Thomas standing guard in case they decided a re-match was required. Neither said a word, Briggs, the boy who always had something to say, watched the water run along the drain. Potts towelled off, dressed and sat on the bench to put his shoes on. On the opposite bench, Briggs did the same; still and reflective, the silence remained. Potts looked at Briggs; he could see his eye already swelling up. He had done that. He had won the fight against the toughest boy in the school. Potts had not thought about the aftermath; he had only thought about the fight; he had achieved what he wanted. But what had he achieved? What now? Who was there left to fight? There was no one left in the school to beat. He could pick a fight with someone he knew and beat them as he had done before, but somehow there was no longer any satisfaction in that.

'You okay?' Potts asked. Briggs, with forehead creased and an eyebrow raised, scoffed. Potts wanted to say more but failed to find words. He picked up his bag and left the changing room.

8

The first lesson of the day had gone well, nothing had been said. Geography with Mr White, but that may have been because there were only a small number of kids from the History class to remind him of last Thursday. It was an easy way to start the week. Mr White would stand and write on the acetate sheets projected onto the whiteboard behind him. Callum never timed the words per minute he could write, probably because he never had time, due to the speed he fired them out. Is that what they taught Mr White at university, speed writing, Callum wondered. An astonishing skill to write so fast yet keep each letter perfectly balanced with the one before. The writing, magically systematic, where robotic letters assiduously appeared on the whiteboard in a constant stream, all perfectly readable, but Callum still felt, despite its wonders, it was a strange method of teaching. Today, Callum was glad of the technique as it kept everybody quiet for an hour. The odd snigger he had encountered when he entered the class had disappeared with attention focused on copy and writing at speed.

An audible sigh of relief swept the classroom as the bell rang at ten-thirty to offer a welcomed respite. It was like running a marathon, not on foot, but with pen and ink. Intent on keeping a low profile during the break, he sat with his back to one of the birch trees that formed the boundary to the school field.

On the way to school that morning, he stopped at Cooke's stores and bought a magazine about battles during the Second World War. After leaving the shop, he took his usual route, doing his double take at the roundabout near the ice cream parlour on Tankerton Road, before heading directly up towards Whitstable. He parked up his bike as always, amongst a mixture of good and not so good bikes, in the rusty corrugated sheds. As he started to walk to his class, he sensed eyes upon him. All about him, fear clutched itself and stuck as all the other kids stood knowing and laughing. Every snigger, every whisper he thought to be about him. He had not been there last Friday; until now, he had been blissfully unaware of what had been said. Word spread quickly when there was news to be told. If he could walk to his classroom with eyes closed, he would. By the time he sat down at his desk he was surprised nobody had said anything. Greater news was to be had, as luck would have it; to his relief, Callum knew nobody wanted yesterday's papers. Last Friday, there was a fire in the science block and the school was evacuated for most of the afternoon. Arson, it was rumoured, but who started it, nobody knew; that was the big story. He was old news, and that suited him fine. This was big, and word had already spread around Whitstable. The thought suddenly occurred, and he worried his mum might hear and question why he had not said anything. That problem, he figured, was the better of two evils and was content to accept.

Callum did a double-take of where he had sat to ensure no ants were climbing up the tree. From his bag, he took out the magazine he had bought in the morning and fanned through it, looking for a good article. *Paris is liberated August Nineteen-Fortyfour*, General Dietrich von Choltitz defied a direct order from Hitler to burn the city to the ground and blow up its famous landmarks. Callum had never been to Paris. He had seen pictures of the famous landmarks of Paris and had a personal goal to go there one day soon after he left school. It was hard to imagine how one man's decision could change the course of history. To be forever known throughout history as the man who blew up the City of Light. It must have played on his mind the consequences of disobeying Hitler's order. The greyness that shrouded the difference between good and evil in a person intrigued him.

'Oi, pisser,' Callum looked up, shielding his eyes from the sun with his forearm, to see three silhouetted giants beaming down on him. He had been so engrossed in his magazine he had not seen Ray and his two mates coming up to him. 'What ya reading?'

'Nothing,' Callum said and got up from where he was sitting and stood face to face with Ray. A place he did not want to be. The shaking in his legs was working its way up to and through the rest of his body.

'Yes ya' are, gives us a look,' Ray snatched the magazine from Callum's grip. 'What ya' planning on joining the army? God help England if we 'ave to rely on ya' to save us. I can see it now with the English army running in the opposite direction of the battle.'

'Give me it back. It's mine,' Callum tried to say forcefully, but his voice shook, along with his body, and it came out more of a begging whimper.

'Come get it, soldier boy,' Ray teased, with Neal and Simon laughing, who stood on either side of him. Unsure what to do, Callum looked around and saw the crowd gathered, hoping for trouble. A fight, some action, anything to keep the school news factory churning over; the murmur of the crowd was intimidating. Scared to try and grab the magazine back in fear it may escalate the situation, but unsure what to say, Callum could think of nothing but repeat the exact words he had said only moments ago.

'Give me it back. It's mine.'

A laugh from the surrounding crowd tensed him further. It was hard enough dealing with Ray by himself, but to have attracted an audience made matters worse. Ray rolled the magazine up and started to use it as a truncheon, hitting

Callum with it. As he did, Callum tried to grab hold but failed. 'Come on, if you want it, you're gonna have to get it.' They started to pass it between the three of them; every time Callum went to take it, they would pass it to the other. Ray took it and held it up above his head with both hands at each end of the magazine, threatening to tear it in half.

'Give it back,' Callum pleaded. Ray started to tear it, 'No, please don't.' He wanted to punch Ray but knew he wouldn't. The magazine, between the bastard's hands, he watched as they slowly ripped it in half. Callum wanted to cry. Ray started to laugh and dance about as if he was Muhammed Ali and dived towards Callum swinging his right arm like a propeller around in the air, ready to throw it down on his target at his choosing. Callum ducked and fell to the floor from the motion that directly led to raptures of laughter from the crowd, which had doubled in size. Where they all came from, Callum could not understand, but if there was a sniff of trouble or entertainment, there was always an express service delivery to them all.

'Give it back to him, you idiot,' came a female voice. Callum opened his eyes, and from the ground, he saw Lucy Curtis between him and Ray. 'You're just a complete moron; nobody thinks you're big.'

Ray looked around him and, with a big smirk on his face, said, 'Not so sure about that, think there's a few people here who found it quite entertaining.' And then threw the two halves of the magazine at Callum's head. Callum flinched. 'Got a girl fighting your battles now, pisser. And do us a favour, never sign up to the army.' Ray spat a string of spittle to the floor that landed so close Callum felt the shrapnel shiver his forearm. 'Come on, guys, let's go.' They walked off. The crowd dispersed, knowing no further action was to be seen.

Kneeling beside him, Lucy picked up the magazine and handed it back to Callum. It was a good feeling to have Lucy next to him, yet at the same time, it made him feel uncomfortable. She was now too close to his failings, manifestly visible for her to see the pathetic creature he was, too weak to stand up for himself. He tried not to look at her in fear of revealing more. 'Don't take any notice of him. He's an idiot, and anyone who thinks otherwise is just as bad as he is.' A few yards behind Lucy stood Jane; Callum caught her eye; it was easier to look at her than Lucy. She stood waiting as if the situation was an inconvenience, interrupting the conversation they must have been having. 'Are you okay, Callum?' Lucy asked. He felt her eyes warming straight into his eyes; he looked down to the ground where the magazine, torn in half, sat sorrowfully. What respect would she have for him after that?

'Yeah, I'm fine, thanks,' he said, totally humiliated; in some ways, it would have been better if he had taken a beating. He knew from experience Ray found one person to pick on, had a fight with them, or more accurately, beat them up, and then moved on to someone else. Callum guessed his time would come at some point, and maybe it would have been better to get it over and done with and still have some self-esteem. But now he had none with Lucy coming to his rescue. The bell rang, Callum still on the floor like the defeated boxer; the end of break called.

'Come on, Lucy, we got French, and we better not be late again.' Lucy said goodbye, and Callum mumbled a goodbye in response and watched Jane and Lucy walk off together. Callum walked back, following the two of them keeping a safe distance of about ten feet, wanting, but not wanting, Lucy to turn her head and look at him again. She did not. He told himself he must put Lucy out of his mind, but how could he? Even the way she walked sent a warm, comforting feeling through him, and he could not help thinking she was the most beautiful thing on this planet.

He had to tell Potts. Uninvited, but not wanting to go straight home, he cycled to see if he was at his hut. There was still a buzz inside him, a good feeling from the conversation if you could call it that, with Lucy. He was unsure if he would tell Potts, but that was not the point. If he went home, there would be arguments between Jim and his mum, murdering the high inside him, which he wanted to hold on to for as long as he could. At Potts', he was confident he could do that.

There was no bell or knocker, so he pushed open the gate and saw the Jeep and boat in the place they had been the other day.

Potts was out the back with Marilyn and friends, collecting eggs they had laid that day. 'You're welcome anytime,' he said when Callum apologised for turning up. 'Did you want to stay for dinner? I have some dabs I caught earlier.' Tempted by the offer but knowing his mum would be making dinner for six o'clock and he needed to get back before, he declined.

'Sorry, can't tonight.'

'Another time then, perhaps,' Potts suggested.

'That'd be great,' Callum responded, excited by the offer.

'I took the boat out today, such a nice day. Maybe, I could take you out fishing one day.'

'Wow, that would be something else,' Callum said, and then was unsure if that was an offer or not, so added. 'Sorry.'

'I'll let you know when I'm next going out, and you're not at school. Officially, that is, can't have you skiving off again. And, Callum, don't apologise for being alive. You have as much right to be on this planet as the next man.'

Callum had not realised it before until Potts pointed it out, in almost every sentence he added - *'Sorry'*. Why was he apologising for everything he did? He did not dwell on it for long, excited by the thought of going out on the boat with Potts fishing. 'Count me in,' he accepted. 'Yes, please, I've never been fishing before.' It was a long time since he had been out with an adult to do something like that. Jim never took him anywhere or showed him how to do anything, the times they were together in public, which were few; Callum got the impression Jim was embarrassed to be seen with him. Callum was an inconvenience to Jim, and he made him aware of it. Not since his dad was alive had he done anything like that. With his real dad, they regularly watched speedway at Canterbury. The grit flying through the air, accompanied by the smell of methanol burning through the two-stroke engines as the bikes raced the corners, the riders leaning to one side, knees almost touching the ground, lap after lap, they circled the track, even now he could still smell and feel it. During the breaks between races, he would have a hot dog and Coca-Cola and his dad would have a cup of tea and a burger. He pictured his dad, the image as clear as yesterday, wiping the ketchup off his jacket, the inevitable result of it regularly squirting out from him overloading the sauce. Callum loved ketchup, and he guessed he got that from his dad. And each time he would now load up a burger, a sausage, or chips with oodles of ketchup, it reminded him of his dad.

After collecting the eggs, Potts poured two glasses of orange squash. There was no running water where he lived. It came from a standpipe half a mile down the path. From the twenty-gallon tanks he would fill and load onto the back of his Jeep, he then replenished the tanks back at the hut he had built to provide his own water system. Water for drinking, the shower and another tank that sat above the bath, a weekly routine giving him all he needed. Hot water boiled in pots on the stove fired up by propane gas as a substitute for the lack of supplied mains for gas or electricity. Connection with the outside world was by radio, no television.

'What do I need a television for?' Potts said when Callum asked. He would spend his nights reading and painting. Several paintings were dumped around the place, which Callum thought that Potts had a talent. The paintings were of the surrounding woodlands, with birds from the wildlife he had seen.

'You could sell these, they're brilliant; you could make

money from them,' Callum suggested.

'What do I need more money for, have enough for what I need,' he said dismissively, 'normally take them to the charity shop. I'm sure their need for money is more than mine. I need nothing. Nothing material, anyway.'

The orange squash was cooling as Callum swallowed in a gulp and was almost gone by the time they sat at the table. Potts looked hot from working hard all day. Digging up lettuces, cucumbers and potatoes stashed high by the kitchen outbuilding, he was pleased for the break.

'How was school?'

'Not so great,' Callum told of Ray and how he cowered and went to the ground when he had pretended to hit him and that it took Lucy to come in.

'There's no shame in being scared, Callum,' Potts told him reassuringly.

'Were you scared in the war?'

'Everybody was scared, and they'd be lying if they said otherwise,' he refilled Callum's empty glass with orange from the jug. 'Who's this Lucy anyway? Sounds a good girl,' Callum hesitated to answer, and Potts caught on quickly, with his face starting to visibly warm, 'Come on, Callum, tell me about this, Lucy?'

'She used to be a friend, but we have lost touch since starting secondary school.'

'But you still like her?'

Callum usually felt awkward answering such questions, but it was easier with Potts. Speaking to his mum would be just embarrassing, and with Jim, he would be ridiculed in his customary way. 'Yeah, I do. A lot, really, but there is no chance she would even look at me after today. And I heard she was going out with Ray Blackman.'

'I'm not so sure, Callum; why else would she have

stepped in like she did? I get the feeling she may like you more than you think.'

'Well, makes no difference; I'd never have the nerve to ask her out.'

'Your loss – but what I would say is don't let a bit of shyness get in your way. What's the worst that can happen? She says no. She sounds to me like the kind of girl that even if she said no, she would not make a big thing about it.'

'Yeah, but I would know. It would be just another knock-back, another rejection that I am useless.' There was a silence for a moment as those words sunk deep in for both: for Callum to express his feeling so openly and for Potts to see the boy's insecurity.

'Callum, we all worry about these things. You are no different from anybody else. There was a young chap I knew once who had a crush on a girl, and he said the same thing as you. He never asked her out. There were plenty of opportunities to ask her to a dance, but he was too shy. War started, and we all got taken in our different directions, and the girl ended marrying someone else, a GI who had come over from the States. They stayed in the same town, and when this chap came back after the war, he lived most of his life, regretting that he had not asked her to a dance. And he wondered how things could have been different every day of his life, but his shyness had left him always regretful.'

Callum listened intently as Potts spoke, 'And,' he pressed, 'what happened to them in the end?'

'The man she married, the GI chap, died quite young, but still, this chap was too timid and shy to speak to her. Then he too became ill and was taken into hospital. One day he had a visitor, the woman he had loved all his life, now in her seventies, she turned up at his hospital bed. She told him that she had always loved him and every day she had wished he had asked her to marry him before he went away to war.' Potts paused and took another drink from his orange, building the suspense. 'He died later that day, but he died a happy man. Three hours of happiness where he could have had a lifetime.'

'Oh wow,' exclaimed Callum, touched by the story. He looked up at Potts to see an enormous grin across his face. Callum realised he had just told him the tallest of yarns, 'bullshit, you're having me on.'

Potts laughed, 'Of course – but I'm sure it's true somewhere in this world. And don't make yourself the person in that story.'

'Yeah, well, I hadn't thought about marrying Lucy – I just think she's nice.'

'Well, maybe not – but don't waste opportunities that come your way, Callum. Life is too short for regrets.'

Before Callum left, Potts filled a brown paper bag with vegetables he had dug up earlier for him to take home.

'Come back again tomorrow and let me know what she says.'

'I'm not going to ask her,' Callum insisted.

He climbed on his bike and cycled down the bumpy dirt track, hearing Potts calling out, 'Ask her, you coward.' Callum laughed as he cycled away with the boost to his confidence he needed.

9

Monday night was always difficult; Rachel struggled to think of what to cook, so the fresh vegetables and potatoes were welcomed. Callum said he had met Potts, the gardener, near the telephone box on Radfall Ride and they got talking. Having more than he could use offered the extras to Callum and his mum asked no further questions. Jim arrived shortly after in a good and civil mood, to everybody's relief.

'I was going to fry up some potatoes and veg if you could carve up the rest of the meat from yesterday.' Jim took the carving knife from the wooden block holder and sliced through the rest of the meat. They sat at the table; Callum thought it strange, almost resembling a normal family.

'I picked up another job today,' said Jim.

'That's great news,' Rachel said, her first thought was he could lend her the money for the car, but she held herself back. 'Callum has made friends with the gardener who cuts Mrs Wickes' lawn. That's where the potatoes and veg came from.'

'What, the crazy man?' Jim responded.

'He's not crazy; you shouldn't say things like that,' Callum defended. In want to keep the mood calm, his mum changed the subject.

'How was school, Callum?' Rachel asked.

'Oh, you know, I had Ray Blackman picking on me again,' Callum said dismissively.

'You need to stick up for yourself,' said Jim.

'He's bigger than me. There's not a lot I can do.'

'Don't be so wet. If you're gonna act like that, don't let anybody know you live in the same house as me.' Callum was not likely to do that. The less association with Jim the better, as far as Callum was concerned. It was as expected; the happy family scenario could not last for more than several minutes; normal service resumed. Callum ate fast, shovelling double-quick-time; he wanted to get out of there as soon as possible. Every minute spent in the presence of that man made him feel sick. The thought occurred to him as he swallowed down the potatoes his mum had fried up, mouthfuls in huge quantities, almost choking. If he were to bring it all back up, he took pleasure in imagining his projectile vomit turbocharged in Jim's direction. Relief finally came with his plate clean; he left the table.

'I'm going out on my bike,' Callum said, directed at his mum, whose anger was still focused on Jim.

'Leave the boy alone,' she said. Callum rose from the table as the two of them continued, oblivious to his exit.

'What, what did I say?' Jim said, bemused by what he had said wrong.

'For God's sake, you should hear yourself sometimes.'

'I'm just saying the boy needs to grow some balls.' Callum picked up his shoes from the cupboard in the hall. The door to the living room he had closed behind him did not silence the arguing from the dining room, still audible and alive.

'You've got something wrong with you,' his mum's voice grew louder.

'Just you watch your fucking mouth,' Jim roared back. Callum shivered at the triggered voice. He knew the signs. He needed to get out of the house as every word screamed made him want to shrink inside himself further.

'I'm going for a ride on my bike,' he called, knowing his words were lost. The fuse already lit. Another night the same as the last. One night without an argument erupting would be a record. They fired each other up. Callum knew his mum was tired of it, and it was her way of letting off steam, but it stoked Jim into a more aggressive and feared mood. He wished he was not such a coward and could protect his mum. The opportunity had come today to stick up for himself, but it was too late to change it, and all he could think of was he simply needed to get out of the house. It had been a rollercoaster day. There was no plan for where to go; he thought about Potts but did not want to trouble him with all his problems. Instead, he headed for the slopes on the seafront at Tankerton.

The dinner plates dropped into the drawer with a crash. How they didn't break she didn't know and, with the same thought, didn't care much either. Wiping the carving knife dry with the tea towel, she stabbed it back into its recessed slot in the wooden block on the window ledge. 'You only make things worse by your pathetic remarks all the time,' she spoke tersely and glared at Jim.

'Oh well, whatever, it's not my problem if he's a wimp. The problem is from you keep fussing him all the time,' Jim responded, uninterested and dismissive, gripping his half empty pint glass of beer. 'Anyway, I don't wanna talk about it anymore, so just leave it. That's it, subject closed.'

'But that's the point, not everybody's as insensitive as you. Some of us have feelings.'

'What d'ya say? Who'd ya think you are?' Jim stood up; his voice raised to a neighbour-hearing decibel level. He knocked back the last swig of his beer. Eyes wide, popping and wild, the switch flicked and screamed, 'Bitch.' And relieving the sudden anger inside, launched his glass at Rachel. She ducked, the glass smashed on the wall behind her. 'Clean it up, you fuckin' bitch and don't start again. I'm not in the mood.

I'm going out for a drink.'

Rachel got the dustpan and brush from the under-sink cupboard, knelt down and started to clear up the shattered glass. The front door slammed closed, she curled up on the floor, shaking with tears flowing down over her broken life.

***

The rolling slopes of Tankerton, the grass bank overlooking the beach huts offering an array of vibrant colours and the sea sung out below, Callum breathed in the sea air and sat with his back against the cannons with his bike to the side of him. The large black cannons hinted at the defensive history Whitstable played in the past. The Maunsell Seaforts, visible alien structures in the sea, looked out to provide protection during the Second World War. Callum tried to imagine what it must have been like in those days. He thought of Potts and the things he must have gone through. Anything in comparison would seem trivial to him. The problems he had were nothing in comparison, he told himself. But it was hard to accept anybody's could be greater than his own, and with no solution forthcoming, it made him angry. It was his last year at school, exams to be taken next June, and then he could find a job. Unemployment was on the rise, but he would take anything. And, with a job, he could leave home. Get a small room somewhere. Anywhere would do. Then he would be free. Able to escape from the hell hole that suffocated him. But then there was his mum. Sometimes he felt having him around was the only thing that kept her sane. How could he desert his mum, leaving her trapped alone with Jim? He feared for her. Thousands, if not millions, of times, he had played the various scenarios around in his head. Each time he came back with the same answer. There were none.

Any job he got would not pay enough to look after his mum. Trapped in the house, paid for by his dad's life insurance policy but now partly owned by Jim through marriage. At times he blamed his mum; he tried not to but struggled to understand what she saw in the man. It must have been hard, he recognised. How different it would have been if his dad had been alive. It never made sense how his dad died. At the age of nine, it was hard to know someone, but he knew his dad was sensible and careful. His mum had told him he did not drink excessively and definitely not when driving. The car was only six months old, and no faults were found with the brakes or steering that would have caused him to have lost control of the car the way he did. It felt to Callum unfair that he had been deprived of knowing his dad and losing him at such a young age.

The evening offered a generously cool temperature issuing relief from the sun's heat from earlier in the day. On Tankerton slopes, Callum straddled the cannon and watched couples walk by holding hands in their perfect worlds. The sun dropped out of the sky and fell behind the end of the sea, giving a red hue. A picture of beauty contrasted the horrors of Callum's world. A father attempted to fly a kite with his son whilst the mum looked on, failing due to the calm evening, much to his son's disappointment. A young couple came into view and sat further down the slope from him. He recognised the boy, an ex-pupil from his school, a couple of years older. The newspaper wrapping the boy held he unfolded and shared the fish and chips contained inside. Both spiked-haired, rebelling or fashion-led, Callum did not know but could see they were clearly in love. Even from that distance, he could see the glint in her eyes as she looked at the boy with a radiant smile emanating happiness far removed from Callum's world. It made him think of Lucy. It made him sad. It made him think of Potts telling him to ask her out. It made him think he was not good enough for her. Never would he experience such a thing, he had convinced himself.

With a deep breath filling his lungs with the salty sea air, he looked out onto The Street. An aisle that became visible at low tide made it possible for people to walk out onto with the sea parted at either side. Matchstick figures strolled the half-mile stretch of pebbly sand to the end. In his story mode, Potts told him of a man who fell in love with a mermaid in the sea. He built up the ground day by day to reach her, adding more shingle and sand, raising the ground up to where the mermaid swam. Eventually, once he had built the path long enough, he walked the entire length to talk to her at the end. Nothing should get in your way if you want something badly enough in life, Potts had said. A car drove past with windows open and radio on full blast, where Bowie screamed out we had *Five Years left to Cry In*, which smashed the calm and obliterated the beauty around Callum and reminded him he needed to head home.

***

It was silent when he entered the house in contrast to the calm he had experienced at the seafront. Instead, an eerie stillness fogged the room. No television or music. The kitchen had been tidied, all plates and glasses washed and stored away, but no sign of his mum or Jim. He went back through to the hall and climbed the stairs with ears perked, listening for a clue to the whereabouts of everybody. It was too early for them to have gone to bed. 'Mum,' he called, 'are you there?' Still, there came no response; just silence captured the house. At the top of the stairs, he put his ear to his mum's and Jim's bedroom door. 'Mum,' he whispered. He heard a movement from within but no reply. There was someone in there, he was sure, so he edged the door open. Sitting on the bed with her back to Callum, she didn't turn. 'Mum, why didn't you answer?'

'I didn't hear you.' Confused, Callum knew she must have heard. She slowly turned to face him.

Callum gasped, 'Mum, my God, what happened?' Moving over to his mum, he sat beside her on the bed and put his arm around her. Against her nose, she held a tissue, red with the blood that had soaked through it. Her left eye, swollen and black.

'Jim hit me,' she said, 'he went to the pub and came back half hour later screaming and shouting. Calling me trash and accusing me of spending all his money. We argued, and then he started hitting me.' She started to cry before she finished her sentence. 'And then stormed off out again.'

'Oh, mum, we have to get out of here.'

'If only we could,' she said, defeated as a prisoner on death row, 'we have no money and nowhere to go.'

'I was thinking when I finish school we could rent somewhere.' She smiled sympathetically, and Callum knew as he had spoken the words, they held no strength but hoped they could have provided some comfort. But they did not, and he knew there was no point in pretending.

'It will be all right, Callum. He goes like this and then calms down. He always apologises, realising he was wrong.' Callum removed his arm from around her in the horror of her acceptance of the situation.

'Mum, it's not okay; we have to leave and get out of here. Away from him, we can't live like this. Can't you sell the house?'

'It's not just mine, Callum, Jim owns half, and he wouldn't agree. It's okay; we'll be fine,' she tried to reassure him. 'You go and have a bath and get an early night.' Callum didn't want to leave her but could think of nothing else to say that would help or change the situation. 'And not a word to Jim when he gets back. It will only make things worse.' Callum left her room feeling helpless. There was nothing he could do even if he wanted to; if he confronted him, Jim would probably end up hitting him. But one thing remained true. He knew his mum was wrong about it. It will not be all right.

Jim didn't return home that night, and Rachel, in some ways, was relieved. There was still an overhanging feeling, a sense of guilt that somehow it had been her fault. The more she thought about it, the more she heard what he accused her of - Wanting a car, Wanting the house decorated, Wanting a holiday, All of it, Want, Want, Want. No wonder he lost his temper; he was the one earning the money, out working all day. She hadn't worked since Jim moved in. With her eyes closed, trying to sleep but failing, she lay there alone, convinced it was her fault. And, now by herself, she touched the empty pillow next to her where Jim would have been. If only she had not been so stupid. Tomorrow, she would make it up to him and put things right.

10

Breakfast the following morning, Jim had not returned. Rachel made light of the previous night, telling Callum that it was nothing to worry about and that she had overreacted.

'I shouldn't have got you involved. When people are together, they sometimes have arguments.'

'Mum,' Callum pleaded, in fear for his mum.

'It's okay, just Jim overreacted this time.'

'But it's not the first time, is it, mum?'

Rachel, after some thought, replied, 'It's okay. There's nothing to worry about.'

The bruising around the eye was still visible, but hidden with her best attempts using her makeup to conceal it. The short black skirt and pink low-cut blouse she was wearing would have been more in fitting at a nightclub. It was obvious to Callum his mum wanted Jim back, but on his way to school, he wished he never saw him again.

***

Three desks from the front of the class by the window provided the perfect view of the field outside. It was difficult to concentrate on the lesson, with his mind wandering off every few minutes, thinking about his mum. Maths was straightforward. A lesson revising what they had done last year, which Callum received an A star grade for, so drifting out of the lecture would not do any harm. Mr Bell, dressed in his green jacket and flower power shirt, looked five years behind the times. In this school, that made him one of the most vogue of teachers, and he liked to tell everybody too. Often he would divert off into topics on music, great bands like Steely Dan and Jefferson Airplane and the like.

'Sir, those bands are dead and buried,' the kids would argue back. 'You should be listening to The Jam or The Pistols,' they would say.

'Nowhere near as good,' he would argue. Callum had not been big on music and didn't follow who was making the charts. Most of the music played in his house was from the fifties, Elvis and Eddie Cochran, dictated by Jim's choice. He didn't know what his mum liked. She would have the radio on when Jim was not around but owned no records of her own.

'Have you heard of The Clash, sir?' Callum had been watching a man walk his dog on the field adjacent to the school past the cedar trees. The soft voice that accompanied the question brought his attention back to the class. It was Lucy's.

'No, never heard of them,' Mr Bell replied.

'Great band, sir, you should listen to them; move you into the twentieth century,'

'What are they? One of these punk bands that scream out the words you can't even hear what they're saying.'

'They are punk, sir,' Callum listened intently at how Lucy spoke eloquently with enthusiasm and passion, 'the words are poetry. They have something to say, something about society and the injustices between the rich and the poor. They're protest songs. That's what art is for to make a difference. Not just a load of love songs about the boy getting the girl.'

'Maybe, Lucy, but I think we need to get back to our Maths lesson,' Mr Bell said, realising that he had spent half the lesson talking music. Callum looked back out the window.

The man with the dog had gone.

'For homework,' Callum's attention returned to the classroom to make a note of the homework. 'Please answer all the questions on pages twenty and twenty-five for the next lesson.' At the end of the lesson, Callum, not keeping with his usual routine, was one of the first to the door. He needed some fresh air but suddenly feared he had left too early, so he looked back to the classroom where half the class were still at their desks, packing their books into bags. As he surveyed the room, his eyes met Lucy's, who was still at her desk writing but had looked up just at that time. She smiled at him, throwing him off-kilter; he didn't know where to look and couldn't understand what was meant by it. Last term, whenever he saw Lucy, she looked the other way. It was like she was trying to avoid any contact with him. Yet, now in the space of a few days, they had come into contact again. Quickly he turned away, embarrassed to retain eye contact, and ran down the corridor to the exit.

On the school field, he found a more secluded place further up from where he had been yesterday. Hidden away, as his mind circulated the thought that maybe he could hide away for the rest of the school year. Maybe he could hide for the rest of his life. He had a great view from where he sat and watched the other kids filter out.

One group of boys formed two sets of football teams, and a game started with twenty players per side. In his previous school, he would have been with them, but now, he had got used to being on his own. Some girls played netball, and others snuggled up in small friendship groups. The rest were the smokers who hovered, mostly hidden, by the boundary line of the cedar trees. Puffs of smoke would appear from behind the trees like smoke signals from clandestine meeting points. The secret smokers featured as low priority on the teachers' crime list; investigating something they already knew the culprits for was not required. If you wanted to smoke, you smoked; inconspicuously was the only unwritten rule. The usual hum of the school playground was turned on.

Alert systems moved to medium. Ray, Neal and Simon followed the puff of smoke from behind one of the cedar trees. Callum shrunk in himself so as not to be seen. Alert system returned to normal as they walked off in the other direction. In their path was Richard Knightley. Was he to be their victim today? Another lamb to the slaughter; what was it with them that they got from bullying and terrifying the other kids? Richard Knightley was one of the smallest boys in the year; if people did not know him, they would have thought he was in one of the lower years. Possibly two years below. A friendly, harmless, wouldn't hurt a fly type of boy, willing to help anyone who needed it. Callum wanted to help him but knew that the direction of fun would be turned towards him if he said anything. Guilt again tormented him. He kept his eyes focused on them, ensuring they didn't change their direction and headed back his way. Then it began; Neal started running and executed a grab and run with Richard's bag. Before Richard knew what had happened, Neal was twenty yards away. Richard gave chase. Callum could not help but see the humorous side of the smallest boy in the school, five-foot tops chasing one of the tallest and strongest boys.

'Run, Neal, he's after you,' a shout bellowed from Simon, both he and Ray in fits of laughter at what they were witnessing. Callum felt an extra pang of guilt, realising he was no better than them, joining them in their sick humour because he was not the one on the receiving end this time. Neal approached the main building, helicopter propelled his arms, and let Richard's bag fly up on top of the single-story block. The bag landed in full view, and a cheer went up from the majority of onlookers, like a valiantly displayed flag or a symbol of their ignorance.

'Hi, Callum, you all right?' It made him jump. He had been so focused on the Neal and Richard incident he had not seen Lucy coming towards him. There was no Jane, just Lucy, standing there.

'Yeah, I'm fine,' he said after a long pause, confused and forgetting how to use words.

'Can I sit down?' Lucy didn't wait for a reply, and Callum never gave one. She was so confident he wished he could bottle some of it from her and use it himself. So beautiful, sitting there next to him; he wanted to kiss her. 'Did you understand the homework?'

'What homework?' Dumb answer, he realised as soon as the words left his mouth. Maths, of course, they had just had maths, so he went to correct and redeem himself, and both in sync said. '*Maths.*'

'Yeah, I think so. I haven't looked at it, really, but it's what we did last year.'

'I don't understand. I can never understand old ding dong.' Mr Bell's pet name – he got off lightly, comparing it to what the rest of the teachers got called. 'Is there any chance you could help me with it?'

'Yeah, of course, sure', he said eagerly and panicked that he had sounded too eager, and Lucy gave out one of those smiles that made him want to melt.

'Great, did you want to come round my house Thursday and we can go through it?' It was getting better by the minute. Not only was she asking to spend time with him, but she had now invited him to her house. Callum's mind was spinning around like a fairground Waltzer, totally out of control. A lightning bolt struck home; that was why she had been so nice to him recently. She needed his help. It was nothing to do with her liking him. It was simply down to her needing her maths homework done. How stupid could he have been to have had such a thought? 'What do you think?' She prompted, and Callum realised he had forgotten to answer her question. Whatever the reason she wanted him to go around her house, he figured he would take it.

'Sure, what time?'

'Say about seven. You remember where I live, don't you? I would have had dinner by then if that's okay?' He remembered where she lived. He felt foolish, but he had played and replayed the time at her house in his mind over and over. The kiss, what he would do for a game of Ludo now.

'Yeah, that's great.'

'Brilliant, see you at seven then.' She got up and walked off. He watched her walk away gracefully, sexy; her blonde hair floated in the wind like a hair shampoo advert.

***

He couldn't contain his excitement when he met up with Potts. 'I got a date with Lucy,' Callum said, beaming from ear to ear as he balanced like a tightrope artist on the breakwaters wooden strut where Potts was fishing. Line cast, nothing biting.

'You asked her out, good lad,' Potts said, looking out to sea, with the legs of his khaki army trousers rolled up and waves splashing against his bare legs, hung invitingly above the water level as he sat on one of the supporting posts of the breakwater. The sea was lively, and at every fifth wave, it jumped higher, spraying his upper half.

'Not exactly,' Callum confessed. Intrigued, Potts turned his focus to Callum and looked him in the eye for a moment before reverting back to the sea's horizon. 'She asked me if I could help her with her homework. So I won't see you Thursday.' Potts smiled to himself. He was not aware there was an arrangement for them to see each other every day but, strangely enough, was happy and drew comfort with the idea. There was a chill from the sea's spray as it hit, but Callum's words sent warmth through him, providing a refreshing welcome.

'That's okay, you go and enjoy yourself, but I wanna know all the details when I next see you,' Potts said.

'Friday, I could come around then,' Callum said, enforcing their new friendship.

'Friday is good,' Potts replied. Over the last few days, Potts had got used to seeing Callum and, to his surprise, had looked forward to it. It had been a long time since he had had company, and on the occasions, it had happened, he had rejected it. With Callum, it felt different; he enjoyed their chats and giving his advice when the boy asked. For what it was worth, he had never been great at providing advice, and there were probably good reasons for it. Few people would ask him for it, and he probably wasn't qualified to give any, the mess his life had been, he considered for a moment. And rather than giving, he could do with some himself.

'What you fishing for?' Callum asked.

'Dinner,' Potts stated the obvious.

'What have you caught?' Callum probed, knowing the answer, smiling at the empty bucket at Potts' side.

'Nothing,' Potts said, defensive of his fishing skills. 'Now, don't change the subject. This Lucy sounds to me as if she likes you more than you think.'

'Nah, she just wants me for my mind,' Callum had perched down next to Potts.

'Well, that's a shame, but probably just as well from what I've seen,' Potts replied, and they both laughed. As they laughed together, there was a big tug on Potts' line. A healthy sea bass, he reeled in and dropped in the bucket. The smile on Potts' face expressed happiness and relief. 'Did you want to join me for dinner?'

'Can do, mum and Jim are going out tonight, so I've gotta get my own dinner, perfect timing.' Twenty minutes later and another bass bit, the dinner menu was ready. Potts drove them back to the hut with Callum's bike in the back of the Jeep.

It took Potts minutes to scale, gut and fillet the fish. An expert skill perfected from a weekly exercise over many years. His chef skills were equal to the job, and with a cold breeze in the air they decided to sit indoors. It was the first time Callum spent any time inside his hut. It was divided into two rooms. The living area and a bedroom were separated by a tapestry of tartan picnic blankets sewn together hung over a wooden beam that spanned the width of the hut. It was clean but untidy. Bookcases lined the wall, floor to ceiling, apart from where the two windows let beams of light in and viewed the front garden area. The bookcases were of different designs; some purchased from what Callum thought were probably second-hand or charity shops, and others hand-built. They had a unique carpentry design with uneven shelving and various types of wood. There was a mix of books, fiction and non-fiction.   Hemingway and Orwell appeared to be the most popular. Directly behind where Potts sat, the shelf was stacked high, full of historical war books.

'Did you fight in the war?' Callum asked.

'I was there, yeah, North Africa.'

'Field Marshal Montgomery, eighth army?' Callum had read all about Monty's desert rats. The changing point of the war, without General Montgomery and his battles with Rommel, Britain would have lost. That was what fascinated Callum about history: how everything could change from one event or the action of a single person. Lives changed forever, a bit like his own.

'Yeah, never met him, but that's the guy.'

Callum continued to speak with enthusiasm about the individual battles that took place.

'What did you do in the war?'

'Infantry.'

'Wow!' Callum could not comprehend the suffering,

the hardship and the danger of it all. 'That must have been tough?'

'Must 'av 'er,' Potts repeated Callum's words and mulled them over as he continued chewing on the meat of the fish. 'You don't know how right you are. It was tough for everyone.' Those words put Potts in a daze, maybe from a memory of something he had wanted to forget, and for a short time, he was no longer in the conversation but somewhere far away.

'Did they teach you how to fight? I mean, like, hand to hand combat and boxing, that sort of thing.'

'I learnt to fight at a young age. I was brought up in London. Everybody learnt how to fight. And boxing, yeah, we used to box at school.' He replied with dry enthusiasm.

'I can't imagine what it would 'ave been like to be there.'

'Best that way,' Potts responded. It was now Callum's turn to venture off into some reverie of war, battles and conflict.

'Would you teach me how to box?' Potts' eyes looked to the open door at Callum's side and beyond and breathed in deep as if in pain before answering.

'No,' Potts' voice was slightly raised as if Callum's question had angered him; after a few seconds, he continued, 'best you read books. You'll learn more that way than from being able to lay a man out with your fists.' Callum did not follow it up. He knew Potts was right in part. Books will teach him more about the world than learning how to fight. But he liked the thought of being able to lay a man out with his fists. Nobody would push him around if he had the strength and skill to fight; then, he would walk with confidence. From his plate, he skewered the final piece of fish onto his fork and put it in his mouth. His eyes were drawn to the spine of a book resting horizontally on top of the others, *Monty - Field*

Marshall Bernard Law Montgomery. And the thought came to him; nobody changed the world without knowing how to fight. And no books were ever written about men who did nothing.

11

At the Marine Hotel Rachel and Jim had a couple of drinks outside looking out to sea waiting to be called to their table. The temperature had dropped, and the air had a definite chill. Rachel regretted her decision only to wear a cardigan. In his leather jacket, Jim wrapped his arm around her to keep her warm. It was good to go out, and after Jim's apology, the hope of change filled her heart. It was just after three o'clock; he returned home from work and said he was sorry. He had booked a table for them to go and eat tonight. With guilt written over Jim's face from the actions of the previous night, pain and regret clearly stabbing away at him, it made it impossible for Rachel not to forgive. Rachel knew people made mistakes. Rachel knew she had made enough herself. There was no point in continuing the argument, creating an atmosphere when he had tried so hard to make it up to her with the gesture of a meal out. She struggled to remember the last time they had eaten out. It felt odd, but it was good to clear the air. Watching the sea brought a calming effect, its waves rolling on the shore, the sound absorbing and forgiving; they needed tonight, a break from being locked up in the house. She knew it was hard for Jim to find work with unemployment at its highest for many years, but he was bringing in the money and supporting the family. Last night and throughout today, she reflected, realising it did no good to push continually for more.

When he arrived home, Milk Tray chocolates in hand, sorry eyed, 'Because the lady loves,' he said and handed the box to her. His voice choked with how sorry he was and begging forgiveness for the mistake he had made. Then when he said he had booked the table, her body filled with excitement, and the previous night's events were brushed aside. Washed and changed, Jim drove them down to the seafront and parked in Marine Parade opposite the hotel.

Table ready, the waiter called them, and they followed him into the restaurant. The majority of diners wore suits and ties. She had on the skirt and blouse she had been wearing throughout the day. They were the best clothes she had. Smart and acceptable, but with Jim in jeans and his leather jacket, Rachel felt awkward, as if everybody was looking at them. Suddenly, she remembered that it was not what they were wearing that caused such interest and lowered her face to the floor, having forgotten her black eye. She tried to conceal it as best she could with makeup, but it was still clearly visible. And to Rachel, it felt like the whole restaurant was looking, burning their eyes into her, opinionated and knowing what had gone on behind closed doors. She tried to shrug it off. Were they all so perfect? Probably not, but she could not get rid of the inferior feeling telling her she was not welcome there. They were seated in the corner by a window which looked out to the front. Waves continued to roll in against the shore in their never ending cycle. The table was private; it pleased her, relaxing her from the thought the rest of the restaurant's guests were talking about them.

Scanning the menu, 'D'ya wanna have starters as well?' He was really pushing the boat out. The guilt must be so intense. Rachel stretched her arm across the table, and with her hand, she touched his to reassure him she had forgiven him.

Having not been out to a restaurant for a good few years she was going to make the most of it, but at the same time, nerves tingled about spending too much money and ruining the evening. It was too tempting, and she conceded to her greed.

'Yeah, I'd love a prawn cocktail,' she said and smiled at

him.

'I'll have the oysters.' The Whitstable Oysters that he always raved about when they first met. 'You know what they do to me,' he said, a cheeky grin spread across his face for inference to their aphrodisiac qualities.

'I hope so,' she replied, still her hand on his as she played her finger, smiling back in acceptance.

Rachel remembered the days Jim came into the Pearson's Arms when she worked there and regularly ordered a plate of oysters. She smiled to herself – life was so simple, with her problems behind and the future to look forward to.

Service was good, with the starters arriving not long after placing their order. A young girl served them, who smiled pleasantly and commented that the prawn cocktail was her favourite too as she served; memories came flooding back to Rachel of what it was like to be normal and socialise with other people. 'Thanks, Jim, this is so good,' she said, savouring the taste of the Marie Rose sauce that Rachel had created many times at home from her Fanny Cradock cookbook, but it tasted so much better when someone else had prepared it.

'It's good, init,' Jim said, as he popped his last oyster into his mouth, 'maybe we should do this more often.' Rachel's ears and heart perked up at those words.

'You're right; we really should spend more time together.' She stretched out her leg and rubbed it up against his, "Just the two of us.' He smiled back at her in agreement. They ordered more drinks, a glass of the Portuguese Mateus Rosé wine (large) for Rachel and a pint of bitter (Watneys Special Brew) for Jim.

'Well, looks like work's picking up, so money shouldn't be a problem.' Further work had come in today on a new housing development in Herne Bay, only a few miles from home. 'It's a big job; they're building over two-hundred new homes on this estate.' Jim looked relaxed and pleased about the statement, pleased with himself that he would have a regular source of income, able to provide comfortably for them. 'Should last six months or possibly more.'

'Really, that's fantastic news.' Money was the cause of all evil or something like that, Rachel recalled. Where did that come from, and where had she heard it? At the back of her mind, she connected it with a lesson many years ago at school relating to the bible. Evil recently, she tried to think of it with those words, had entered their house when they had no money, but somehow that made no sense. However hard she tried, she could not, for the life of her, think why it came to her now as she was trying to enjoy her meal. And then it hit her. When she and Michael had money, EVIL came to visit them and took him away from her. She remembered back to before the accident and how good things were when Michael was around.

'What's the matter? Why you got that great big grin on your face?' Rachel hadn't realised in her reverie thinking of Michael a smile had spread across her face.

'Oh, I'm just happy to be here.' She picked up her glass of Mateus Rosé wine, 'Cheers,' she replied, chinking glasses, clicking herself out of it. Main meal arrived, Steak and Chips, rare for Jim and Chicken Kiev with garlic oozing out of its crisp bread-crumbed coat.

'Listen, I was thinking about what you said.'

'About what?'

'The car, about getting you a car.' She hadn't wanted to bring it up. She had accepted it was selfish of her and had tried to put it out of her mind, 'maybe in a few months, we could think about it. You're right; it would be good for you to get out more.' The evening was turning out better than could be expected. Wild garlic sauce melted in her mouth as she looked out the window, the waves slept, and the sun waved goodbye as it slowly dropped out of view.

'It's old Jimmy Thorne? It is, Jimmy. Shit, I don't believe it, 'avent seen you in years,' slurred the man, who made Jim's leather jacket and jeans look like he was a millionaire. 'Don't you remember me, Harry, it's Harry...' he slurred, swaying on his feet man waited for Jim to remind him of his own name.

It took Jim some time to make the connection to who the drunken man was, maybe in part from the distraction of trying to work out what he had ordered in the restaurant from the various fresh food stains down his grubby t-shirt that looked like he had been living in it for a week. 'Harry White, yeah, Christ, it's been a few years.'

'Yeah, good old days. Mind – Probably saved me a lot of money,' he continued to slur and looked at Rachel. 'Luckiest bastard ever when it came to cards.' He swayed back as he adjusted and focused hard, concentrating on Rachel, 'Sorry, you two having a romantic evening,' he joked.

'This is my wife, Rachel,' Jim introduced, 'this is Harry White, used to work with him. And, play cards a lot.' Harry White stopped dead still as if paralysed, immediately followed by recognition as he stared at Rachel.

'You're kidding me, right,' Harry said. 'Rachel McNab, is this Mickey McNab's wife?' Rachel looked confused and horrified to hear Michael's surname. 'You always said you were gonna bang this one, can't believe you did it, but never bet against Jimmy Thorne.' Harry White burst into manic laughter as he finished the sentence.

'Yeah, thanks, Harry,' Jim said, looking awkward, something Rachel had never seen of him before, 'think you've had one too many, mate.' Jim told Harry they had planned a quiet evening together and after repeating himself several times, he eventually took the hint. Jim watched Harry walk away until out of view. 'Sorry 'bout that, the guy's pissed as a skunk left in charge of a brewery.' Rachel sensed Jim's anger at the intrusion.

'That's okay,' Rachel let out a nervous laugh, and with

her hand, she brushed her hair that fell across her face, 'don't worry, he was well gone, wasn't he,' she said, dismissing it as nothing important.

***

Callum didn't want to make it obvious he had been at home in his bedroom trying on three different shirts before deciding he looked best in the blue one with the big white collar. It was just maths homework, not a date. By telling himself that repeatedly, he believed it would make him less nervous. It hadn't worked. Earlier in the day, Lucy had checked he was still coming over in the evening, which removed the fear it was true and not something he had started to believe he had dreamt up. Not only had he checked himself in the mirror fifteen times (who was he kidding) it was fifteen before losing count, then double checked he had his maths book and then headed out. It was six-fifty when he arrived and hung about on the corner for ten minutes until his Timex watch clocked seven. Being too early would have shown him to be too keen, and she could get suspicious and think he read into it something more than she meant and send him packing.

Lucy's house was by Whitstable station, just off Old Bridge Road. Although the house was smaller than Callum's and semi-detached, it was a nice area. The approach and house were just as he remembered it. Same red door, paint a little more peeled, and the same green Ford Escort that now showed patches of rust with age. He pushed his bike past the car and at the top end of the drive saw it had dripped oil, which was now stained into the concrete. One more deep breath. Keep calm. Try to relax. He pressed the doorbell. The chimes blasted with fury which made his heart race. Twenty seconds later Lucy opened the door wearing blue jeans and a white t-shirt with a picture of a band with the words, The CLASH, in bold red writing across it. Pig-tailed hair at the sides made her look cuter than ever. Callum was not sure if his mouth had dropped jawed or not, but he made a conscious effort to ensure it was now closed.

'Hi, Callum, great you made it,' she said and opened the door wider, standing to one side to proffer the entrance of the hall for Callum, 'come in.' They went through to the kitchen, where Lucy offered coffee and biscuits which Callum turned down saying he was fine. 'Come and say hello to my dad,' she said. Callum followed her out of the kitchen, cup of coffee in her right hand, and then into the front room, where her dad was watching television in a wheelchair.

Callum was taken aback before managing to regain his manners, 'Hello, Mr Curtis,' he hoped he was not staring from the shock.

'Hello, Callum, how are you? We haven't seen you in a long time,' Callum was surprised he remembered him, but pleased. 'Look how you've grown.'

'I'm good, thank you, Mr Curtis,' Callum replied, unsure if he should ask after his wellbeing, so he decided not to. When they left the room, Callum asked Lucy, 'What happened to your dad? Why's he in a wheelchair?'

'I thought you knew; it must have been shortly after you were here last time. Seems to me as if it were forever.' She said un-fazed, 'It was an accident at work years back; a crate fell on him, paralysing his legs. He's okay, but makes it easier if someone's around, so I look after him most evenings whilst mum's at work, and she looks after him during the day.' A deep feeling of pain struck Callum remembering how Lucy spoke about her dad and how he was so good at sports. At one point, he was close to making the national swimming team. 'It was probably shortly after your dad's accident,' Lucy added.

'Right,' thought Callum, which was probably why he didn't know. He had shut himself off from the world for a time and guessed Lucy may have done similar, 'guess you had it pretty tough too.'

'Well, it wasn't easy, but not as bad as you.' They went upstairs without saying anymore and entered Lucy's bedroom. Posters of the Sex Pistols, The Clash, The Ramones and The Cure plastered her bedroom wall. On top of a chest of drawers, a portable black and white television was on quietly, and the opening credits and theme tune played Top Of The Pops starting as they entered. 'Shall we watch this before we start?'

'Yeah, great,' Callum said as if he watched it every week. Rarely did Callum get to watch Top of the Pops, as Jim's dictated the viewing in their house when he was in, so he jumped at the chance. And, to watch it with Lucy made it even better.

Lucy turned the volume up. They sat on the floor with their backs rested against Lucy's bed. For every artist or band that came on, Lucy had her opinion and something to say about them. David Soul – *Boring*, Brotherhood of Man – *What the hell*, The Boomtown Rats – *That's a bit more like it*, and Elvis Costello – *This guy gets it*. Callum was unsure what the guy got, but he liked the music and was happy to agree with her.

'What about The Clash?' Callum asked after the program finished remembering Lucy's enthusiasm for them in class.

'Nothing in the charts at the moment. But they're gonna be big. Bigger than the Pistols, wait and see.'

'Does Ray like them?' Callum didn't know where the question came from, maybe he had started to relax, or his worry about what Ray might say if he found out festered in the back of his mind.

'What?' Lucy sounded shocked and surprised. Callum was dumbstruck; he didn't know what to say to redeem the situation. Maybe it was time to pick up his bag and leave. He had been on autopilot. He was always so careful usually, but the words had just slipped out without prior censorship. Everything had been going so well. 'What did you mean about

Ray? Why ask about him?'

He had to reply but was unsure what the best response would be, so he just spoke the only words that came to mind, 'Well, aren't you going out with him?'

'No,' she said and looked upset or maybe even annoyed, and Callum regretted asking the stupid question.

'Sorry, I didn't mean to upset you. I just heard you were…'

'He's an arsehole, yeah I did for a week. Biggest mistake of my life. Not sure why I agreed in the first place.' Watching Top Of The Pops with Lucy, the chatting and laughter they had shared that had been so great; now turned to an awkward silence.

'What happened?' Callum said to fill the void.

'He came around here, saw my dad and started referring to him as the cripple,' Lucy looked as if she was about to cry. Callum wanted to put his arm around her to comfort her, as he had with his mum, but didn't feel confident enough and worried it would only worsen the situation.

'Sorry, I shouldn't have asked.'

'Nah, it's not your fault – I told him to piss off after that. Stupid idiot, I am. Still, we're all allowed to make mistakes,' she looked at Callum for confirmation, 'aren't we?'

'It's okay. I think he's an arsehole as well,' they laughed, 'along with the rest of the school.'

'Thanks, Callum, for being normal and not judging me,' Callum, confused by Lucy's words thinking he was the one who was constantly being judged. 'Don't wanna be boring, but shall we do some maths?'

'Sure,' Callum agreed, and they spent the rest of the night working through the maths homework.

12

The door to the hut was open, but nobody was home. It was the same with the outbuildings.

'Potts,' Callum called out but heard no response. Marilyn, running loose, came to greet him with Sophia not far behind, but she kept her distance still a little unsure of Callum. He bent down and stroked the back of Marilyn's neck; affectionately she pushed her head into his hand, wanting more, 'Hello Marilyn, How are you? Do ya' know where Potts is?' Marilyn provided no help. He walked past the chicken coop, which was open, with Doris and Lizzie showing no interest in venturing out but sitting happily in their slumber. Callum knew Potts must be near or he would not have left the coop open. Trees grew denser as he went past the outbuildings and the vegetable patches; much easier to lose someone there. There was no sound but the woods. No vehicles, television or music, just the trees creaking as their branches touched each other in the soft breeze and birds called out. A hundred yards further, he crossed a stream that ran through Potts' plot of land. The stream provided irrigation to the crops and the tracks that Potts had neatly dug trickled with water down to the vegetation. At that part of the stream, it was shallow and narrowed enough to jump, which Callum did. He looked around and still saw no sign of anybody; again, he called out, only this time louder than before with hands bellowed around his mouth. The birds stopped their song to listen to interruption before, to Callum's relief, he heard Potts shout back.

'Over here.' He looked around to where the call had

come from but could not see Potts. 'Up here,' he realised he was looking at ground level, but Potts' voice had come from higher. Looking twenty yards forward and twenty yards up, he saw Potts swinging from the branch of a silver birch with a rope looped around his waist and slung between the branch and trunk. A bow saw in his right hand cutting the final strands of bark that were suspending the branch in mid-air; Potts yelled with joy, 'Timber.' Callum watched it hit the ground with a rustling sound, cushioned by a pile of other branches previously cut, which broke its fall.

Potts descended from the tree with surprising speed and ease for a man who walked stooped and slow. 'Morning Callum, how are you?' Even his voice seemed energised, 'Do you wanna give us a hand cutting these up?' Callum happily agreed. Saturday morning was spent cutting through the branches Potts had sawn down before he had arrived. Autumn was coming, and with winter on its heels, Potts would start clearing several trees at the rear of his plot for firewood. The area was too dense to bring the Jeep out so they loaded the foot-long logs they'd cut into a hand cart that, when fully loaded, needed the two of them to drag over the uneven ground. They laid two planks of wood across the stream, lined the wheels up with precision and slowly guided the cart across and then along the final stretch to the bunker where they unloaded the stock. By the time they had finished loading and unloading the cart Callum's arms, back and legs were aching as they had never done before. He was unsure why his legs would hurt as they did. There was the matter that he did little sport and spent the rest of his time sitting in his bedroom studying, so he figured this was an influential factor. He took a strange pleasure from the pain of his aching muscles, realising how he had enjoyed being outside in the fresh air and sharing time with someone else. The sun shone, and although the heat it omitted was not as intense as the previous days, it did not stop them both from sweating buckets.

They stopped for a drink by the bunker and had a long

glass of lemonade; Callum needed only a couple of large gulps before it was gone. They formed a small chain, with Callum passing the logs from the cart to Potts, who piled them into the bunker the size of a small shed. It was a slow process, and Callum was glad for the rest each time Potts rearranged them to make room and neatly stacked the logs on top of each other.

'How was Thursday?' Potts asked as Callum passed him another batch of logs.

'Thursday,' Callum replied, with a knowing smirk on his face, pretending he did not know what Potts was referencing.

'Come on; you know exactly what I'm talking about. How did it go at Lucy's?'

'She's a quick learner, so I'm sure she'll do well in her maths exam?'

'Callum!'

'Okay, it was a good night. We watched some TV, talked a bit about music, school, all that sort of stuff.'

'And what about that kid, Ray? Did you ask her about him?'

'Yep, she's no longer going out with him, it only lasted a few days and she realised she'd made a mistake.'

'Good news, so you asked her out?'

'No, it wasn't like that.'

'I'm telling you, Callum, she's interested in you and remember what I told you about my friend who didn't ask the girl and ended up with only a few hours happiness instead of a lifetime.'

'Yeah, and he wasn't real.'

'Not the point,' Potts nodded and eyed the heavily loaded cart, 'and pass those logs. You're slacking, boy.' Which was true; Callum had gone into a beautiful world thinking about Lucy.

By the time they finished, it was half-past-one.

'Hungry?' Potts asked. Callum was starving; he had not worked so hard physically for as long as he could remember and concluded - Never. They sat on a couple of tree trunks that Potts had cut and carved into seats. The seats were ornate and Callum saw Potts' artistic element in them, something he must have taken care of over a period of time. There were four of them circling a fire pit which Potts set alight.

'Four seats,' Callum said quizzically and intrigued, 'thought you said you didn't have much company.'

'Always be prepared,' Potts said with a grin, 'you're not the only man who can take an interest in the ladies.'

'Oh yeah, anybody in mind?'

'Not at the moment. I'm taking a rest.'

'So when was the last time you had a lady visit?'

Potts thought for a time, calculations working in his head, looking up to the skies for help, before responding, 'Nineteen-fifty-six.' Callum laughed, 'Yeah, and it was after that I made these seats. Always kept them cleaned up 'cause you never know, and you, my friend, are the first to use them.' The flame had eased on the fire pit, so Potts threw a couple of sausages and two steaks on the metal grill resting above the fire that caused it to burst back into life before settling down for the meat to cook.

'Will you tell me more about your days in the army?' Callum asked Potts as he cut the sausage that Potts had dished out with jacket potatoes and beans, all cooked on the fire pit.

'I don't like to talk about it, Callum. The army was not what I thought it would be. It ain't like in the films; bullets and guns are real. They kill people.' Callum said nothing. A part of him was slightly disappointed and thought it had shown on his face as Potts continued after a tortured silence. 'When I was your age, I thought I wanted to join the army, but I had nothing else to offer. Or the world had nothing to offer me, or so I thought. But you are different, Callum. You're intelligent, and you live in a different time. It may not seem it but there are plenty of opportunities out there for you.'

'Nearly two million unemployed, a nuclear war could kick off any day. I don't see it like you. I have my stepdad, who I hate and hates me, my mum, a prisoner in her own home, and I'm a shivering cowardly wreck. No future, as The Pistols say. I ain't so convinced as you.' Callum was impressed by his own conviction and ability to express his opinion. Normally never wanting to be controversial and always accepting what people would say, he wondered if it was Lucy's influence.

'I think you'll find the song finishes with, 'We're the future,' Callum looked at Potts, amazed he even knew the band and the lyrics as well, which astounded him, considering he had not listened to any of these bands until after his evening with Lucy. 'What!' Potts chuffed, 'I may not have a TV, but I've got a radio and can read a newspaper.' He cut another piece of meat off his steak and chewed on it thoughtfully. 'Things change, Callum. Life is not static.'

Callum hoped he was right but saw no way out of his problems. Even if he did get a job, he remained as much a prisoner as his mum. 'What do you think of a man that hits a woman?'

'What makes you ask that question? Nothing to do with Lucy and that little git Ray, I hope.'

'No, just something I read, just wondered what you thought.'

'Any man who hits a woman is a coward, scum, lowest of the low.'

'If you knew a man who hit a woman, what would you do then?'

'That's why I live here, Callum, away from people. I

like it like that. Nobody bothers me, and I don't bother other folk.'

Nineteen-Thirty-Nine

A couple of days off training came as a welcome break for many of the lads. Potts leant against the bar and took a cigarette from his packet of Players, sparking it up and adding more fog to the already smoke-filled bar. Only ever known as Woody, Christopher Woods ordered two pints of ale to replenish their now empty pint jugs.

'Thanks, beautiful.' He winked at Mags, the barmaid of The George public house who passed the two pints to Woody. On nights off from training and when they had the money, Woody and Potts spent most of their time there and became good friends with Mags.

Woody liked to think he was in with a chance with Mags, but Potts knew he was delusional as Mags only had one man in her life who was serving with the British Army on the France-Belgium border, sent out the day war was declared. But Mags liked to tease Woody, and he knew the limits and if not Potts would give him a slap round the head to bring him in line. Potts had met Woody when he had joined the infantry training at Aldershot after serving in the T.A. Both were fit young men but army training put them through their paces.

After leaving school at fourteen Potts had done manual work, carrying goods and freight from riverboats to the warehouses on the Thames near his home in Putney or collecting glasses in the local pub, The Bricklayers Arms. As soon as he reached sixteen, he joined the T.A's as a way out, an opportunity to get away from his father, who never had any time for him. And away from his mother, who had provided other services to the men at The Bricklayers Arms public house. It was a new life in Aldershot. A life which he welcomed, and his friendship with Woody had given it something extra he had never experienced. Brothers in arms, true friendship – To care and look out for someone for the first time gave him a purpose to live.

Woody came from a small village called Roborough in Cornwall and had only joined up when parliament introduced National Service on the 3rd September at the declaration of war. The timing could not have been more inopportune, one month before he had had a trial for Plymouth Argyle football club. A week later, news arrived he had passed and the club wanted him. He signed a contract as a professional footballer. The proudest day of his life. A dream from a small boy was now dashed.

The two of them had hit it off on the first day they met. London and Aldershot were the only places Potts had known and he was fascinated by the stories Woody spoke of his home village with such affection. Potts learnt how the RAF fighter planes had a runway nearby and when they took off, you could almost jump up and grab hold of them. In contrast to that was the tranquil countryside and coastline where Woody and his family would spend time by the sea in the summer months. His mum, his dad and his sister Mary, it all sounded perfect and idyllic - the complete opposite of his own upbringing. Potts had never seen the sea and didn't know how to swim. Woody promised that he would take him down to the beach in the summer and teach him to swim. And watch him play football once the damned war was over. Potts knew Woody wanted it to end, and the sooner, the better. Woody had something to go back to.

For Potts it was different. He didn't know what he would do after the war; he didn't want to go back to his life in London. Potts had found a new family in the army and one he enjoyed. At times, he would think back to his school days in London. The pointless fights he had got into at school. The boxing fight with Briggs. It was that fight he continually replayed in his mind. After defeating Briggs, he had not got into any other fights. Boxing in the army – yes, but no fights to prove he was the toughest, the hardest. He never felt the need after that; the need for that recognition had faded and held no importance. Another strange thing happened after that; his father never hit him again. He never worked it out, the reason, whether it was that he stood taller and looked more confident or just a timely coincidence.

'Cheers, mate,' Potts shouted as he struggled to hear Woody over the increased noise as more squaddies filled the pub. A cold October air entered the pub as a group of new recruits made their way into the pub. The doors opened and sucked the smoke out of the smog filled room and then closed again, replacing it with the odour of nicotine that infested the wallpaper and ceiling.

The group of four made their way to the end of the bar and ordered their beers from Mags who by now was rushed off her feet. As she turned her back on them to get their drinks, Potts saw the three of them joking and eyeing her up, with the fourth making lewd actions by thrusting his hips in Mags' direction. It was not unusual, it was part of army life, but it saddened Potts to witness it.

'Come on, Woody, let's grab that table by the fire'. The two of them went and sat at a small round oak table that had become available, and Potts quizzed Woody further to learn more about Cornwall. The pub thinned out which Potts was happy about for they could now talk without the need to shout. The main noise now came from the four young squaddies who had entered earlier and were getting louder with each drink consumed.

'What you going to do, Potts?' Woody asked. 'When all this is over, I mean.'

'Don't know. Haven't given it much thought, unlike you. You have a clear vision with your football and all that. Me, maybe I'll stay in the army, work me way up, maybe 'come a Sarge or something.'

'Best of luck with that one, mate. Soon as I can get out of here, I am. Don't like the idea of killing someone.' Potts looked at Woody; the concern on his face gave Potts the distinct impression that it was not some random statement. It was something he had been thinking about, and it had occurred to

Potts that it was something he had not. War was not killing another man. It was about defeating the enemy, and he had not given much thought that the enemy was made up of men like him and Woody.

'I guess that's just the shit we'll have to deal with,' Potts said, trying to dismiss the thought from his head.

'Yeah, well, as I say. The sooner that shit is over the better and we can all return to normal life. Playing football, teasing my sister, helping my mum and dad, that's all I want.' As Woody continued Potts' attention was drawn to the four squaddies larking about jumping on each other and calling out across the bar to Mags.

'Any other services you offer, luv?' The tall one called out; Potts, using his own six-foot-two height as a measure, estimated the loud one to be another two inches on him.

'Enough, lads,' Mags said sternly. She had a way with the boys who came in the pub; she had learned from experience how to control them, 'Behave yourselves or you'll be out.' The rebuff had a dampening effect, but Potts convinced that was not the end of their fun, decided to keep an eye on them. The group moved away from the bar, angry that Mags had not responded to their games as they had hoped; they rested their beers on the mantelpiece near where Potts and Woody sat.

The door opened and the cold night air took a firmer grip. One of the group, which Potts had his eye on, the one with the acne babyface, must have felt the cold bite as well as he took the poker and stoked the fire, enraging the flames to bring a welcomed heat to the room. Babyface made eye contact with Potts and gave him an acknowledging nod.

With the pub at its quietest since they had arrived, Mags came out from behind the bar, collected the empty glasses from the tables around the pub and lined them up along the counter where Jack, the landlord, collected them and took them to the back of the pub for cleaning. Mags approached a table full of empty glasses. Stacking one inside another, with both hands full, the squaddies started again.

'Come on, luv, don't you wanna do a service for your country,' the tall one was back on it, with full force, 'us brave soldiers going off to save you.'

'I've told you, boys, enough is enough.' Mags turned to walk away when the tall one slapped her bum. She turned immediately, 'I warned you, now get out of here and don't come back.' The tall one grabbed hold of her and pushed her against the wall; she dropped the glasses as he forced his lips onto hers. She managed to break free and slapped him around the face. Both Potts and Woody stood up from the table. The tall one punched Mags in the face; she fell back but did not go down.

'Get out now,' she demanded.

'Whose gonna make us?'

'You heard the lady; time to leave, guys,' Potts said, drawing the attention of all four of them towards him. Potts had already decided he would take the tall one out first, hoping to deter the others from more trouble. That was his plan. To get nearer to the tall one, Potts moved past Woody and now had his back to the fire, facing the bar. The bar was empty; he thought maybe he could stall any trouble until Jack returned from the kitchen out the back of the pub. But there was no sign of Jack when the tall one grabbed an empty bottle from the table, smashed it, and pointed the jagged edges toward Potts' face.

'I asked you a question, whose gonna ...' before the tall one finished the sentence Potts struck him hard around the head with the poker he had taken fast from the coal bucket. The tall one went down with blood leaking from his head. Potts was relieved to see him still moving as he lay on the floor and not dead. The other three stared open-mouthed.

'Go on, get your friend outta here, and don't come back.' Mags said. They watched the three help the tall one to his feet and cradled him out of the pub. 'Thanks, guys,' Mags smiled, 'for that, I think, you two deserve a drink on the house.' They accepted gratefully.

Potts and Woody drank the beers on the house offered

by Mags by way of thanks. They said little. Woody had never seen such aggression. Potts was just pleased he had not killed his first man.

13

Outside the van choked into life on the second attempt, Rachel lay in bed listening to him drive off to work for an early start to the new job he had spoken about with enthusiasm. As she lay on the bed, his love still warm leaked out onto her inner thigh. There had always been something special about that part of their relationship. For every fight, there was the making up with added animal passion. She smiled, rolled onto her side, and snuggled up, deep into his pillow, opening her senses to draw in his scent. When it was good, it was good. It made up for those moments he lost control. Nobody was perfect; she knew that, and he had told her so himself. But now, it made it worthwhile through those times of wariness, holding her thoughts; maybe we all have to walk on eggshells at times, knowing things can always change.

***

Potts crouched down and petted Sophia for providing her first egg in three days. 'Good girl,' he said. She clucked in response. The red comb on her neck springy as he ran his fingers over it. He planned to have bacon for lunch and was jubilant to now be able to add a fried egg to it.

Sophia went quiet, enjoying the attention as Potts continued to stroke her. Early morning brought the dew to the ground, dampening the sound of the woods around him. The odd whisper of trees and the birds taking turns to call out. Then, the bird song fell silent, replaced by a crackling in the woods, the sound of an intruder in its natural world blasting a twelve-bore shotgun signalling the opening of the season for the pheasants to hide or run. An inherent decision they would make without thought. Another shot fired, sparking recognition and fear in Potts. The muscles in his hand contracted tight and crushed the shell of the egg; the translucent orange liquid ran down his gripped hand, clinging on until dribbling to the floor. Sophia moved away, sensing death around.

***

Callum could not remember when he last felt so good. Spending time with Potts out in the fresh air and helping him work on many jobs on his plot of land had given him a new interest. When he woke, his first thoughts were of excitement in greeting the day instead of dread.

He didn't see Lucy on Monday but was in the same lesson for history on Tuesday. During the lesson, she thanked him for helping her last Thursday and asked if he wanted to come around again this week to do more. It was great to know it was not a one-off, and he couldn't help but think about it all week. He had been left alone at school and had not seen Ray and his gang, which was always a blessing. But the strangest of it all was Jim had been friendly to him. Callum knew there were degrees of friendly with Jim; not shouting at him or ridiculing him was the level of it, and he was happy to accept that.

His mum seemed happier; at times, even laughter between her and Jim visited their house. Callum still spent most of his time in his bedroom when he was not at Potts', and whilst sitting at his desk or lying on his bed a few times he heard them laughing downstairs. The sound reminded him of new lovers, young and innocent getting to know each other. He did not believe it to be true. When he heard them the first time, the unusual and rare sound frightened him. He hoped the situation remained but doubted it to be possible.

They had gone through periods before when they had kissed and made up, and over time, each day, the façade slid away. A layer followed by another stripped away the mask revealing the monster beneath. Tensions would then return, his mum timid and scared, Callum's anxiety heightened, and Jim a tinderbox ready to explode.

***

Thursday and Mr Bell should have marked the test Callum had helped Lucy revise. Nerves were greater for Lucy's mark than his own. If she did well, it would be an endorsement of his help, but if there was no improvement? The thought occurred to him that if her score was no better than normal, she might give up, and there would be no need for him and, worse, no more evenings around her house.

Break finished and there was the regular pandemonium in the corridor. Pupils rushed in all directions pushing and shoving each other as they went. When Callum arrived there was the usual hum of the other kids chatting. Some sat on desks waiting for the class to begin. It was unusual for Callum to be one of the last to enter the classroom. He was nearly always the first and would be waiting by the door when Mr Bell arrived. There was little else for him to do, but today his mind had been wandering. Scanning the classroom, he spotted Lucy. The seat next to her was empty. The opportune moment to sit next to her and see her results, but hesitation played the strings. Panic gripped; what if she told him he couldn't sit there? The embarrassment would be too much to take. Especially with the class now near to full. As he moved towards the desk nearer to the rear, he was convinced she looked up at him with a smile; he was unsure how to interpret. Was she asking him to go and sit next to her? Instead, he continued in the opposite direction to the other side of the class and sat at a diagonal to her. As he settled down, Mr Bell moved to close the door, and Jane came running in and went to join Lucy. He felt relief in making the right decision. Jane and Lucy always sat together. What was he thinking?

A double period of maths; in the first half, they worked through trigonometry. Callum had already worked through the book twice before and found it easy. He could not believe they were still struggling to understand the basics and the questions raised in class by some pupils.

'Okay, class,' said Mr Bell. Everybody went quiet. They all knew what was coming as he picked up the answer papers from his desk. There was a worry painted on faces and Callum looked over at Lucy. She was biting her lip but Callum saw a glint in her eye expressing optimism. With her right hand, she drummed her fingers on her other. It surprised Callum that he was usually the one who was drumming his fingers or with his foot rapidly beating out a rhythm on the floor, but today he was still. A rare calm and confidence struck without any conscious effort. The fact alone, he thought made him nervous. But most of that nervousness was for Lucy, not for him. Not the constant thoughts of what people were thinking about him and the fear of him doing something wrong or upsetting someone.

Conversations with Potts had naturally flowed, and he had asked him questions that he would never have dared ask anyone else. They were perfectly ordinary questions that people asked daily, but for Callum, it took courage. *'What did you do in the war?', 'Have you ever been in a fight?'* and somehow boosted his confidence now in the school classroom.

'I have your test result,' Mr Bell said while he walked to the back of the class and started handing out the test papers with their results. That meant Lucy, near the front, would be one of the last to receive hers. Callum tried not to look towards her but failed to evade his eyes. Her eyes were now closed, praying, he guessed.

'Well done, Callum,' Mr Bell said, whom Callum had not seen approach, placed his test paper on his desk in front of him. Ninety-one out of a hundred, an A grade again. As expected, his test results had consistently come in around the ninety mark, give or take five. He ran a quick check over his paper where he had dropped marks and then looked up to see Mr Bell, one row of desks behind Lucy.

He placed the paper face down on Lucy's desk. For a few seconds, she left it there, not wanting to turn it over. Slowly she eased it over to reveal the result, like unwrapping a present and hoping it was what she wanted. With the paper turned, she studied it, her face hard to read. Slowly an ear to ear smile crept across her; she whacked Jane on the arm in excitement and showed her the result. Jane looked shocked; Callum lip read the 'Well done, you lucky cow.'

Lucy twisted in her chair, tracked down Callum sat on the other side of the classroom, and mouthed the words. 'Thank you.' A shiver shot through him and then a rush of joy absorbed him. She turned back and continued to talk to Jane where they exchanged papers and reviewed each question.

At the end of the lesson, the crash of chairs accompanied voices of joy and disappointment as they shared the results. Callum, in no rush, with nowhere to go, packed his books into his bag from his chair and was putting his coat on when he saw Lucy coming towards him with Jane watching and waiting by the door.

'Callum, you'll never guess what I got.' He didn't guess but knew she was pleased by her face. 'Sixty-five. That is the best I have ever had,' she said and then seemed to lean towards him, and for a mad fantasy of a moment, he thought she was going to kiss him - but she didn't. 'Thank you so much. It made so much sense after going through it with you.'

'That's great, Lucy. I'm really pleased for you.'

'Amazing, absolutely brilliant. Are you still okay for tonight?'

'Yeah, of course.'

'Good, 'coz I'm not letting you go now.' And then she was gone with those words ringing musically in his ears.

***

Bacon sizzled on the gas burner in the kitchen outbuilding. Potts tonged it from the pan onto the homemade bread, buttered and roughly cut. The ketchup, he fork spread across the bacon and kissed the second slice of bread on top. Leaving the kitchen, he looked left and right cautiously before taking his mug of tea from the counter and sitting down on the chair at the table outside.

For a minute, he listened and enjoyed the natural sounds around him before picking up his mug to take a sip of tea. An uncontrolled spasm attacked his hand, and the shaking made it impossible to hold the tea in one hand, so, in support, he raised his left to steady himself. Still, the tea spilt down his shirt. Replacing the cup onto the table next to the bacon sandwich, he saw a fly crawling on it. A second fly joined, and they sat on top of the sandwich, feasting. Potts' eyes opened wide, focused intently on those flies, memories tormenting again.

Nineteen-Forty-Two

Three flies landed on Potts' spoon as he lifted the bully beef to his lips. Incessant flies, damn well never giving up; after two years in the North African desert, Potts knew you had to hold the tin close to your mouth and quickly scoop the beef. The barren wilderness was wearing him down. Word was that they were getting the edge on the Jerries', but he had heard it before. He had been there before. New soldiers brought in like on a conveyor belt to strengthen the lines to replace the dead and injured. Somehow, he and Woody had escaped injury or worse. He did not know how. This inveterate war would never end until they were all dead, Potts was convinced. The only true goodness that had come out of any of this was his friendship with Woody. From the beginning to now, they remained friends and the bond between them strengthened every day. Potts had never had a true friend. At school and for his brief period at work before joining the army, he had not mixed with others. Until now, he had been a loner. There were the kids he hung out with on the estates where he had lived, but that was for causing mischief in some form. Never was there any one person he classed a true friend. Potts and Woody had changed since their first meeting at Salamanca Barracks in Aldershot a couple of years back. They had seen things that no man should. With the horrors, death and mutilation all around, Potts had learnt to appreciate life, although as a trained soldier, he would do his duty; all he wanted now was for it to end and for them to go home. Woody never wanted to be there in the first place but had proved himself a strong, brave and competent soldier, yet each day, he still dreamt and talked about playing football again, walking out in front of a cheering crowd. Perhaps it was that vision that kept Woody sane. The belief, one day, things would return to normal. For Potts, if that day was ever to come, there was no dream. The question always remained what he would do with his life after all this was over.

Potts looked out to the vast, empty space ahead. Nothing but desert with the odd spray of camel thorn and tamarisk bushes was to be seen. A dune blocked any further view a thousand yards to the south, but Potts guessed it was much the same. They had taken the position from the Italians yesterday. There was little resistance from them; with the British having superior weapons and outnumbering forces, the job was made easy. Potts began to believe it was true about the rumours circulating the camp; the Italians were losing the will to fight.

Potts and Woody had dug trenches around the perimeter of the area they had taken. Their job was to control the area whilst the bulk of the platoon was due to take the region to the south held again by a dilapidated Italian army.

'Candy from a baby,' some of the men had joked. When those two areas were secured, the enemy mines could be disabled, and the force of the Eighth Army tanks could file through to smash Rommel to oblivion.

Early morning Potts watched the men leave heading toward the southern region. He silently prayed and wished them good luck. Sun rose in the desert sky and the temperature adjusted itself from the freezing cold of the night to the blistering heat of the day.

In the distance, the sound of guns fired where the British advanced. It was impossible to tell how it was going, but there was growing confidence in the men since Monty had taken charge. Men whistled, sang and chatted; hope had been rekindled as they secured the area.

Through his field glasses, Potts looked to the south for any signs of victory. There was nothing as he had known would be the case. He turned to his right and looked northwest with the crazy idea of seeing England through his binoculars. England was not in his sights; instead, he saw a large number of Panzer tanks and armoured vehicles heading in their direction.

'Jerries,' he yelled out to the men in the trenches below. From the relaxed whistling and singing, the men immediately adopted readily alert positions. Grabbing sandbags, they quickly threw them up to increase the height of the defensive wall and lined the Bren guns waiting for the Jerries to attack. A strike from the front and their defences could hold, but Potts knew it would be the end for them if they got around the back.

The small number of soldiers left to secure the position was now to be tested to its limits. Surprise was their crucial weapon, hoping the Germans believed Axis forces still held the position. They calculated they were outnumbered by at least two, maybe even three to one, as the German tanks drew closer. Four Panzer tanks, ten armoured vehicles loaded with Spandau guns ready to release hell's fury upon them. German troops within range, the British held their fire nervously, resting their fingers on the triggers. Four hundred yards, Potts felt his heart pounding, he had been here before, but it made no difference. They waited for the order to be given to open fire. Then the approaching enemy stopped in their tracks.

'Get ready, men. I think they know we're here.' Sergeant Cripps called out. 'Harves, what you got?' He called to Stephen Harvey, eyeing them through his Enfield's 3.5x telescopic sight.

'Serge, I got the Obergruppenführer as if he's standing next to me, and the bastard looks like he's smilin' back.'

'Get ready to fire, gents; let's take them out before they have a chance.' Outnumbered as in Tobruk, where they were ripped apart and escaped with their lives only by luck. How much more luck had he got left? 'Fire,' Sergeant Cripps gave the order. Two six-pounder anti-tank guns fired missing their target by a country mile. 'Sort that range out,' screamed Sergeant Cripps. Two snipers fired, doing damage as the Germans panicked from the initial surprise. But within minutes return fire was coming back heavy.

In the newly dug out trench, Potts and Woody gave each other a familiar look. Next to Woody, Private Peter Cullen, frozen to the spot, looked out to the enemy before curling up in a ball, crying. Woody grabbed him by the scruff of the neck shouting for him to pull himself together. Potts looked on; the boy's uniform still fresh and unbleached from the tortures of the desert sun; the new boy at school, who got his first kicking and sudden realities of truth behind the glamour and honour of war sank in. Bullets and shells fired overhead, getting nearer each time. Woody left the boy crying in a ball and began to fire back through the gaps in the sandbags they had piled up a few moments earlier. One shell hit to the right of them, the screams of dying men haunted as it ripped the bunker and men to shreds. Behind them, the six-pounders anti-tank gun launched its shell, hitting one Panzer. The hatch opened and two men started to crawl out. Potts aimed and fired, killing the first one. Out the hatch followed the second whom Woody took out. The others did not appear, assumed to be burnt alive inside.

The heavy sounds of shells exploding around shook his body violently. Two more tanks advanced with their tracks crunching the bones of dead soldiers ahead of them. Spandau's fired twenty-five rounds per second, taking out three more British troops. They were running desperately low on ammo and men. Again, machine gunfire came in from all directions. There was a scream from behind. Jack Hawkins, operating the anti-tank gun, had been shot through the head. Without someone on the anti-tank gun, they had no chance. Potts was the closest, but he would have to climb out of the bunker and run a hundred yards to the gun. He would make himself an open target. There was no choice; without further thought, he climbed up and headed towards the gun. As he started running, he could feel the bullets dancing around him. Any minute, any second now, one of those was going to have his name on it, but he kept on running. There was no turning back; every step he took sank him into the deep sand, reducing any speed he ever gained. He finally made it to the gun. Two men lay there dead. He looked and paused momentarily in shock at the blood and brains splattered across the gun. A shell from the German attack landed nearby, reminding Potts if he did not get back into action, he would be joining them. There were about twenty shells in boxes to his side. He loaded a shell, fired and missed. Again, another miss.

Ahead he saw the attacking force start to split. Two tanks manoeuvred to the right. They were planning to get to the rear, where the British defences were non-existent. Woody joined Potts, knowing it would be impossible to move the gun alone. The two of them changed the angle and aimed at the tank, moving to their rear. After two further shots, they got a direct hit, they wanted to celebrate, but the job was not done. Heavy fire was coming in from the other two tanks. Fire was burning all around where vehicles had been hit. They repositioned the gun towards the front where the bulk of the enemy was attacking. Woody loaded another shell and screamed, 'Fire.'

But Potts did not fire. He stood staring down below where he and Woody had been moments earlier. Private Peter Cullen stood up in the bunker with his hands in the air, tears streaming down his face, his head above the sandbags, fixed to the spot. Target practice for the Germans. Potts watched as a bullet entered his forehead and exited out the back. Peter Cullen fell to the ground - dead.

'Potts, fire the damn gun,' Woody screamed. Again, he fired, another hit. By now, they were almost out of ammo, but relief came with perfect timing from their rear when the lead Platoon of the Company, dispatched earlier, was sighted coming back. Within thirty minutes, the Germans had retreated. Peace had resumed.

Potts sat with his back against the armoured protection plate. Private Peter Cullen, probably not reached his nineteenth birthday, dead. It was not the first time Potts had seen men give up, through fear so intense, something telling them they'd be better off dead. It made no sense. For Potts, he would always fight to the death. Is that not what life was about? He asked himself, but failed to answer.

From the inside of his breast pocket, he pulled out a packet of Players and took a cigarette. He struck a match and went to hold the flame to it, but his hand started to shake, making it impossible to light his cigarette. He tried to steady his right hand with his left, but both went into an uncontrollable spasm. He threw the match to the floor and looked to the sky, wondering what had become of him.

14

It wasn't new; Callum had seen it all before. Kiss and make up routine. When will his mum learn it will not last? He hoped he was wrong, but too many times he had seen it played out before his eyes. *Leave the bastard*, repeated itself over and over in his head as they sat at the dining room table, eating bangers and mash in the happy family façade. His fork stabbed the sausage; its juices bubbled through the pierced skin. Again he stabbed, this time with more aggression, imaging it to be Jim.

In search of more pleasant thoughts, he brought Lucy into his mind eye. After dinner, he planned to cycle to her house where they would continue working through the homework set by Mr Bell.

'I can give you a lift to Lucy's if you want?' Jim offered.

Callum wanted to throw up; he may be able to convince his mum that he had changed, but it would not work with him. He wanted to say as much but instead simply said, 'No, it's fine, I'll cycle.'

He left his plate by the sink in the kitchen; his mum said she would wash up; grateful he didn't have to stay any longer than needed, he left the house.

Rachel took the plates to the kitchen and started to clear up. Jim stayed at the table with a pint glass of lager that had just under half left.

'Thanks for offering to take Callum,' Rachel called out as she scraped the remains of Callum's mashed potato into the bin.

'I thought it was a good idea.'

'You know, I was thinking it was times like that when you're not around, it would be good for me to have a car.' There was silence.

***

At Lucy's, Callum said hello to her dad. Lucy got her coffee from the kitchen as they had last week, but this time, unlike last week, Callum had one also. They went upstairs to watch Top Of The Pops. They talked about all the bands and rated them as they had done last week. On the bed was a copy of Melody Maker and NME that Lucy bought every week.

'I really want to go to one of these gigs in Canterbury, and there are a few in Margate, but mum and dad say I can't go unless I have someone to go with,' Lucy said, pointing Callum to the page inside that listed the gig guide.

Bands and venues with dates, Callum wondered if that was his cue, his opportunity, the moment he had been waiting for to ask her out. Worry and insecurities took hold, assisted by fear of her laughing at him and the probable rejection.

'How about Jane? Doesn't she want to go with you?' He regretted his weakness and lack of confidence. *Damn you. You idiot,* the voice screamed in his head. They could have gone together. It didn't have to be as boyfriend and girlfriend. As they were now friends, helping each other out, there was nothing to be embarrassed about. Everybody had friends except Callum; he chose to remind himself. Why could he not think quicker? Every time the need arose, his brain would freeze. Quick at maths, history and science, but when it came to thinking on the spot when talking to someone, especially Lucy, he was bottom of the class.

Had she told anyone he came around on Thursday

nights, he wondered? Other than her parents, someone like Jane. Had she told Jane? Or was he a secret, which was why they didn't speak much at school? Maybe she was embarrassed to be seen with him. But Callum tried to dismiss the thought. Lucy was perfect in every way; she wouldn't do that, he told himself, not entirely convinced.

'Nah, she's not really into music, prefers her horses, she goes horse riding every weekend, and she has no money left after that.' Callum grunted. 'Here, take these if you want.' Lucy handed him the two magazines. 'They're last week's, but they got some good articles in there.'

'Thanks.' Callum took the magazines and put them in his bag, wanting to say more, but again failed and ended with, 'I'll have a read of them later.' The music conversation ended so they moved on to maths. A subject Callum was comfortable with and could talk about for hours. Problem was - nobody wanted to listen.

'Where does your mum work?' Callum asked after about half an hour of maths revision when he thought Lucy looked a little bored. It was the last thing he wanted to do; what good would he be to her if that happened? And that would mean no more Thursday nights watching Top Of The Pops together. It was the best night of the week, and from the second he left her house last Thursday, he had been waiting for the following Thursday to come around.

'Oh, she cleans offices down near the High Street.'

'Okay,' Callum gave it some thought, 'so who uses the car?'

'That's mine, for when I'm seventeen. Mum doesn't drive. She was going to learn but never did, and as time went by, they decided to keep it for me.' There was a look of excitement on her face. And, Callum had to agree, it was pretty exciting to have your own car. 'Cool ah? Maybe I'll take you for a drive when I've passed my test; what d'ya think?' He didn't have to think; he was up for that. Images flashed manically of the two of them driving over to Margate. A night out at Dreamland, the amusement park, sitting side by side on the rollercoaster. Lucy screaming from fear and Callum holding her hand comforting her, telling her it'll be all right. He laughed out loud. The thought was crazy; she didn't mean it; it was just one of those things people say, and secondly, she would be the one holding his hand, trying to comfort him. 'Why d'ya laugh?'

'No reason, just think the idea's cool,' Callum replied and felt blood rushing to his head, embarrassed by his amorous thoughts.

'Me too,' she agreed. He was pleased she didn't question him further into why and how his mind had run off in a million fantasies. 'You know you said you liked The Clash.'

'Yeah, they sounded great.'

'Well, I made you a present. I hope that's okay.' Beneath the poster of The Clash was her dressing table. She opened the drawer and started to search for something. 'For helping me with my maths homework, I recorded an album of theirs on this cassette.' She handed the homemade cassette to Callum.

'Thanks,' he said, 'that's really cool. You didn't have to, ya' know.'

'No, it was a real help.' She spoke about the songs on the tape, 'have a listen and tell me what your favourite song is, and then I'll tell you mine.'

'I'll listen to it when I get home.' They spoke more about music, school, and the kids and teachers at school.

'What do you do at the weekend?' Callum was surprised by the question. Although they had spoken a lot and the conversation had flowed effortlessly, it had been on more general things, nothing personal; this was a direct question about him to him.

'You'll think it a bit weird,' he said, regretting the intrigue roused and the fear she would be disappointed or simply plain weird.

'This sounds interesting; come on, tell me more?' She crossed her legs, swivelled around and looked straight at him, making Callum very nervous.

'Well, I have this friend who lives in the woods that I go and visit.'

'What you mean like, he lives in a tree or something?'

'No, of course not,' Callum laughed at the thought and the impression he had given, 'nothing like that, he's got his own bit of land and a hut, and it's just in the middle of nowhere.'

'Go on,' she said, totally absorbed in Callum's mysterious weekend adventures.

'He's got chickens and lots of crops and a crab pool. He basically lives there away from people as much as he can, apart from some basic things he buys, he lives from things he grows or catches, fish, rabbits, crab.'

'So, how d'ya meet him?' Lucy continued to fire question after question, excited to learn more. He told about the Friday he skived off school and how he recognised Potts from being the gardener to one of Callum's neighbours; Potts found him sleeping with all the ants crawling all over his body. And the shower. Lucy rolled up in laughter at that, which made Callum smile tentatively - unsure if the joke was on him. 'Can I come with you?'

'Sure,' he answered without thinking which he was pleased he had. Knowing if he had given it any thought, he would have stumbled and mumbled and messed up a great opportunity to spend more time with her.

***

On the way home, he pedalled like crazy in desperation to get home and play the cassette Lucy had given him. He wanted to listen to it before Saturday to tell her what he thought about each song. Both Melody Maker and NME, he would read from cover to cover. He would learn the names of every member of The Clash and find out something interesting about the band that maybe she didn't know. Determined to impress her, it would be his homework. By the time he reached his front drive, he was sweating and out of breath. The garage was full of junk, so he rested his bike against a mountain of empty paint tins. He pulled down the metal doors that creaked in a request for some oil that he ignored and instead clanged it closed. He let himself in the front door.

'Mum, I'm home,' he called out, sitting on the stairs in the hall whilst taking his shoes off. 'Mum,' again he called, excited to tell her his news about Lucy and him going out on Saturday. They weren't going out, it wasn't a date, he had to keep reminding himself, but it was not just maths homework and he couldn't wait to tell his mum. She knew how much Lucy meant to him and he knew she would be pleased. In recent weeks things had changed a lot for Callum. With meeting Potts and the time spent with Lucy, his confidence grew back. Something he had many years ago and had lost. Maybe it was possible to return to what he was before and be just like everyone else.

From the hall, he entered the lounge, where a blanket of evil covered him: clear as the change in temperature from walking out of the cold into a heated room. But here, the heat was as hot as hell.

'Mum,' he called again, this time without excitement and energy but trepidation and fear.

Then he heard the muffled voice, 'Callum,' rising in tone towards the end of his name in hope and salvation. Following the sound, he went through into the kitchen. Jim stood suspiciously with his back against the door to the storage cupboard.

'Where's mum?' Jim stared at Callum, eyes wide and wild.

There was a bang on the cupboard from inside, 'Callum,' came the beaten voice from behind the door.

'Mum?' Callum looked to the cupboard and then back to Jim, where he saw the blood glistening around his gums as he smiled manically, his eyes popping with madness.

'Go on, Callum, go up to your bedroom. Me and your mum are having a little disagreement,' Jim said in a calm, calculating way Callum had not witnessed before. Rage he had seen many times, but here there was a difference. Clear evil speared Callum with impending doom.

'Let her out,' Callum said as sternly as he could, knowing that his voice quivered as he spoke. At the same time, his mum banged again on the cupboard door.

Weeping, she called out, 'Please, Jim, let me out.'

'You're not going anywhere, now shut up, bitch,' Jim spat the words out, rage had returned, and he turned and started banging at the door with the soft outer part of his fist ferociously screaming, 'SHUT UP, SHUT THE FUCK UP.' Then with his foot, he started kicking at the cupboard door over and over, a hole appeared with splitters of wood flying out. The sound of the door vibrating, coupled with the level of Jim's screams, left Callum standing there staring in shock and fear. Jim stopped for a moment and returned his wild gaze towards Callum, 'What you doing here, boy?' the sound of Rachel's weeping behind the door, 'well, go to your bedroom.'

Callum did not know what to do. His mum was trapped and in danger; he wanted to protect her, but he knew Jim could easily throw him to the floor. 'Potts says men who hit women are cowards,' Jim looked at him, confused and impatient with Callum's statement.

'What, who the hell is Potts? One of your little weedy school friends?'

'No, he fought in the Second World War; he's a hero, not someone who goes around beating women.'

'What the fuck,' Jim laughed in disbelief that he was having this conversation with Callum. 'Rachel, I don't know what your boy is on, but ya' better tell him to go to his room, or he's gonna be in a lot of trouble.'

A few seconds passed and Callum could see Jim was about to explode. Callum was shaking all over, helpless 'Callum, darling, go to your room,' the timid voice of his mum came from behind the cupboard door.

'I can't leave you, mum, not like this.'

'It's okay. I'll be all right; it's just one of those arguments that got out of hand. I'll be okay.' There was a threatening silence as Callum tried to assess the situation on what the best move was. All options were bad. 'Tell him, Jim, it'll be okay, that you have calmed down now.'

Jim looked at Callum; white foamed spittle had gathered in the corners of his mouth like a rabid animal about to attack, 'Sure, she'll be all right.' And then he indicated with a threatening nod of his head for Callum to go upstairs and leave them alone.

'Okay,' Callum said gently, 'mum, I'm gonna go upstairs, but shout out if you need me.' Jim scoffed at Callum's pathetic threat. He left the kitchen, but doubt grew whether he had made the right decision with each step. In the hall was his bag with magazines and Lucy's cassette. He picked them up and walked up the stairs, with ears attuned to any sounds coming from the kitchen.

On his bed, he opened his bag and dropped the two magazines and a cassette of The Clash onto the floor. Fifty minutes ago, he could not have been in a better place, yet now he could not be anywhere worse. Impossible to read, but tempted to turn on his tape player, turn up the volume and put the cassette on to hide any noises from below. That would make it easier. What he could not hear, he could not be blamed. Hear no evil, see no evil. Guilt magically taken away, but he knew it would be the opposite. It would be amplified.

Every sinew tensed, muscles taut and rigidity paralysing his body to the bed. The screams from his mum downstairs pierced the ceiling, biting its way through the carpet and crawling its way onto Callum. Again with more intensity they came. He rolled onto his side and cried. He wanted to believe there was something else he could do, but there was nothing.

15

They took the bus. Lucy was not keen on cycling. She had a bike, but living closer to the town centre she rarely used it and was adamant she would not cycle the two miles outside Whitstable. They had planned for Lucy to board the bus at nine-fifty and for Callum to get on at the Chestfield stop and then get off at Tyler Hill. It was still a mile walk from there, with most through the woodland where cedar, ash and oak separated the outside world that Callum had grown to love. He hoped Lucy would too. On Friday they confirmed the arrangements, but other than that, they had not spoken. Callum was not in the mood to talk to anyone. Leaving for school that morning, he had seen nobody. His mum had not appeared from her bedroom, and he was too afraid to call out or go in and see her. Jim had already left for work. He had heard him in the bathroom, singing to himself as if nothing had happened; Callum waited until he heard the front door close before getting up to wash and go to school.

Friday night, all three sat at the dining room table. Nobody said a word, just deadly looks, with his mum occasionally finding a smile to reassure Callum everything was all right. It wasn't, he knew as much, and any pretence of hiding the situation was far gone. His mum had no visible bruises, no black eye this time, but that was not unusual. Jim knew where to inflict pain that did not show to the outside world.

Callum had not told Lucy, and as the bus pulled away, he looked out of the window, sitting next to her, wondering if he should. It was the first time they had been together that he had not wanted to talk. Withdrawn into his shell, reflective of the world and his life, he watched the houses disappear and turn to fields that turned to trees and woodland as they grew closer to their stop.

'You okay?' Lucy asked, sensing something wrong. She wrapped the fingers of her hand around his arm, squeezing gently. The sign of affection almost made him burst into tears, but he managed to control himself. 'A problem shared is a problem halved,' her smile penetrated him. She was perfect; he wanted to hold her tight until all his troubles disappeared. But when that would be, he did not know, if they ever would.

Feeling claustrophobic, Callum was grateful to see the bus pull up at their stop. Fresh air was welcome as they left the bus. Lucy first, followed by Callum. 'Is it something I said?' Lucy asked.

'Oh, no, sorry, it's just I have a few problems at home,' Callum said, looking at the ground ahead as they walked towards Potts' hut, which was a good half hour away. Outside, Callum's mood changed, the air gave him a release and with the open space around him, he opened up to Lucy, who was both sympathetic and horrified at the same time. She offered no solution other than she would always be there for him if he ever needed to talk. 'Thanks, Lucy, I appreciate that,' he said, as if hers meant nothing, words said and lost in the breeze, but inside they meant more than she could imagine.

Deciding not to spoil the day, he changed the conversation, 'Okay, enough about that, let's have a fun day.' She smiled as they walked further into the woods. 'Up that path is where I first went. And got lost and ended up sleeping in an anthill,' he pointed to their right, 'but Potts lives up here a few more minutes' walk.' Lucy was amazed and loved the wilderness surrounding her. She was glad to be wearing her DM boots, which Callum had advised, from the muddy terrain that was amassed from the overnight rain.

Tire tracks from Potts' Jeep were visible and were dug

deep into the earth that most vehicles would struggle to drive through. They eventually came to the wooded fence panels that shut Potts' land off from the rest of the world, although very few of the outside world ever ventured this way. Callum twisted the iron ring pull handle to open the gate and they both entered. Lucy was amazed at what she saw as Callum had been that first time. A clatter and chorus of clucks erupted as they approached the hut, with Marilyn, in the lead as usual, with Sophia not far behind.

'Hello,' Callum knelt down and greeted his friends who had come to see who was visiting, 'meet Marilyn and Sophia,' Lucy joined Callum, crouched down, and stroked the two chickens. 'Marilyn and Sophia, say hello to Lucy.'

'Hello, Callum,' Potts appeared, his vest soaked from where he had been washing. His hair was still wet, and towelling it dry as he spoke, Callum thought he looked like he had stolen the style of an absent-minded university professor, 'and you, I assume, are Lucy.' Potts knew her name, and if he knew her name, it was because Callum had spoken about her, which pleased her.

'Hi, how you doing?'

'I'm fine, young lady, but I would have dressed proper if Callum had told me he was bringing a friend. So please, excuse my attire.'

'Short notice, sorry,' Callum added. Potts grabbed a shirt, slung over the back of the chair from the shower room, and put it on. Callum showed Lucy around, and whilst he did, Potts lit the fire pit for them to sit around for lunch.

'You hungry, Lucy?' Potts asked as they returned and joined him while he sat on one of the carved chairs by the fire pit.

'Always,' she said as she and Callum settled into the adjacent carved-out chairs, 'this place is fantastic.'

'Thank you. I do like it, find it very peaceful – relaxing,'

Potts said, pulling out a string of sausages from a bag on the chair next to him, gently placing them on the grid on the fire. They talked about school; the sausages sizzled invitingly, providing hunger-inducing music in the background. Lucy told of how Callum has been excellent in helping her with maths and reckoned he should be a teacher.

'Do you want us to help you with anything after lunch?' Lucy asked.

'No, nothing to do now, so you can just sit back and relax. Maybe we could go and pick some blackberries later, but that's about it. There's still a few left, might get another blackberry pie, Callum's favourite.' Potts was as easy to get on with as Callum had said. It was almost twenty years since Potts' last guest, and now he had two; it was then as they chatted and laughed, that he realised how much he had missed the company of people. They talked about fishing, and Lucy was keen to join them. They spoke about school and how Lucy was impressed that Callum was so clever and top in most classes.

'Well, Lucy, I have to say from your school, you are much nicer than that other individual I hear about.'

'Who's that?' She asked, wondering who else Potts knew from school.

'Ray Blackman, a right little git and bully by all accounts.'

'Oh him, yeah he is, but there's bullies closer to home than him, aren't there, Callum?' Lucy knew Callum wanted to tell Potts. On the walk up there he had told her Potts would know what to do, and he would have some advice. It seemed the perfect way to broach the conversation.

'Yeah, well, it's Jim,' Callum spoke hesitantly in a quiet mumble.

'What, your stepdad, what's happened, Callum?' Potts asked with concern, sensing something wrong.

'I don't know, not sure where to begin, or what the point is anyway, but Jim hit my mum last Thursday.' Once he started, it easily rolled off. The cupboard, the threats and the madness in his eyes. The full history.

'Shit, I didn't realise,' Potts said as he stabbed the ashes in the fire pit with the poker while he absorbed what Callum told him, 'I guessed your relationship with him wasn't great. You never really spoke about him, but didn't realise it was as serious as this.' Both Lucy and Callum looked at Potts, waiting for an answer, a solution. He looked from the red glow of dying coals; he realised they were waiting for him to speak, as some great philosopher who had the key to the world's problems. How wrong they were, he didn't have the answers to his own problems, and it felt wrong to advise others on how to sort theirs. Not wanting to let Callum down, he responded with the best he could, 'You need to contact the police about this, Callum.'

'My mum wouldn't do that,' Callum said, resigned to the fate he knew would be the outcome if she did, 'one is they wouldn't take much notice; they think there are more important things to deal with, and' he paused not wanting to continue, 'Jim would kill my mum if she did – And, afterwards he would probably kill me.'

'Speak to your mum at least; see what she says.'

'Can't you, I mean, can't you talk to Jim? Tell him to leave her alone.'

Potts was thrown. It was the last thing he had expected to hear, 'I can't get involved, Callum. It would make things worse.'

'But you've done boxing and been a soldier in the war. It might scare him,' Callum sounded desperate, 'or make him think twice at least.' Potts looked down again, his attention drawn to his hand that had gone into a wild spasm; shaking uncontrollably while holding the poker, he dropped it instantly as if he had been burnt, hoping Callum and Lucy had not noticed.

'You can't ask Potts that,' Lucy interrupted. Potts was unsure if she had noticed his reaction or if it was good timing, either way, he welcomed her interjection.

'You need to speak to your mum, Callum. It would only make things worse if I got involved.'

'It makes sense, Callum,' Lucy backed up Potts' suggestion.

'Let's go and pick some fruits,' Potts suggested, desperately wanting to move the subject onto something else. They all agreed and Potts went and collected some bags from the hut before they set off.

Blackberries were scarce, and they found barely enough to make a small pie between them. Potts had been wrong, but in a way, it had served its purpose. Their hunt for fruits, the conversation had moved on. The mood had lightened; there had been laughter and a general sense of ease. On route, they passed by where Potts and Callum first met, and they pointed out the spot to Lucy. Potts took great pleasure in describing, in detail, how Callum was dancing about in his underpants. Lucy laughed; Callum went red-faced. The anthill was still there, more giant than ever, with thousands upon thousands of ants going about their business. Callum wondered if they had recognised him. Although their find had been small, they had been gone three hours.

'Tea, shall we have tea?' They all agreed, 'You make the tea, Callum, and I'll get the biscuits, and me and Lucy will rest our legs.' Potts collected the biscuit barrel from the kitchen outbuilding and left Callum boiling the kettle on the stove. The two of them returned to the carved seats, unscrewed the top of the biscuit barrel, and offered them to Lucy, 'Don't stand on parade here, Lucy, take another unless you don't like my biscuits.' His homemade biscuits were the best, better than any mass-produced biscuits bought from the supermarket. She took another. 'Help yourself if you want more,' he offered and put the barrel on the empty seat between them.

It was easy to like Potts; Lucy immediately took to him and saw why he and Callum had become friends. Having learnt today about Callum's problems, she felt it even more important for Callum to have someone he could trust. She, too, wanted to be a part of that. Having a stepdad like that, after his real dad had passed away, must have been difficult; she understood why he had hidden away. Taking another bite of her biscuit, she looked around the woodland and realised this was Potts' hideaway and wondered if he too was hiding from something.

'Lucy, I'm not usually the nosey person, but I have to know,' Lucy's thoughts were interrupted and now intrigued by his comments, 'what's happening with you and Callum? Are you boyfriend and girlfriend yet?'

A nervous laugh escaped her before she responded, 'No, I keep waiting for him to ask. I keep dropping hints, but he's a bit slow on the uptake,' spoken as if she found his shyness and naivety endearing.

'Yeah, well, he lacks a bit of confidence, does our Callum. As you can see, he hasn't had it easy.'

'I know, I understand, but it must be obvious I like him, don't know what he's scared of.'

'Obvious to me,' Potts said, looking towards the kitchen outbuilding where Callum appeared with a tray of tea. 'Come on, Callum, the biscuits will all be gone if you don't hurry up. I think Lucy has taken a liking to them.'

It was getting dark when they had finished tea and had talked for another hour. Instead of the long walk and the bus, Potts said he would take them home. Down the muddy track, the Jeep's wheels spun and slid, but somehow they managed to get out onto better ground; after that the journey was less fairground ride style. They pulled up at Lucy's house first.

'Go on, Callum, be the gentlemen and take Lucy to the door.' Callum jumped out and walked Lucy to the house. Potts watched the two of them from the driver's seat, silently urging Callum to ask her out. He could see Lucy dragging the conversation out, wanting and waiting for the same; Potts could also see the disappointment on her face as they parted. Callum got back into the Jeep, and Potts started the engine heading off to Callum's house.

***

In front of the mirror, Rachel rubbed cream across her stomach, standing with her blouse off, and wearing just her bra. She grimaced at what she saw. Black patches of various shades merged into each other. Slowly and gently with each movement, her hand ignited pain. Touching her ribs; her eyes released a tear from the pain and sadness. Convinced one of her ribs was broken, she knew from experience it would mean four or five weeks before it healed. She hoped it would be the last time, but how many times could she hang on to such belief? Outside she heard a diesel engine rumble. Fear returned with the thought Jim had come home early. She looked out the window to see a Jeep with Callum climbing out of the passenger's side. The only thing she could wear, the loose-fitting blouse, lay on the bed. She put it on, wincing as it touched her skin, wiped the tear from her face and went downstairs.

16

The lawnmower regularly jammed with clogged-up grass from lack of use where growth enjoyed the neglect over the spring and summer months. He was exhausted already, and the job was not even half done in the front garden. There was still the back to conquer, how easy it would be to break his promise to himself, but he did not want to let down his mum, so he continued, determined to honour his commitment only he knew of. Guilt came with jagged teeth and nagged him over the last week. Since last Thursday night he knew he had to do more for his mum. Nobody else would, and it was wrong he had done so much with Potts but left his mum to do everything. The lawn had been left in disarray all summer, and although it was late in the season, it would look better for the winter months. His mum would know he was trying to help, and it would give hope and lift her spirits. She cooked, cleaned the house, and did his washing; cutting the grass was the least he could do, so from now, he was determined to do more in future. Over the recent weeks since meeting Potts and spending time with Lucy, he had ventured out of his room and realised there was more to life than just study. His mum was an important part of that. She was always there for him no matter what he did or whatever his problems; he realised how hard that must be with all she had to go through.

Radio Two sang out through the lounge window at the front of the house, where Callum continued to fight with the lawnmower. The strong identifiable scent of a Marlboro cigarette escaping from the window ajar told Callum it was Jim in the front room. When the lawn was fully cut, a passerby would have thought it was just like any other house on a Sunday morning. Nobody would know of the problems within those four walls. They would walk right past, nobody coming to the rescue, busy with their own lives in their own worlds. The neighbours, who kept their distance, may suspect but would not know half of what went on. Like most people, they didn't want to know. It was easier to turn and look the other way as he had the other night, ignoring the screams of his mum, lying on his bed, wanting it to go away. Wanting was a useless action, for, with wanting, nothing changed.

***

'Who's this Potts?' Jim asked, looking out to the front garden watching Callum push the lawnmower up and down leaving tufts of grass behind him. Rachel didn't answer immediately; instead, from the coffee table in front of the settee, she picked up her packet of Rothmans and lit a cigarette. It was needed before she could speak to Jim. Since Thursday, she had avoided any conversation. It seemed to make no difference to Jim. Apologies came, as before, on the Friday and Saturday, but when she had not accepted them as she had so often done before, he shrugged it off as if to say. *Your loss. Makes no difference to me.* A million thoughts now went through her head. Too many to process, and she needed time to work them out. The cigarette helped; it calmed her and gave her time to respond without immediate reaction.

Rachel didn't look at him; she hadn't for the last few days. The bruises remained sore and her ribs spat shards of pain each time she moved. Hatred remained vivid and virulent. Friday was the day she cleaned the house, but the agony that twisted within her was too great. She waited for the comments to come, the complaints from Jim that she did nothing and he was the one bringing the money in to keep them all. The usual song she had accepted so many times before, but this time it had to be different. But the question of how was the thing that nagged away repeatedly. They could separate and divorce but he would take half the property. A part of her accepted that, although at the same time, she told herself if she did, she would have been robbed. It had been with Michael when they bought the house. With Michael, they made a home, and it was with him that a sizable chunk of the property had already been paid. She wanted to count all the bricks that made up the house and then count how many were paid for when Michael was alive to justify her confused reasoning. When she thought harder and longer, the mortgage was paid off with life insurance before Jim had moved in. The only thing he had paid for was the ongoing bills. It made her even angrier to think he was entitled to any of it. But there was Callum to think of, and she knew they were safer without him, poorer maybe, but safer.

'He's a friend of Callum's,' she said.

'What from school?' Jim pressed.

'No, he's an old boy, somebody he met in the woods, off Radfall Hill one day.'

'He meets an old man in the woods and you're okay with that. What kind of mum are you?'

She wanted to answer. *What kind of dad are you?* But held back to avoid further confrontation, 'It's not like that, he's Mrs Wickes' gardener from over the road. He's always around.' The front garden now cut; Callum pushed the lawnmower to the back. A sense of pride came over her watching Callum outside cutting the grass. She stubbed her cigarette out in the glass ashtray on the coffee table and left the lounge to go to the kitchen. Away from Jim, she watched Callum continue cutting the grass in the back garden.

Rachel took a deep breath to remain calm as Jim followed her into the kitchen, annoying her further. Everything about him she detested, his scent, his voice, and his breath touching her wherever she stood. She lit another cigarette. He did the same; the kitchen filled with smoke.

'What do they talk about?'

'I don't know. Why don't you ask him? He's your stepson,' her voice terse, but again she calmed herself and continued. 'I think they talk about the war or something.'

'What is he? Some kind of war hero,' Jim laughed at what he thought was a joke.

'I think he did stuff in Africa. Callum didn't say much.'

'So,' Jim said pensively; Rachel looked at him, trying to work out what was going through his mind. Wondering if she had said something she shouldn't. He took a long draw on the cigarette and blew the smoke out slowly as he watched Callum working in the back garden. 'Okay, I'm going out. I'm meeting someone,' Jim suddenly announced. Nothing was said; he stubbed his half smoked cigarette into the ashtray and left the room. The smoke whirled with purpose upwards, towards the ceiling, from the still part-lit cigarette. Rachel moved into the dining room, sat at the table and watched Callum through the patio doors.

The first weekend of October was still warm and Callum was finding it hard work. It would have taken half the time if he had done this every week.

An hour later, he had finished; he sat on the bench that looked out from the patio area at the back of the house and congratulated himself on a job well done. The flowerbeds that bordered the garden, which lacked flowers, still needed weeding, but there was a clear visible line between them and the grass that rewarded his efforts. Tiredness overcame him while he sat and relaxed. It was not just from working in the garden, although he felt it from that too, but a different kind of fatigue. Physical work brought satisfaction. It was the other that drove worry and anxiety with it. The fact he had not slept well for the last three nights had caught up with him. Stretching legs out with his back straight on the bench he closed his eyes; through his eyelids, the sun was bright, and his mind drifted away.

Nineteen-Forty-Two

Potts closed his eyes. It had been a long night keeping watch, which had taken its toll without him realising. The whole war was beginning to drain him of energy and life. Joining the army gave him a reason to live, where now it had taken his only hope. The continued suffering and pain it all caused. Keep focused, and it will be over eventually, he told himself, but in the same thought was at a loss for what would happen to him then.

Jennings had worked his way through fifty yards of mines, along with twenty other men. How long Potts' eyes had been shut, he was not sure, but the bang shook him back awake. Jennings' body sliced into two halves; Potts watched his upper half, still alive, slithering in pain. His first thoughts were that Jennings had stepped on and activated a mine, but immediately following the explosion, there was a barrage of fire. The initial fire had hit one of the mines, which exploded next to Jennings.

Recognising the danger, Potts looked to where the shots had come from and returned fire. The men clearing the mines were falling like flies where an incessant fury of bullets rained down, followed by grenades igniting the anti-tank and anti-personnel landmines around. Potts, on higher ground, and three others were helpless to provide any defence from the speed of the attack. Another mine exploded, catapulting an army transporter onto its side, crushing and trapping the legs of one of the engineers underneath. Bullets from a Spandau machine gun splattered around the trapped man before one hit him in the shoulder, launching the man with force upwards, only to be jerked hard back down to the ground from his trapped legs. Potts watched on, helpless, too far away and with the German attack hidden behind a hill with an angle impossible to target, he got up from his position and ran to the side to try and take them from the flank.

'Woody,' Potts screamed over the noise. 'Cover me,' Woody looked up to see Potts pointing to where he planned to go. Woody gave a thumbs up and started to fire towards the German position to cause a distraction. As Potts made his move, the engineers tried to return fire but were in open ground and vulnerable to the attack. The Spandau was spraying ammo recklessly all over, and was the only reason half of them remained alive. Potts made it to a mound on higher ground and lay down to get a better view of the German attack party. From that angle, he could see a party of about fifteen men. He fired into the crowd and saw one go down, some turned their attention in Potts' direction whilst the majority continued the onslaught on the engineers, who were now down to three, maybe four left alive.

Within less than a minute, the last engineer was dead. Twenty men spread lifeless on the desert sand. Deadly silence melted the dawn air. A moment of remembrance. Potts laid his head into the sand wanting his body to be sucked deep down and buried beneath. A noise from someone shouting from the area he had come from made him lift his head to see what was happening. Two stretcher bearers came into view with a white handkerchief in each hand, waving nervously.

'Go. Okay,' a voice with a strong accent from the German side called out. The two British ambulance men walked out into the dead zone moving between the men laid out on the ground, checking for any remaining life. The Germans, Woody, Potts and the British lower down looked on an unreal world where moments before there was life until they had all started killing each other.

One of the medics went over to the truck that was on its side with the trapped man beneath. Frantically he called to the other. From his reaction, it was clear the man trapped under the vehicle was still alive. The other medic ran over and joined him and tried to lift the truck off the man. They did not have the strength to move the two-ton truck between them. Potts watched the men straining with all their strength, but it was no good. He wanted to go down and join them. Guilt flooded over him for the lack of help he had provided to those men; maybe with three, it would be possible, but going down there with a red cross on your arm is one thing; for him, it could be another. The Germans would know that it was from that position their men had been shot dead, and it was Potts who was responsible.

'Wait.' The same accent as before sounded another call from the German quarter. Then five German soldiers appeared with white scarves held high and made their way slowly and cautiously to join the British medics. When they reached the truck, they each took hold and, with the combined strength of all of them, and on the count of *'drei'*, lifted the truck pushing it to one side, freeing the trapped British engineer below.

The German soldiers returned to where they had come from and resumed their positions. The medic called out, 'Danke schon.' and lifted the wounded man onto the stretcher. As they carried him back to the ambulance behind the British line, Potts watched on. It was hard to comprehend what had just happened. The complete and absolute absurdity of it all made no sense. Potts rolled back down the hill and re-joined Woody and the other men.

17

The house quiet, Callum at school and Jim gone to work, bruises fading, but Rachel's wounds remained deep. The pain, violent and vindictive, she tried to understand. Trapped in her house, she thought of the grass slopes at Tankerton and imagined herself looking onto the seas, powerful waves breaking the shoreline as they crashed down. A bustling crescendo as the waters gathered and rolled themselves together, howling and calling out as they travelled away again, holding the secret so well kept. Questioning every action, a history of her life played out in her mind, desperately trying to justify why she was to blame.

Tufts of cut grass in mounds made her smile, thinking of Callum cutting the lawn yesterday. She opened the patio door; it scraped on its worn runners. The autumn air was real, but she was not as she breathed it in deeply. Unscripted and unexpected, a tear rolled down her cheek from subconscious memories that played like a movie in the background of her mind.

***

Wendy Crouch, her best friend. Friends for life was what they would be. That is what they promised.

'Let's make a pact,' Wendy said as she slurped her strawberry milkshake, purposely exaggerating the noise to bring the attention of the two boys sitting at the table next to them. Rachel looked down to the table to hide her blushes as Wendy smiled cheekily, encouraging them more. Both virgins, both waiting for princes to arrive, Rachel dared to look up towards the table and saw a tall blonde quiffed-haired handsome prince smiling at her. Quickly she turned away to look out of the floor-to-ceiling window that opened up to the world from Valente's ice cream parlour as blood rushed through her heart, pumping ferociously. She liked the feeling and secretly wanted it to last forever, nerves tingling through her body, exciting her.

'Always friends! No matter what?' Wendy questioned. Her smile was more fantastic, knowing they had caught the two boys' attention at the adjacent table.

'No matter what,' Rachel agreed, and they both giggled out a teenage laugh. Avoiding eye contact with the two boys, she focused on the row of motorbikes lined up on the road outside, displaying their prowess. Which ones, she wondered, belonged to the boys next to them? A chair brought her attention back inside as it scraped the floor, with the blonde boy rising from it and making his way to the jukebox on the far side and then to the counter to place an order. Rachel watched as he walked; her excitement inside continued to race.

Fats Domino flooded out of the speakers, Blueberry Hill sang, and Rachel, having diverted her look, felt his eyes on her as he returned to his seat. A minute later, the waitress approached the boys' table with a Knickerbocker Glory, chocolate layered, glistening invitingly over the vanilla ice cream. The boys redirected the waitress away from their table with the ice cream who then served it to Rachel and Wendy's table. Both raised their heads in synchronised movement and looked at the two boys and, in unison, smiled and giggled together in a perfectly timed dance.

The blonde one held up four spoons, 'Would you like to share with us?'

Before Rachel, still in shock at this time and still not giggled out, had a chance to respond, Wendy jumped in with the response, 'Sure thing, come and join us.'

The two boys jumped up and sat on the two empty chairs next to Rachel and Wendy, smiling and excited. Michael, the blond one, who sat next to Rachel, was the quieter and more sensible of the two. Harry, the one with all the jokes, sat next to Wendy and led the conversation. By chance or by fate, the pairing was the perfect match. After that night, Wendy was no longer a virgin, Rachel waited a little longer, and Michael, the perfect and considerate gentleman, never pushed the matter.

Fairy tales did happen. It was true. She could not believe it, and one year later, Harry and Wendy were married, and the summer after, it was Rachel and Michael's turn. Both Harry and Michael were builders and spent most of their time together at work and out of work. Both were football mad, Michael was Arsenal, and Harry was Chelsea. Wendy and Rachel had no interest in football but spent most days at each other's houses. Both talked about the future, the day they would own their own houses, and both knew that dream would happen soon.

***

Rachel went into the garden, wiped a tear, sat at the patio bench, lit a cigarette and wanted to reverse time. Nothing was constant except for bad things that repeated.

***

They celebrated when Wendy fell pregnant again, but Rachel didn't think about the glaringly obvious, having two children cost more money than having one. She and Michael spoke about it.

'Maybe we should have another baby? It would be nice to have a girl, a little sister, for Callum. What do you think?'

'We can't afford it; we need to buy a house first, get out of this rented place,' Michael said, sticking to their plan. Rachel agreed; she knew Michael was right, always logical, always sensible. A new baby cost extra pounds, and extra pounds came from London. Harry found work in London, and Wendy moved away.

They exchanged letter after letter, but it was not the same. Nothing could replace those days they spent together. Afternoon tea, talking about their dreams, what they would do together in the years to come, it was talking about it as much as having it that Rachel enjoyed.

Without Wendy around, boredom hit and Rachel took a job a couple of nights a week at The Pearson's Arms, a popular pub on the seafront in Whitstable. They kept in touch and would visit each other, and on Michael's thirtieth birthday, they came back to celebrate the occasion, but it was not the same. The distance between them had severed the bond of friendship. Every mile from Whitstable to London and every day apart stretched it further. Rachel remembered their pact that night at Michael's birthday. *Always friends, no matter what* - They were still friends, but other things in life had come along that made their friendship not so important. Children, bills, work, and life got busy, and the things that used to be important slipped from their minds. Letters became fewer, visits fewer, and the value of their friendship depleted. Their teenage fantasy replaced by adulthood reality.

***

'Thank you, I don't know what I would do without

you here,' Rachel cried onto Wendy's shoulder at Michael's funeral. But Wendy went home to London. The distance seemed greater, and her friend now might as well have been a million miles away. Alone to bring up Callum by herself, she turned to Jim. He was there for her when she needed it, not Wendy. True friends show their cards when most needed. Jim asked nothing in return. Not even sex. But after a few months, Rachel needed more than just a friend. She needed to feel attractive again; she needed to be wanted, and she needed a physical connection. One thing led to another taking its natural course; it was good, something she had never experienced before, something she didn't know was possible. It helped. Michael would never be forgotten; he would always be a part of her, her first love, but Jim sometimes made her forget. At first, there was guilt, but it faded after a while. She told Wendy, but she had been poisoned by words Harry had spoken to her about Jim.

'What things?' Rachel quizzed.

'Oh, it doesn't matter,' never revealing, that made it worse, 'I just don't trust him.'

'You can't just say that and not tell me what Harry said about him.'

'Oh, forget I said anything,' Wendy said, exasperated. 'All I'm saying is you're vulnerable at the moment. Some men will take advantage.'

'Jim's not like that. He has been there when I needed someone,' Rachel said with bitterness.

'What do you mean by that?' Wendy said, shocked and horrified as if it was aimed at her. Rachel didn't admit it, but it was.

And, now, as she stood in the garden, a chill hit her; she wished she had listened. If only Wendy had told her what Harry had said, it would have made it much easier, although at the time, she was unsure if she would have listened. She was so desperate. Had he done this before? Had he hit his partner in a previous relationship? Surely Wendy would have told her if that had been the case. They had been friends long enough to say something like that. Maybe there was something else so dark it would be impossible to say without sounding mad. Rachel played with it in her mind and thought she was getting carried away as she had that day when she had last spoken to Wendy.

'Just leave it, Wendy. You can't handle the fact that I have found someone else. You just want it to be like it was before. I thought you would be happy for me. Don't bother coming to the wedding.'

'I won't if that's how you feel.' A little off thirty years of friendship gone, both too stubborn to contact the other. They never spoke again. Jim protected her during that time too, telling her she was not worth it if that was how she acted. That was at the time, but now looking back, she wondered if that was Jim's plan all along, to take her away from her friends. No job now at The Pearson's Arms and no contact with Wendy, her only real friend. At the time, being with Jim was what she wanted. It was hard enough looking after Callum. He was struggling, and all her efforts were put towards him. Facing people was hard, and Jim protected her from them, but she became lonely and trapped as time passed.

Things had to change, she told herself as she looked out onto the garden that Callum, her son, had worked so hard on. She knew he had done it for her, and her toxic relationship with Jim would eventually kill him as it would kill her. She was on her own. Her only true friend lost. It was her fault, which was a mistake she could not repeat for Callum's sake, and somehow she needed to put right the wrongs of the last few years.

Nineteen-Forty-Two

Fires from hell were unleashed. With the second battle of El Alamein, the sleeping morning sky was broken by fury and denouement. The moon no longer looked down upon the peaceful desert resting below but hid with fear behind the white sheet of flames that cloaked it from its sacrificial lamb.

In the trench, Potts looked at Woody; his eyes focused forward towards enemy lines. His eyes wide in disbelief at the enormity of it all, Potts read fear in Woody's face or perhaps a reflection of his own mind.

All around, noise blasted deafening booms and cracks, but Potts lowered the volume around him and tried to comprehend the reason for it all. No answers came to him, only a fear of death. Reports and rumours had circulated; this was the big one. The Axis forces were near to being on their knees and, with one final push, would see them taken down. There was no doubt he was on the side which was now to suffer fewer casualties. Yet there was no escaping; fear moving inside his body increased its hold with every crack or boom that smashed the sky. If this was what it was like on their side, what were they experiencing on the other?

They waited for their orders to advance. Anytime soon, they would be called upon to do their duty again. Their duty again - to kill another German and to defeat and rid this world of the tyranny that gripped it. Another German soldier, in all probabilities, was of a similar age as Potts, conscripted to kill a British soldier for the cause they too had been directed. A German soldier, who at home had a mother, a father or a wife and children. Children, boys and girls of an age too young to understand, waiting, praying each night for their father to return home. With another burst of fire the volume snapped back in with a vengeance. Potts watched on, and he wanted to know how many children would never see their fathers again with each shell launched and exploded into enemy territory. Why didn't they just give up? and save themselves from the inevitable horrors to come. A choice to be killed and buried in these desert sands or to return home to live the life they have been given. That was the choice; if they chose to remain, he would become the executioner of their judged sin.

The bombardment went on too long. Potts wanted to move; he needed to get active to stop him from thinking. Eventually, the whistle came for them to advance. Woody moved first and Potts was quick to follow. Tanks fired ahead clearing the lines and causing confusion in enemy lines for Potts and the infantry to capitalise. Potts and Woody marched forward, scarves wrapped around their faces to protect them from smoke and sand that suffocated the area from the shells launched, leaving abandoned Axis vehicles in flames. As they moved forward, bodies appeared strewn on the sands and in burnt-out vehicles. Potts' scarf slipped from his face allowing him to breathe the waft of death from around. He had become accustomed to the recognisable smell of burning; reminding him of roast pork. Rumours may be correct; he was beginning to suspect that the enemy was retreating. And then all this could end. A burst of fire came in their direction. The squad moved forward, opening fire. Potts and Woody were to the rear of the advance, and he could see some of their forward men going down from pockets of small resistance that pointlessly remained. By the time they reached the German line, they were already dead, wiped out by the forward section.

Woody and Potts were ordered to check the trench and rifle pits whilst the rest of the squad checked the vehicles and nearby areas. First trench they jumped into was a long passage that seemed to continue forever. Every twenty yards there were groups of dead German soldiers mangled together. Some whole and some in pieces, the ones whole or those still with faces looked at Potts with twisted expressions of confusion and eyes looking for answers. Each body Potts passed, he slowed, each holding his own story. He knelt by one of the soldiers and put his hand on his arm. He wanted to talk to and comfort him, 'It will be okay, you see. It will soon be over.' He was not sure if he had spoken the words out loud or not. Madness surrounded him.

'Potts, come on, mate, all clear here, let's move on to the next and get the fuck out of here.' Woody viewed Potts' pensive stance, adding words of encouragement. 'Be home for tea before you know it.' Potts heard the words but did not believe them. They checked around before climbing out of the trench. All was clear, nothing but their own troops above, so they moved onto the next trench, a short distance away to the side.

Again they jumped down, and this time Woody, for the first time, looked more relaxed and said, 'Hey, Potts, do ya' recon the rumours are true,' Potts did not respond to Woody's voice that felt distant. 'It gotta end soon; it can't go on forever. I can feel it, mate,' in Woody's voice there was a confidence and excitement that brought Potts back into the world of hell they were living, 'I have a strange sense it's gotta end. Really can this time.'

'Well, it's over for them.' Potts looked at the German bodies. Three years of war and the suffocation of death were taking their toll. He could face it no more; it made his skin crawl. Nobody would win, even if they were turning the tables.

'Yeah, guess so.' Woody agreed, looking at yet another dead body but failing to recognise the disconnection in Potts' voice. Potts wondered if Woody remembered what he had said when they were in training about not wanting to kill anyone. How many men had they killed between them? Did Woody still feel the same, or had he, as most men, accepted killing as second nature? Part of the job, with no thought of who that person was and who they themselves had become. Were they the same men they had been those few years back? Potts knew the answer, and he knew he was not and, by conclusion, realised that no man could be. But Woody had a point. There had to be an end.

The trench they were in was shorter than the previous one, but the number of dead was equally as great. Potts looked down at his boots submerged in a pool of blood where the trench undulated. His eyes fixed and his body frozen; he watched the blood gently ripple over and around his boots from the wave he had created.

'Put the gun down,' Woody shouted.

From the inside of Potts' boots, blood had found its way in, soaking his socks, warm and hypnagogic from being inside those bodies, now dead around him, only moments ago. Potts wanted to be sick. He wanted to lie down with them and accept the end.

'Put the fucking gun down,' Woody shouted again.

Disorientated, Potts looked up to see a German officer with a Luger pointed at Woody. The world moved in slow motion as Potts watched the man crumpled up on the floor as he applied pressure to the trigger of his gun before the blast of the bullet fired from the barrel. Woody was thrust upright against the trench wall and screamed in pain. He had been hit in his right leg, the shock forcing Woody to drop his gun. The German officer aimed his Luger back at Woody.

Woody turned to face Potts, 'Shoot the bastard,' he yelled in desperation and pain. Potts lifted his gun fast and pointed it toward the German officer. Potts rested his index finger on the trigger and started to squeeze. The officer's face focused on Woody only. Potts aimed his gun with a clear and easy shot to take him out. There was blood over the officer's face, and Potts knew he was looking at an already dying man. The officer fired again. This time hitting Woody in the left leg bringing him down to the ground, level and only yards from the officer's face.

'Shoot him,' Woody screamed, spitting out the words. Potts' finger locked; he could not pull the trigger, he willed it, but a force outside of his conscious thought control would not let him pull the trigger to fire the bullet and kill another man. The German officer fired. This time hitting Woody, splitting his face in two. The officer turned and looked at Potts. The

Luger fell limp at the officer's side. Potts, still having the officer in his aim, watched a pointless smile appear upon his face.

'You win,' the German officer said. Those were the last words of the officer before he closed his eyes. Potts sunk down in the pool of blood that had now been topped up by the officer's and, Woody's.

18

Callum's life might have been submerged with problems he had no solutions to, but he was on a high. Like the mermaid from The Street by Tankerton slopes, Lucy often swam into his thoughts. He too would build a pathway to get to her. Protect her and never let her go. To love her forever and for her to love him back for eternity. Dreams were rare for Callum, normally, he experienced only nightmares. The last lesson of the day and he found it hard to focus. Physics, he was usually taking in every word, but today he wanted to dream. He knew he could afford to dream. It was a lesson he could let his mind drift without fear of hurting his grades. Already he had put enough work in to ensure success. The class had not settled down yet, with the normal misbehaviour occurring at the start of every lesson.

'Draw the magnetic,' Mr Cunningham said, but no one listened. He breathed in deeply and raised his voice to try again to get everybody's attention. 'Draw the magnetic field pattern of a bar magnet showing how strength and direction change from one point to another.' Mr Cunningham tried setting the homework to an uninterested classroom. It was something he always did at the beginning and the end of each lesson in the hope that, by repetition, some of the class would take notice. Callum made a note, content it was something they had already covered and he could do comfortably.

Mr Cunningham acquired the nickname Mr Magoo on account of the television cartoon character with poor eyesight. The difference between the two was Mr Magoo refused to admit he had a problem, whereas Mr Cunningham was fully aware but, up to this time, had failed to find a pair of glasses strong enough to see both close up and distance. It meant he could not see past the first two rows of desks in the classroom. This led to the disintegration of order when controlling the class. And those who wanted to cause trouble sat towards the back.

'Please make sure you have it completed by ...' He stopped mid-sentence. Everybody in the classroom was now aware of the cause of the sudden pause and expression of concern on his face. 'Don't be alarmed, boys, girls, but I can smell fire. Does anybody else smell it?' His eyes squinted to improve vision, a fruitless and ineffectual action, his neck stretched and nose poked forward, looking in vain, sniffing in the hope of identifying the location of the fire.

'No, can't smell anything, sir,' Neal Tarrant called from the back row of desks, cigarette in hand as he spoke, followed up by a long drag before passing on to Simon Clegg. Simon sat by the window and took an exaggerated, dramatic drag (Oscar nomination pending) before blowing the smoke sky bound with force and then disposing of it with a flick, sending sparks flying as it hit the open glass window before falling to the ground outside.

'No, I can definitely smell something,' Mr Cunningham confirmed as he followed his nose. The trail led him to the open window where the cigarette had taken its journey before concluding. 'Okay, must have come from outside. False alarm,' he said, relieved they did not have to evacuate the building and find the emergency evacuation gathering points. Fifteen minutes at the start of each lesson was always consumed by some prank, ultimately leading the class into fits of laughter. Last week Mr Cunningham spent five minutes asking 'Jimmy No Bones' questions who of course provided no response. 'Jimmy No Bones' had lots of bones; he was the skeleton from the biology lab that mysteriously had been sat in the second row from the back of the class and was dressed in Richard Knightley's school jumper, which was stolen from him earlier

157

in the day.

'Who has done that? It's not funny,' Mr Cunningham angered. This was not the general consensus of the class, some of whom were in tears from laughter.

'This is an abuse of school property.' After no one admitted to stealing 'Jimmy No Bones', and because he was wearing Richard Knightley's jumper, it was Richard who was told to take him back to the biology lab. Fifteen minutes after the class was meant to start and Richard had returned to his desk, the lesson began.

Callum left the mayhem of the classroom and returned his thoughts to Lucy, remembering before class waiting in the corridor, there amongst the noise, the pushing and the shoving as people rushed around late for lessons. Waiting for Mr Cunningham to arrive and open the door, he saw Lucy waiting outside her class just down the corridor for Mrs Price, the drama teacher. Lucy was unaware Callum was watching her. He studied every crevice in her face, every muscle that moved in perfect symmetry, and as he looked, a crescent-mooned smile appeared, elevating her beauty with dynamic force somewhere incredible he struggled to believe could exist. Thursday nights could not come fast enough. He wanted more and wondered if there ever would be, but he remained too embarrassed and worried to ask at the risk of breaking the status quo.

In his bag beside the desk was the copy of the Melody Maker she had given him the week before. Already he had read almost every article from cover to cover, and halfway through the one that said *The Clash Planning Tour*, he noticed dates for next year to be announced soon. Maybe he could offer to take Lucy. It was her favourite band; she would have to say "yes" - wouldn't she? He questioned himself. The physics lesson was boring in comparison to his thoughts. The topic already familiar and read up on; it was done three times before over the last two years. He remained with his thoughts. The ringing of the bell called for the end of the lesson and an end to the day, which he welcomed. It was strange how he didn't want school to end a few months ago. Preferring to stay there and learn more instead of going home, he now had other things to entertain his mind.

He plugged in the combination (314159) to pop open the padlock and pulled his bike out, releasing it from the stand. He pushed his bike outside the school, through the gates, and then sat down on the field outside. There was no rush, so he decided to finish the article he had started to read about The Clash. Secretly he also knew, although he tried not to admit it to even himself, Lucy would pass by that route on her way home. Maybe she would come over, and they could talk about music and what was in the Melody Maker.

No venues, along with no dates, were listed, just the expected geographical locations. Most of the gigs were in the big cities, London, Manchester and even Paris. There was no chance they were coming to Whitstable, but he had hoped they might play at Canterbury. Disappointed, he turned the page and looked at the gig guide. Bands he had never heard of were playing locally. They could go there if he could find a decent punk band playing. He scanned the names of the bands with revived hope when the paper was snatched from him.

The print on the page of the bands in the gig guide his eyes had been focused on was replaced by two brown Doc Marten boots. Beside them were two other pairs. He looked skyward; above him, grinning, was Ray Blackman.

'What ya' reading? Didn't think nerds like you read magazines like this? Thought it was more Physics Weekly you read.' Callum stood up. His heart pounded and blood thumped around his body causing him to physically shake. 'What's your favourite band then?'

'The Clash,' Callum responded impulsively.

'Fancy yourself a bit of a Punk Rocker, do ya'?' Ray slapped the rolled-up Melody Maker hard against Callum's chest.

'It's good music,' Callum said, trying to diffuse the situation. People started to gather around, ready for the show.

'You Punk Rockers are meant to be tough, aren't you?' Callum didn't respond. His eyes fixed on the Melody Maker in Ray's hand. Lucy's Melody Maker - He had to get it back. What would she think of him if he said Ray Blackman had stolen it? 'Come on then, Syd Fucking Vicious or are you known as Calamity Callum.' Ray smacked the rolled-up magazine against Callum's head, harder this time. 'Come on then, Punks against Skins', Ray rolled up his sleeves, 'if you think you're so tough.' Callum feared the worst. The inevitable. His time had come. Heart pumping faster, blood racing, fear immeasurable.

'I don't want any trouble. I just want my magazine back,' Callum said, knowing his request to be pointless.

'No, if you want it, you're gonna have to fight me for it.' Ray unrolled the magazine and held it between his two hands. 'Well, Mr Punk Rocker, you'd better fight me for it before I tear it into a thousand pieces.'

Callum had to have that magazine back. For Lucy. He had to have it. Unplanned and outside his control he threw his right fist and caught Ray in the face. The magazine fell to the floor. Calum thought to grab it and run but he froze, looking at Ray's face. Total disbelief masked Ray. It was true Callum himself did not believe what he had done. A silence ensued all around, yet he knew there stood thirty or forty kids gathered waiting - wanting. He looked to the crowd for an explanation and reason for his actions. They had none but confirmation from everyone, painted with the same expression. Shocked with disbelief Callum would dare hit Ray Blackman, and then their expression, in regimented fashion, changed to a look of realisation of what was to come next - *oh yeah, this is gonna be good*, knowing there would be a repercussion to what Callum had done. He didn't have to wait long. Ray's fist hit hard and then again. One after another they came, too fast for Callum to do anything but try to protect his face, which was now a punch ball for Ray's entertainment. The taste of blood lacquered his lip and his eye closed from the force of blow after blow. Callum went down. In his ribs, the power of Ray's DM boot wreaked pain. Callum was about to die.

'Tough guy,' Ray spat out. Seconds passed before Callum dared open his eyes, lying on the floor, grateful to see Ray and the other two walking away. The Melody Maker lay in front of him; he stretched his hand out to pull it near as consolation for his humiliating defeat. The hum of voices faded into the distance. As the crowd dispersed, pushing through them and running in his direction, he saw Lucy. He sat himself up before she arrived and knelt beside him.

'Callum, what the hell you doin'? Are you all right?' She said with concern clearly in her voice.

'He nicked your magazine.' He laid the palm of his hand against his jaw to check that the shape was the same as before Ray had used him as a punch ball. 'So I told him to give it back.'

'Are you mad? You know what he's like, always looking for a reason to pick a fight. It's only a magazine.' Callum's eyes opened wider, feeling Lucy's gentle touch against his face where kindness replaced the soreness. A frisson of excitement leapt through him with her hand softly against his skin.

'Don't you want someone who can look after you? Someone who's tough and not a coward like me.'

'What? Someone like Ray Blackman picking fights with someone smaller than him all the time? You're not a coward, Callum; he's the coward. You stood up to him. But aren't you ever gonna understand?'

'What?'

'I like you as you are, always have, and just want you to ask me out, for God's sake.' Callum was shocked by Lucy's words; it was the last thing he expected. 'Well, go on then.' She waited silently - before deciding further prompting was needed, 'If you want to?'

'Will you go out with me?' Eventually, Callum got the

words out, each one attached with doubt.

'Yes - At last, for someone who is top of the class you're not that bright at times at reading body signals, are you?' She wrapped her arms around him and hugged him. He considered the pain throbbing on his face a worthwhile outcome for making him and Lucy an item. Boyfriend and girlfriend; that sounded good, his first girlfriend, and he would never have wanted anyone else. She leant back and looked at his eye. Already the swelling had started to show. 'Come on, Callum, let's go back to my house and I will put some cream on your eye.'

He pushed his bike as they walked back to Lucy's, talking about The Clash and how next year they were planning another tour. From the time of leaving the field to arriving at Lucy's front door, they had already arranged their first date. It may not be until next year, but even if they had to travel to London, it was what they would do.

This was a moment in his life he wanted to remember forever. All his senses were heightened as he sat on the bed in Lucy's bedroom. The tap from the bathroom gushed with the crashing sound of Niagara Falls, with Lucy dampening a flannel for Callum's face. As he waited for her to return, he absorbed the scent of her perfume left behind while she made her way to the bathroom. The sheet on the bed he sat on was soft and cool, and he imagined Lucy sleeping there at night. Her eyes closed, dreaming of the future, and he wondered if he was ever part of those dreams. The poster on the wall of The Clash reminded him it was true and they had agreed to go and watch them next year. The world from that moment on was going to be perfect and he couldn't wait to tell his mum and Potts. The need to share his happiness was overloading and spilling out.

Lucy returned from the bathroom with a bowl of cold water with added ice she got from the kitchen. Gently with the flannel she dabbed Callum's cheek and eye. It stung, accentuating the pain, but Callum enjoyed Lucy's touch. She wiped the blood that was still wet around his lip.

'I had planned to go and see Potts tomorrow night. Did you want to come with me?'

'Yeah, sure. Straight after school?'

'Yeah,' he confirmed and there it was, as easy as that, their actual first date. He knew he would have to think of other ideas about things to do and places to go, but it was a good start.

'Your lip won't stop bleeding.' With the flannel, she grabbed some ice cubes, wrapped them inside and placed them again on Callum's lip. Pulling the flannel away she looked at his lip, 'Damn it, Callum, it won't stop. There's only one cure I know of.'

'What's that?' Lucy moved her face closer to his and kissed him on the lips. Callum laughed with nervous embarrassment, 'What are you, a vampire?' It was the best or maybe the only thing that came to mind.

'Are you complaining?'

'No,' he said, and she kissed him again.

Cycling home, he could not remove the smile from his face. His first kiss plus the first date were arranged with the most beautiful girl in the school. No – He corrected himself, the most beautiful girl in the world. The cool wind on his face helped soothe the pain that was now a long way from his mind.

When he arrived home, he was pleased to see that Jim's van was not on the drive, which meant his mum would be on her own. Nobody to spoil his day, it was not possible anyway, but he wanted to tell his mum when she was alone. He hurriedly parked his bike in the garage and entered the house.

'Hi, mum,' excitement in his voice as he called out.

'Hi, Callum,' his mum called from the kitchen. He rushed into the kitchen, taking his coat off as he walked. As he entered, he stopped in horror. His mum sat on the kitchen stool surrounded by glasses and plates shattered all around.

'Mum, what the hell happened?'

'Jim,' she said, 'Jim is what happened,' her voice empty. 'Lost it again. This time he didn't hit me, though, which is something, some kind of blessing, I guess.' With her head surrendered to the floor, it took a while before she looked up to see Callum's face. 'Oh, my God, what's happened to you?'

'Ray Blackman is what happened to me. But I'm all right. I've got loads to tell you. It's all good news, but let me help you clear this away first.' His mum didn't move from the shock, he guessed. He got the dustpan and brush from the kitchen cupboard and cleared the broken glasses and plates splintered across the floor. 'Mum, you gotta do something about this. He's getting worse; one day, he's gonna go too far.' On the countertop, cutlery was manically scattered in chaos. His mum sat staring at the wall, her index finger on the handle of the carving knife, rotating the blade around and around, lost in a trance. Callum moved the knife slowly away from her and placed it back in the wooden block.

'So what's the good news?' she asked, which gave Callum some relief to hear her speak but still concerned she did not answer his question. He started to tell her about his day, about Lucy, explaining that she was now his girlfriend. Callum hoped his mum would relax and open up. Instead, she said nothing but continued to stare at the wall.

'Mum, I am serious; you have to snap out of this and start working out how you are going to leave Jim.'

Noticeably her breathing had grown louder, quick sucky sounds as if hyperventilating; Callum was growing concerned, thinking he might have to call an ambulance. Slowly she raised her head and looked Callum in the eyes, 'Leave Jim, are you crazy? He'd kill me.'

Callum took her hand and felt her shake; he moved in

closer and wrapped his arms around her, trying all he could to bring comfort. Her whole body was in the same state. Fear had taken its grip, a fear ten times greater than he had experienced earlier when confronted by Ray Blackman. There was little he could do but hold her until she started to calm down. For as long as it would take, he knew he had to stay there.

19

'What's up with you?' Steely Stan asked as he crane-handled the salt and vinegar crisps into his mouth, as sustenance, from the large glass bowl in the centre of the table and munched on them loudly. He brushed away the crumbs that had escaped his mouth from his yellow-stained t-shirt.

'Nothing, just get on and play your hand,' Jim said, sitting opposite, frustrated and annoyed at the question. There were four players tonight, not the regular five, due to Pete Fisher, Jim's usual drinking partner, having consumed too much alcohol the night before and having missed work now also missed the game. They played each week and alternated between Frank and Steve's house. It was at Frank's, which Jim preferred because it was closer to home, and he could take the back roads with less risk of being stopped by the old bill. It was also cleaner and stored less of an odour. If there was an odour, it was masked out by the Camel cigarettes he smoked by the truckload, in Jim's opinion, a preferred scent. Jim looked at the five cards in his hand as Eric Clapton bent notes for Cream in the background on the Fidelity stereo in the corner of the room.

Four aces and a pot of only seven pounds were not going to be much of a life changer. He looked at Steely munching on his crisps; the sound aggravated Jim's already heightened temper. 'Hurry up, Steely.'

'All right, keep your hair on.' Steely laid his cards. Three eights, Jim scooped up his seven pounds. 'Jim, come on, mate, you looked like your gaskets about to blow. Seriously mate, you worry me, not trouble with Rachel again, is it.'

'She's doin' my head, keeps on 'bout wantin' a car.' He picked up the cards; Steve, sitting to his right, had been dealing. Not so good. 'Love the girl to bits, but she pushes it too far sometimes.' Fifty pence in the pot with three cards returned in the hope of a miracle to change his luck. Life was unfair. Why some people had so much and others so little didn't make sense. It made him think back to a few years ago when he would find people to play in big games. Starting bids were five pounds and no one was allowed to play unless they had a hundred pounds to start and were prepared to lose it. It was a different world. Being the finder, he would sit in on games every so often. Tonight, seven pounds was the highest win so far and unlikely to be topped. By the end of the night, he knew he would have lost most of that and walked away with two or three pounds up or down as usual. He scanned the faces around the table. Rough, distant people who had lost their way. All with nothing. Empty people. Of the four around the table he was the only one still married and owned his own property - was that his success story?

The house they sat in now was rented. Frank's ex-wife lived with another man in Margate. Steve divorced twice with two kids he never saw. Steely never married; no surprise there, Jim thought. What woman would put up with a man who didn't know what a bath was? But maybe they had it right. Perhaps he would be better off alone; what did Rachel bring to his life? Sex, but he could get that elsewhere. He would lose half the house, Rachel thought it was hers, but he had kept her for the last six years, so he deserved at least half by his reckoning. And he earned at least that for her constant nagging. Steve dealt him another three equally bad cards.

He threw his cards into the centre of the table, 'I fold, pile of crap. I need another beer. Anyone else?' Three yeses, so Jim got up from the table, went to the kitchen, and got them from the fridge.

On returning to the table, Steely was cussing again

from another loss, the only one so far who hadn't won a game, now six hands into the night.

'Cheers, Jim,' Steely said, as he took the can of lager from Jim, 'maybe you should cut her some slack.' Jim sat back down and took a long swig enjoying the beer rolling down his throat, thinking about the answer.

'Maybe, but it ain't just that.'

'What's that? She got another man?' Steely laughed at his own joke, knowing Rachel could not have another man. Everybody around the table knew how possessive and controlling Jim was, and Rachel's opportunities of meeting another man were as slim as Steely dating Raquel Welch. And the chances of Jim allowing her a car was even weaker.

'Nah, course not. What woman would need another man if she had me.' They all laughed at the ridiculousness of his comment, but for Jim, he partly believed it to be true. 'Callum's becoming a bit lippy now - Needs to be put in his place at times, so that causes extra friction.'

'Callum, don't believe it,' piped in Steve, 'he's such a quiet boy, scared of his own shadow.'

'Yeah, well, he made friends with this crazy grey-wired haired old war hero or something.'

'What? He's thinking of joining the army now, is he?' Steve joked as he dealt the hand.

'Nah, this guy's a gardener or something like that, they just talk a lot, but I think he's giving him ideas above his station.'

'He's a gardener you say?' Steely jumped back into the conversation.

'So Rachel says.'

'And he's got grey wiring hair? Like Einstein?

'Think so – why, do you know him?'

'Not Potts, lives up Radfall Ride?' Steely found humour in his question.

'Yeah, that's the guy - why?' Jim, now intrigued to find out more.

'He ain't no war hero. He was in the war – sure! But he ran away. He was a deserter. He's well known round here. Thought you'd know that.'

'No,' Jim smiled, 'no, I didn't.' The news had made his night. He looked at his hand, two black aces and two black eights, never one for superstition and not wanting to tempt fate. He asked himself the question. What would Wild Bill Hickok do? But it was too good not to. 'Count me in,' and added his fifty pence to the pot. The best hand of the night for Jim, he banked twenty-five pounds; his luck was in, coming out with cash in his pocket whilst Steely went the whole night without one win.

Nineteen-Forty-Two

Fear had taken its stranglehold around his throat cutting off the rancid desert air. Potts walked away, unaware of the allied forces advancing forward against his path pushing past him. His gun left behind, the symbolic symbol, sacrificed in the bunker. The sun started to rise in front of him. Behind him, chaos triumphed, guns fired, men fell to the ground. Dead or injured, it was not important. But Potts heard nothing. His mind shut off from the horrors he had experienced too many times. Advancing soldiers grabbed his arm occasionally and shouted in raised voices in an effort to be heard over this maddening world to ask him, 'What you doing?' And then move on, too busy to care or wait for an answer. And then there were others who did not grab his arm. They asked no question. They already knew the answer. They too had questioned the stupidity of it all. They too had considered the alternative, but they failed to do anything about it, and when the next order came, they followed as they had before. The noise around muffled, the lights bright and flashed, but it made no difference. The war was over. No longer could he kill another man.

To his right, walking parallel, another soldier marched in the same direction as Potts. Neither man was aware of the other. The only man in Potts' mind was Woody. Dead at the age of twenty, never again will he kick a football. His mother and father at home, unaware they no longer had a son. His sister, still hoping with pointless hope he would return after the war. Potts knew he would not. The friend he could not protect, the only true friend Potts had ever had in his life, lay dead because of him. One day earlier, shooting that German officer would have been easy. Just another life to be taken, but he had reached his limit. There were only so many he could kill. Those before who had suffered his bullets mattered not, and with each step from the killing ground, he wished he had saved just one.

He walked for thirty minutes. Still, the lines of armoured vehicles loaded with men moving forward, queuing up, waiting to get to the front. Each man trained and ready to fight. But no one told them how the reflection of reality could affect the mind, holding the pain within. After another thirty minutes, the lines started to thin, but he kept walking. Nobody spoke to him now; he did not look anybody in the face. He knew what he would see if he did. Dead men walking, men with scars so deep they would never be healed. For the rest of their lives, memories remaining poisonous, killing each and everyone of them slowly each day.

The smell of the desert was full of death and hell penetrating his pores. He walked, trying to escape that stench but knew he never would.

'Hey mate, where you going?' A private in the scout car drove alongside Potts. 'Do you wanna lift?' Again the private called to Potts, who did not respond. 'I'm heading back to fifth division quarters. Need to pass some intel back to the Sergeant there. Give you a lift if you want?' Potts looked at the Private in the driver's seat. Eighteen years old, Potts estimated him to be, barely old enough to shave. The private stopped the scout car. Potts climbed in.

'How far is it?' Potts asked, his body and voice drained of energy. The further away he could get the better in Potts' opinion. Still, the noise was loud with the bombardment but not deafening as it had been.

'It's about twenty minutes away from all the hell that's going on there, at least. Do you smoke?' The private offered a cigarette to Potts, which he took and put in his mouth without lighting.

'Do you want a light for that, mate?' Potts continued to stare ahead without a word. 'You don't say much,' the private said, trying to create a conversation that he was beginning to believe was not going to happen. The sound of the bombardment faded away, and Potts sat in the scout car, thinking he was heading in the wrong direction. Not that he wanted to return to the mayhem which was back there. But back there, it would have been easy to end the questions and problems he knew would never leave him. There had been no conscious decision to walk in one direction or the other, and with logical thought returning, he wished he had walked the other way, for he was sure there would have been a bullet deservedly waiting for him. There was no fear, no hate, no emotion; he just wanted it to end, for he could see no point in anything anymore.

'Almost there,' said the private. Potts looked at him and realised that he knew he had deserted. Already at his age of innocence, the boy understood. 'I can drop you here,' he said, knowing that if he took Potts into camp he would be arrested for desertion.

Potts thought for a moment; not scared of arrest or death, he needed to continue walking. 'Drop me here, appreciate the lift, thanks.' Potts climbed down onto the sandy road below. 'Look after yourself. Make sure you get back to see your family when this is all over.'

'You too, mate,' the private replied. The engine revved as he pulled away and Potts watched him disappear into the distance before he started walking again.

20

The number twenty-two bus sailed along Radfall Hill and on their way to Potts' they held hands. It emitted an excitement Callum had not experienced before and a warm, invigorating feeling of completeness. Not completeness in the end but at the beginning of change. The change he had waited for to escape the labyrinth that always brought him back to where he started. Now a sense of hope ensconced around him since he and Lucy had been together. Break time at school and lessons they'd shared, sitting together, talking about this and that, and anything that came to mind, and at the end of each day, when no one was looking, they kissed to say goodbye. Callum liked that bit. It was the seal of confirmation, and he knew now it was no prank. No elaborate joke the other kids had concocted to make him look the fool. His confidence had grown whilst being with Lucy. Someone other than his mum cared for him, and he cared for her and then, of course, there was Potts. If someone had told him two months ago how different life would be now, he would not have believed them. Potts was like the father he lost six years back. Although Potts was different from his father, he liked to think they both shared similar traits. Thoughtful, caring, non-judgemental and understanding in accepting we all have our own faults. Callum realised now it was the faults in us all that made life interesting. Before, he would hide from the differences in people, but now that fear waned with each day that passed. Lucy rested her head on Callum's shoulder. Two new people in his life had changed it all.

In the fields to his right, men walked with sticks

and dogs, waxed jackets and cloth caps beating bushes where pheasants fled. The sound of shotguns reverberating disturbed Callum's thoughts. The sound numbed by the glass from the bus' window. Callum watched some pheasants escape while others' fates were not so lucky.

Lucy entered Potts' front garden first, and Callum closed the gate and dropped the latch clunking the gate closed. They approached the hut when a noise erupted from the chicken coop to celebrate Lizzie laying some eggs. Lizzie was always the reluctant one. As her cries of joy died down, Lucy looked at Callum to see if he heard what she had. They looked in the direction of the hut, and confirmation of a faint whimpering sound drifted towards them. Callum acknowledged her, and they crept slowly towards the door, nervous about what they may find. A distinctive crying was, without any doubt, coming from inside. The door was ajar; Callum moved in front of Lucy and peered inside. On the floor, in the corner, curled up in a ball, crying and weeping, was Potts. Callum ran towards him and knelt down beside him followed by Lucy.

'Potts, what's the matter? Are you okay?' Confused and concerned, unsure what to do. Oblivious to Callum and Lucy's presence, Potts ignored them and continued to weep.

'Potts, it's me and Callum,' Lucy said, trying to bring him back to some recognition of normality. Still, they received no response. He remained with his head wrapped with his arms shielding himself and looking only to the floor with his face hardly visible. Callum put his hand on Potts' shoulder, and at the same time, from the woods outside, a shotgun fired on its hunt. Potts jerked, screamed and threw his arm outward hitting Callum across the chest and knocking him to the floor. Callum held himself in pain.

'You okay?' Lucy checked to see the pain on Callum's face inflicted by the force of Potts' arm.

'Yeah, I'm fine,' Callum confirmed. 'What's the hell's

wrong with him?'

'Don't know, should we leave him? Let him calm down,' Lucy said as she moved away, scared and nervous.

'I'm not leaving him,' Callum said, dragging himself off the floor. 'He needs our help.' A sense of duty, a sense of care, a sense of debt, Callum did not know which it was and had not the time to think but held the conviction he knew he could not leave his friend in the state he was. He owed Potts too much. If it were not for him, he would still be hiding in his own little world, and there would be no Lucy with him now. He was sure and did not doubt that fact. And without suppression of fear, a natural and uninhibited urge with increased confidence to help another person took control. At that moment, the thought flashed through his mind, and he realised how he had spoken out about Jim and talked to his mum. If it did any good or not, he did not know, but at least he was able to voice an opinion, someone his mum could rely on, someone for her to talk to; he knew he would be there for her now as she had no one else, small things he would never have done before, he owed to Potts. And, now was, perhaps, the time to repay him for all he had done. 'Potts, listen, it's Callum, your friend,' he said, slowly easing his way back towards him. Potts eyed him cautiously.

'Get out of here,' Potts spat venomously. Lucy slotted herself in the open doorway.

'Callum,' she said, quiet and nervous.

'I'm not going, Lucy, you can, but I'm staying.'

'I'm staying with you,' Lucy replied after a moment's consideration.

Callum, reassured by Lucy's support, turned back and looked at Potts shaking and crying, with tears rolling down his face. Another gun fired in the woods, the trees cracked, and a thud as something hit the ground made Potts jerk and look up in fear again. 'It's those damn guns, Lucy,' Callum said, turning to Lucy in realisation. 'Potts, it's okay, they're just hunting, shooting pheasants.' He edged his way closer, and within an arm's distance, he stretched out again to rest his hand on his shoulder. Potts just stared vacantly at Callum. Confusion or recognition Callum was unsure, but there was a definite change from the fearful expression he had displayed before. 'Potts, it's okay; no one's gonna hurt you.' The words felt strange coming from his mouth, but they seemed right. 'It's Callum, your friend,' he said and moved closer and wrapped his arm around Potts. As he held him, he felt Potts shaking. Potts looked up at Callum, the little boy, held by his father after falling off the swing or hurting himself in the playground, looking for reassurance that everything would be all right. Callum said nothing but continued to hold and comfort. Lucy moved back to sit down beside Callum; Potts looked up to check if it was friend or foe. Minutes passed, and after a further ten, the shaking eased; twenty and Potts started to recognise Callum and Lucy. His fear turned to embarrassment, and he pulled out of Callum's arms and sat upright with his back against the wall. Relaxed bodies filled the room as things returned to normal. 'It's okay,' Callum tried to reassure him.

'Sorry,' Potts said, looking to the ceiling, 'I never wanted you to see me like this.' Silence was best; no need for words, Callum decided, and they just sat there breathing slowly. After five more minutes, Lucy stood up.

'I'll go and make some tea,' Lucy said, leaving the hut for the kitchen. Callum offered an arm and helped Potts up and they sat at the table and waited for Lucy to return with the tea. She placed the tray with the teapot, cups and a jug of milk on the table and sat and joined the two of them. 'I'll pour,' Lucy said and placed a cup in front of Potts as she poured milk to start; she remembered from her first meeting with Potts how he had demonstrated how to make the perfect cup of tea.

'Thanks,' he said, 'I'm sorry, didn't want you to worry.'

'Are you feeling all right now?' Lucy asked.

'Yeah, I'm fine. It normally only lasts a short time, five minutes at most, but recently has been getting worse.'

'What caused it?' Callum asked, desperate and worried about the answer.

'Since the war,' Potts explained, 'it was bad shortly after but got better and faded away. Used to go on for half hour or more normally but sometimes hours. But as I say, after a few years it got better, but seems to be getting worse again.'

'Do you know what brings it on?'

'Could be anything, a loud bang, a plane flying overhead. That's why I live here, really. Keeping me-self to me-self, best that way. Only ever go out to earn a bit of money or get food and bits from the shops. I used to go out more, but people started picking on me, calling me names. And, word got out,' he paused, contemplating if to continue, 'that I deserted during the war.'

Callum couldn't help the shame that crawled over him when he heard those words. The man he had looked up to, the man he thought a war hero, he now found out to be a deserter. Yet, before those thoughts passed, guilt swallowed him. Who was he to judge? He had not been there. He remembered his fight with Ray Blackman and how scared he had been then. There were no guns or threats of death, just a black eye. 'It doesn't matter, Potts. What do they know?'

'It's what I know that troubles me most,' Potts continued. Details he had not revealed before. The death of his friend he blamed himself. The death of so many young men's lives wasted, futures obliterated, and fathers, mothers and partners stolen from their loved ones. And, how he could no longer kill, no matter the cause or reason. A war had to be fought, he understood. For the greater good, but he could take no part in killing another man. And then the fear of death took its hold on him. From someone who faced death and danger daily, thrived on it in the early years, and was recognised for his bravery on many occasions, he became the one who would run. There was only so much a man could take.

Both Callum and Lucy listened in disbelief when Potts described, in detail, the carnage he went through. Neither doubted they would not have done the same. He was no coward; he had been braver than most men and saved many lives at the risk of his own. The more Potts talked, the more Callum and Lucy realised what a good man he was and worried about the suffering he had hidden away from them. And, from himself for all those years.

'Have you spoken to anybody about it,' Lucy asked, 'maybe you should see a doctor.'

Potts paused for a moment, 'You're probably right, Lucy,' and then laughed at what Lucy and Callum thought to be a private joke. 'Strange thing is I saw a doctor last week.' Potts said no more about it. They didn't want to upset Potts further by asking more questions, and the conversation moved on.

Tea finished, Potts back to his usual self, Lucy offered to wash the cups and teapot up, but Potts insisted she and Callum had done enough for him and took the empty cups and saucers out to the kitchen.

Callum's thoughts about Potts were distracted by Lucy touching his thigh to get his attention, 'Don't I want someone strong and not a coward? Callum, what you did today showed how strong and brave you are,' she said and leant over and kissed him on the lips, a reward he always welcomed.

**

The smell of authority and officialdom filled the room. It was a world alien to Rachel. It scared her further, and her mind played tricks, making her self-conscious of the other people's looks in the room. All knowing her secrets, knowing her to be the faker, and she had brought it on herself. It was easy to pretend she was the victim, and she had believed it, but her mind had swung like a pendulum the last few days, and now it was stuck pulling off the veil to reveal the truth.

From the small coffee table by the bay window piled high with magazines to pass the time whilst she waited. Woman's Weekly; a story of love and romance, a woman meets a tall, dark stranger, an instant attraction, and love explodes. A pointless story, and pointless to think she would be able to concentrate enough to absorb any of the fiction so far removed from her life that it was almost insulting. She pretended anyway, like one of the two other women sat there reading. A slight cough, a clearing of the throat, from the one with the magazine, who she knew too was not reading. Code between them, a class she will never reach, wearing everyday clothes for their appointment. Not as Rachel had worn her best and only decent dress. The woman at the reception desk who had greeted Rachel on her arrival wore glasses, bifocals that made her look down her nose at everything that moved and eyed the room with suspicion. What am I doing here? She silently asked herself. Her breathing increased with her heart rate, guilty of the mistake she had made. It was not too late. There was still time to leave, but how could she get up and walk out now? Her - with those eyes judging all, all-being, all-seeing, her with the perfect life, her that did no wrong.

Five minutes until the clock struck two-thirty when her appointment was scheduled. There was still time to run, but this was not just for her. It was for Callum; she had no choice, knowing in the depths of truth that something had to change. She must hold on to the strength she had had when she decided to make the appointment. It buzzed rather than rang and jolted her out of her mindless wanderings. The receptionist picked up the phone and listened for a moment before speaking, 'Of course, Mr Pemberton. I will send her in.'

Rachel's heart thumped, knowing it was her turn. Now there was no turning back.

The receptionist stood as she spoke, Mrs Thorne, Mr Pemberton will see you now,' Rachel looked at the clock; dead on two-thirty. The efficiency of it all frightened her further, 'I will show you in.' Rachel fumbled with the magazine, first taking it with her, then putting it on the seat she had been sitting on before finally picking it up to return it to the coffee table. The receptionist waited patiently, without expression, until Rachel followed her through a short corridor. They came to the office with the white clinical door where a plaque proudly displayed Mr Pemberton's name. The receptionist opened the door.

'Ah, Mrs Thorne,' came the cheerful voice that Rachel thought sounded like he must be the happiest man on the planet boomed out, 'come, sit down.'

'Thank you,' Rachel replied apologetically and sheepishly eased herself into the chair in front of his desk.

'Thank you, Mrs Cartwright,' he said as she closed the door, leaving just the two of them in his office.

Books lined the shelves, leather-bound and intimidating; Rachel had never seen so many. Had he really read them all?' She looked at him as he rifled through his desk drawer, eventually revealing an A4-lined paper pad that he placed on the desk in front of him. He smiled, and Rachel thought he had a kind face that made her feel a little more at ease. It was one she could trust; she hoped this time to be correct as so much counted on it. Leaning back in his chair, he ran his fingers up his red braces that had twisted slightly against his blue and white thick striped shirt.

'Mrs Thorne,' Rachel sat upright in her chair as if in front of the headmaster, 'to confirm a few points, the appointment is until three P.M., and in that time, we can assess your situation. Identify the best route forward and the steps to be taken.' He paused and looked out of the window before returning his focus to Rachel. 'Now, the best thing is to tell me in your own words what the situation is and what it is you are looking for, so please – in your own time.' Rachel drew a deep breath. Curtain call, the most critical moment of her life.

'I want to get a divorce, the man I live with attacked me, and I am scared he might hurt me again.' As the words rattled from her mouth, she wanted to cry. She tried to breathe slowly to compose herself.

'It's okay, take your time,' Mr Pemberton kindly voice offered, but Rachel knew a clock was ticking.

'It's not just that, my son lives with me, he is fifteen, and I worry he could be in danger too. Jim, that's my husband; he loses control, doesn't know what he's doing, so I have made the decision to divorce him.'

'Have you ever notified the police about these attacks?' Already, he had found the holes in her story, the faker, as she feared revealed, but so soon, within a sentence. A big mistake she knew it was. Maybe she could leave and forget the whole thing. 'It's okay if you have not; it would assist your case if you had. But please, continue.'

'No, I've always been too scared to. Always thought it would make it worse. I lived in fear of what he would do if I had reported it.'

'I take it your husband is not in agreement with the divorce? I am just trying to establish our best ground for filing for divorce. Has your husband ever been unfaithful?'

'I don't think so, no, he loves me.' Rachel shocked herself with the statement and had always known Jim had loved her. And that was the reason she had stayed with him so long. 'No, I don't think he has,' she concluded, removing the *love part of the statement* that she felt might go against her.

'We can file for divorce on the basis of unreasonable behaviour. This can include physical violence or verbal abuse. You must understand this can be a drawn out process if the other party contests the statements we put forward.

However, my advice in the first instance would be to speak to Jim and get his agreement. It will make the process much easier and less stressful for all parties.' Rachel, with each minute passing, increasing doubt gained momentum too if she had made the right decision. Jim would never agree; she knew that. How naïve she had been, but had she now opened the door to something she could not stop? Thinking of Callum, she had to show strength or else he would suffer. The only thing in the world she really cared about and would find the determination needed to protect him.

'That's fine. I will talk to him, but whatever it takes, I want a divorce,' she said, adamantly with the restored belief it was the right decision.

On her walk home, with every step, she believed she had done the right thing and, with the next, changed her mind. But the ball had been set in motion, and she had no choice but to roll with it.

21

Thursday's night was study night and they had kept it that way. His favourite night of the week, the routine they adopted, Top of The Pops, followed by an hour of revision covering that week's class assignments, and then back to listening to bands Callum had grown to love. The Clash, The Boomtown Rats and The Stranglers all brave enough to call out the wrongs in this world and society. Lyrics he had now memorised as he had poems by Edgar Allen Poe or one of Shakespeare's sonnets (Sonnet 18 - Shall I compare thee to a summer's day – That they spent three months repeating and repeating and repeating – That still half the class could not recite).

'I'll be round at seven,' Callum said, unplugging his bike from the rusty green sheds at the front of the school. Lucy's back leant against the corrugated metal of the stand, wearing her full length leather coat and smiling slyly.

'I have to go somewhere first, in Whitstable, so meet me on Tankerton Slopes, by the canons, at seven-thirty.' Callum looked at Lucy, her smile growing mischievously greater.

'Where ya' going? Don't ya' wanna watch Top of The Pops?'

'Can't tonight, meet me there, and then we'll go to my place.' They kissed goodbye; He knew everybody was looking on with jealousy; for once other kids wanted to be Callum, and it made him feel good.

Intrigue was busting at his seams as he cycled to Tankerton Slopes, thinking about what Lucy was up to, and he couldn't wait to find out the big secret. He trusted her. A feeling unusual but comforting; whatever she was up to, he knew it would not be bad. He had plenty of time as he skipped dinner at home as they had planned to eat together on the seafront. There was half an hour to spare when he arrived and sat on the grass slopes, by the canons looking out to sea, in the regular place they would go after school. The air was clean and fresh and he enjoyed every breath. To think they had their own spot made him feel good. The place he had sat on many times before with feelings of sadness and loneliness, watching others walk by hand in hand, wishing he could be one of those people. And now he was, those old feelings replaced with something he thought he would never experience. Something magical, something so powerful, it smashed those dark days into a distant void of nothingness. The mystery Lucy had left him with had brought on an optimistic excitement. For something good to happen a month ago, the uncertainty would have left him with doubt and fear. Now, the only fear he had was not for himself but for his mum and Potts.

Yesterday Callum and Lucy visited Potts to check he had had no further attacks. He was back to his normal self and shrugged off the incident, but Potts said he was returning to see the doctor in a few days. He didn't want to talk about it, embarrassed, ashamed of memories he had tried to suppress and did not want to relive again, Callum or Lucy were sure. Saturday, they had arranged to go fishing on Potts' boat. He would be working on Mrs Wickes' garden in the morning opposite Callum's house, and after he had finished, they agreed to pick up Lucy and spend the afternoon catching fish for dinner that evening. Callum's mind had wandered away from Lucy for the first time to think of Potts as he checked his watch. Seven-thirty, he looked up the hill towards the

Castle and he saw a girl in the distance approaching. As she got closer, he recognised the gait, it was Lucy, and then her hair, spiked with red and black streaks. When she saw Callum had spotted her she started to run towards him, laughing as she approached; she wrapped herself around him, kissing him as if he was a soldier absent for years returning from war, reunited in their true love.

'What do you think?' Standing back, running her fingers through her hair, posing model-like.

` Wow, you look amazing.' And she did; Callum could not believe it was possible for her to look more beautiful than she already did. He was the luckiest boy on the planet and wanted to kiss her. And he did. As they had missed Top Of The Pops, they made their way into town as planned to buy fish and chips to take back to her house. Lucy's mum was working tonight, so Lucy had said she would look after her dad. They queued up outside the black and white fish and chip shop in Harbour Street.

'Best fish and chips ever,' Lucy told Callum. It was popular, so Callum did not argue, and as they rarely had fish and chips at home, he wouldn't know. The queue went out of the door and snaked up the road. As they stood in line, Callum noticed people looking at them, older couples, unsure what to make of them.

'People keep looking,' he said under his breath to Lucy.

'Let 'em,' she said boldly, and Callum knew she was right. Let them look, and he embraced the moment, not wanting to hide but to stand out. He took hold of Lucy's hand. He wanted the world to know they were together, no longer hiding, knowing he had as much right as anybody else to live his life as he saw fit. With Lucy included in that role, he added to his thoughts.

At Lucy's house he helped in the kitchen. Lucy got three plates from the cupboard, and Callum plated out the fish and chips and served it up at the dining room table, where the three of them sat and ate.

'How's school going, Callum? Lucy tells me you have been a great help,' Mr Curtis said.

'I hope so, but Lucy didn't need much help.' They continued to talk as they ate. A clear and complete contrast to conversations at home with Jim. Not once had Jim ever asked how school was, nor had he shown any interest in what Callum was doing other than to mock. Yet, here Mr Curtis showed a genuine enthusiasm to know. Callum felt awkward to begin, a stranger in a strange town he had never been to before. After a while, he relaxed and felt at ease. It was easy with Mr Curtis, judging no one, and there was no need for competition or putting the other person down. He was full of praise for Lucy, how she was so thoughtful, helping him and her mother when and wherever she could.

'Not sure about the hair, though,' he joked. Ordinary people living ordinary lives, Callum thought and concluded that was what he wanted. They finished the fish and chips, and Callum agreed they were the best he had ever tasted. He and Lucy cleared the table, washed and wiped up, and left Mr Curtis to watch the television whilst they went upstairs to study.

Callum talked algebra whilst Lucy thumbed through the Daily Mirror. 'Are you listening?'

'Yeah, sure,' she said, although the truth was the opposite. 'Oh wow, shall we watch this? It starts in ten minutes, The Exorcist.'

Callum hated horror movies; they sent chills through him every time and he avoided them at all costs, and that film, reports had it was the worst of them all. Trying to avoid and ignore the question, 'Lucy, aren't we meant to be doing maths?'

'Nah, let's watch The Exorcist. Unless you're scared.'

'I'm not scared. Okay, as you obviously have no interest in furthering your education,' he replied with a nervous tagged joke and immediately regretted his impulse to accept the offer.

'Hah, you are so punk rock.' Lucy said and whacked him with the newspaper she had been reading. 'I'll make coffee,' she said and was gone before Callum had a chance to say yes.

The film was starting on her return, and he felt a sense of relief he was no longer alone. She flicked the switch off for the ceiling light, fear returned to Callum's body, leaving just the bedside lamp glow atmospherically spreading itself around the room. Lucy sat next to Callum on the bed hooking her arm through his. From what Callum could work out, Lucy loved every minute of it, the music, the jumps, the scares and the gore. Terrified, he laughed off his fear hoping she didn't catch on to his camouflage. Thoughts of cycling home after watching the film began to play on his mind. He sipped his coffee over and over, quickly and autonomously, before slurping on nothing and replacing it on the bedside table next to Lucy's mug, which was still half full. Adverts arrived, and Callum thanked them privately for the respite. The man from Milk Tray spidered up the wall to prove his love as Lucy leant into Callum's neck resting against his cheek; he turned towards her, and she kissed him. This time she opened her mouth and slid her tongue into his. Each day brought new experiences with Lucy, and everyone good. The restart of the film was an inconvenience for Callum, but the adverts, and more so Lucy's tongue, had brought a welcome distraction from the horrors that filled the screen. Desperately he wanted the next set of adverts to arrive, but he didn't have to wait that long when Lucy again leant forward and pressed her mouth to his. He opened his mouth, expecting and waiting for her tongue but instead received a flood of coffee she had transferred from her mouth to his, laughing hysterically and loudly; she fell back on the bed looking seductively inviting. She pulled Callum towards her and kissed him, no tricks this time. Her hand on his wrist directed him to her breast, where he nervously fumbled to unbutton her blouse and then Lucy, with her hand, unclipped the strap of her bra at the back.

Cycling home, Callum had forgotten the horrors of the film and replaced it with a world of feelings so wonderful his mind sailed on a cloud that could not be touched or hurt in any way.

For that moment, it was a perfect world.

22

Friday night after school, the sun shone. Blue sky and the weather had held gloriously for the end of September. Lucy had endless comments about her hair from the other kids all day at school. All said, she looked really cool and Potts agreed.

'Your hair looks really good, brings out the wild side in you,' Potts commented.

'Thanks,' Lucy replied with an innocent smile as if she did not know what he meant.

'I think I might go for something like that myself,' Potts added.

'You should - It would suit you,' Lucy laughed as she spoke. Callum looked around the woodland and enjoyed the peaceful and relaxed atmosphere the three of them shared. Last night he had little sleep thinking of Lucy. And today at school, they had spoken with excitement about visiting Potts that evening. They walked to the chicken coop, where Potts dropped the large hessian sack full of feed by his side.

'Last gardening rounds of the year,' Potts said, throwing pellets of feed to the chickens that scrabbled and pecked contently; Callum and Lucy helped throw the feed they had taken from the sack by Potts' side. 'Will still 'ave to go a couple of times to clear the leaves in autumn at Mrs Wickes' and general tidy up, but not every week.' Seasons change, as does life. 'I'll bring the boat; if you're still okay to go fishing?'

'Yeah, I'm up for that. What do you think, Lucy?'

Callum said.

'I can't,' Lucy had forgotten to tell Callum, 'my dad has an appointment at the hospital.' Callum said nothing but was disappointed to hear the words. It was only momentarily, as he knew nothing could upset his world, which had become so perfect since yesterday. Although, there were things outside his control. 'Sorry, I forgot to say. I won't be back until after lunch, so I'll wait for you on the slopes for when you get back in.' Although he would have preferred them to have been together on the boat, Lucy waiting on the Tankerton slopes when they returned made Callum feel better. The romanticism about it returned his life to where he wanted it to be.

'Shame, but we will see you when we get back. I should finish Mrs Wickes' by noon, so let's say half an hour after that. And we will be out a few hours, so should get back in about three o'clock.'

'That's great. I will be waiting for you,' Lucy confirmed and threw Callum a smile that made everything all right. Potts threw his last handful of feed to the far corner. Only Marilyn observed, separating herself from the others to feast further.

23

The clinical smell of the waiting room was something Lucy hated. They could kill every germ in every crevice. Throw bleach or disinfectant all over it for all she cared. Every month was the same, test following test, but she knew it made no difference. Dad would never get better. What was the point? It was just a game. But that was just it - it was no game. This was somebody's life they toyed with recklessly. *False hopes – Why not tell us – Put us out of our misery* – That was all she wanted, and everybody can then get on with their lives. But she never said it. Never out loud. It would hurt her mum, instead, she kept quiet, and stayed strong, no point in causing upset when we could all pretend, she thought as she looked at her mum, sat there patiently, hoping for a different response. *No Change, Mrs Curtis.* That is what he would say. Not the miracle her mum had hoped. She sat there with eyes glazed as if permanent tears had formed, Lucy wished she could wipe them away, make it all better, let her mum live and laugh again like she used to, but she knew it was impossible. Some things are best left unsaid. The window to her right offered a view of a finely kept garden. Benches on its periphery, a cedar tree stood proud and central, its roots deep and strong, but one day even that tree will be gone, Lucy thought. A young man tended to the flowers that added colour to the grassed area, beautiful in clusters of yellow and pink, Lucy did not know their names. She made a note to ask Potts when she saw him next.

***

Still blooming and full of colour the Chrysanthemum flourished that Potts planted only a short time back. Potts knelt, pulled the weeds that gathered around them from their roots, and threw them into the wheelbarrow beside him. The flowers, in their short life, had used so much energy in that time, and within a month, they would be gone. In that time, short to some, it had not been wasted, Potts thought. In the blink of a life they had given so much pleasure. Mrs Wickes often commented on how beautiful they looked in the morning and how much she enjoyed looking out at them. They had served their purpose in their complete simplicity. Was that not the purpose of us all, he thought to himself?

It was not yet nine in the morning, and for a moment, Potts remained motionless and breathed in the earthy fragrance of the flowers around him as he had many times before with the sun, unusually bright for an early October morning. Solitude had served him well for many years, but he wondered if he had done right. He looked to Callum's house and at his bedroom window, curtains drawn, shutting out the world. Something Potts had done for most of his life, and it was through Callum he realised he had been a prisoner only from his self-making. Movement jolted his focus to the front door below the window. A man came out, dressed in jeans and a white t-shirt. It was Jim. Although Potts had never seen him, he recognised him immediately from the description Callum had told him. Potts could not help but stare with bitterness at the man that had ruined a young boy's life. He wanted to physically hurt him, to teach him a lesson, a feeling now foreign but justified, he judged. Jim looked up and straight at Potts. Their eyes met for a moment, too long for Potts' comfort, so he dropped his stare to the ground. Fear returned and flooded through him; he sat down on the grass behind the bush to shield himself from Jim's view.

Jim scoffed as he saw Potts fall to the ground. He got

in his van and reversed off the drive. Instead of turning to the left, he went right and put the van into first gear. Slowly he drove the van and stopped it directly outside Mrs Wickes, knowing Potts was behind the bush.

'I know you're there,' Jim teased, 'I'm coming to get you one day – Coward – Deserter.' Revved the engine, kicked down on the accelerator and left the smell of burning rubber and exhaust fumes behind him as he headed towards the end of the cul-de-sac before spinning it around with a screech of tyres screaming with anger against the tarmac and then pulling up again at the point he had stopped before. There was no sign of Potts, but Jim knew he was there hiding, 'And stop playing with the little kids - Pervert.' Again he accelerated away with aggression, leaving Potts behind on the grass behind the bush, shaking, listening to the sound of the engine's growl. At the end of the road, he turned left onto Chestfield Road heading towards the seafront, and from there he would head towards Herne Bay, where he had a small plastering job planned for the morning.

***

Seeing Potts had riled Jim. He did not know why but could not get him out of his head as he drove. He reached for the packet of Marlboros on the lower shelf on the passenger side. And with his eyes off the road for a moment, he veered off to the wrong side. The sound of a car horn coming directly at him alerted him and he swerved, mounting the pavement and narrowly missing the lamppost. A woman with a pram stared, only ten yards from the other side of the lamppost, in fear and shock for the safety of her and her child, and with the window open, Jim leant out and screamed, 'What you staring at, bitch?' Not waiting for an answer, drove off, lit the last cigarette, and threw the empty packet out the window in a rage. He drew in the smoke hoping for a shot of calm that failed to arrive.

Instead of going straight to his job he stopped at the seafront and got out of the van. There was plenty of time, the job would not take him long, and he needed to gather his thoughts. From Cookes Stores he bought another pack of twenty. He walked across the road, sat on the concrete slab surround of the miniature boating lake and looked out to sea. The second cigarette still brought no calm, and the anger grew. What had he done wrong?

He had tried his best. His life was Rachel, and why could she not understand? She had been the only woman for him, a love so unbelievably strong even he was surprised how powerful. Never before or since had he experienced such a force, and from the moment he met her at Michael's thirtieth birthday party had there been any doubt. Rachel was the only woman he ever wanted, and would spend a life together. He was the only one who could make her happy he knew that. Everything he did was for her. Protecting her from the outside world littered full of so many bad people. He slapped the concrete border next to him; his hand stung from the force, and anger returned towards Rachel; it was her fault again for not understanding. If only she knew what he had been through to keep her and to get her in the first place, risking everything, but she would not understand. And then there was Callum. The boy was not his, but he had looked after him. It was his money that paid for his clothes, his food, his books. His Goddamn books, all those physics books and maths books, what good were they, but he had never complained. It wasn't normal for a boy his age to want to read things like that. He should be reading football books and men's magazines. He just wasn't right, but he had said nothing, kept quiet for Rachel. Recent days had been harder than most; there had been a change, something he had not recognised in her. When they had argued before they would make up. Sex was their reunification, their sign of forgiveness for what each had done, but this time it had not happened. No sex, and now the silence. When he spoke, she would walk away without acknowledging his existence, as if he were a ghost in his own house. It was a beautiful morning and it grieved him to have such thoughts. Count to ten, the voice inside his head spoke. Count to ten, so many times he had heard that. Ten, nine, eight, slowly he did, and with each declining number, he took a larger gap between each one, trying to self-hypnotise himself. On five – Flowers – He would buy her flowers. This time he would be the one to back down. For once, even though he knew it was her fault, she was too precious to him to let it continue. The calm he had been seeking arrived, and he got up and walked back to his van, content with the answer he had found, knowing Rachel always loved flowers.

***

Doubt came back to torment Rachel as she paced up and down, cigarette in hand. She was eager to talk to Callum but decided to let him sleep longer. Her mind jumped about from here to there. The need for confirmation she was doing the right thing nagged her hard. All those years together would mean nothing. Was she giving up too easily and quickly? Her second marriage gone wrong, and what would people say? She knew how people liked to talk. The life she had craved so much. To be with someone was not asking too much, but now it would be ruined. Nobody would want her after this. First husband dead, and second divorced. Maybe she had jumped too quickly and had read the situation wrong. She knew Jim loved her. Like no other, *I could never love anyone like I love you, Rachel; never forget that*, those words he spoke, not just once, but many times.

A tear rolled down her face. It gave her strength from the memories of all the tears before that had fallen, all the tears of hurt and pain she had lived. And just like the tear that ran down her face and rested on her lips, she would wipe him away too. Wipe him from her life, whatever that meant; life had to be better without him. She looked out onto the garden from the dining room chair where she sat. Weeds had grown where there was once perfect lawn. It seemed only yesterday that she and Michael had come to look at the property. A new house with just topsoil as a garden where the seeds had not yet grown, and three months later they moved in where the lush green grass had grown. Michael had always cut the grass; it was his passion outside work, so house-proud; she smiled and looked upwards, wanting to speak to him now. *The other man's grass is always greener,* he would say. It was his favourite saying, but is that what he would say now? Would he think she was running away from her problems, something he would never do? The grass elsewhere had never been greener when she had been with Michael. They had argued occasionally but never to the point of thinking she would be better off without him. Or was it time that blurred her memory? Confusion, fear and insecurity played tricks on her. She looked at the clock on the kitchen wall, twenty minutes before ten. If Callum was not up by ten, she would wake him.

***

The familiar hum of the lawnmower welcomed Callum out of a long night's sleep. He curled up and snuggled into his pillow, comforted by the thought his friend was nearby. His mum was downstairs, and Lucy, so real she was with him wherever he was. The morning sun paraded itself through the drawn curtains, and Callum's eyes focused on a fly, tired and weak, that made flight in stop-overs from the curtains to the wall. Too tired to fly, it trod the path from the patterned circles from one to another; it made the journey before it fell on its back and gave up life. Callum hauled himself out of bed and opened the curtains. The boat hooked up to the back of Potts' jeep excited him with the thought of the day ahead. He watched Potts clear the weeds from the flowerbeds at the garden's front.

He worried about Potts. Concerned about the stress, all those years since the war still affected him, he told himself to make a note to check Potts kept those doctor's appointments. He worried about his mum. What would become of her? In a few years, he would move out and leave her alone with Jim. He worried about Lucy and her dad and decided he would help her where he could. And then he realised how he had changed over the last few weeks, with time to consider other people, time to look out for them. Before, he had spent all his time fighting the problems he had, but now that burden had been offloaded. The thought of looking out for others gave him an extra boost, a bigger reason for life.

By ten o'clock, he had washed and changed and made his way downstairs, where his mum was waiting with tea and jam on toast already prepared for him.

'Thanks, mum,' he said with a smile and joined his mum at the table where she sat with her tea and cigarette.

'What you got planned today?' she asked.

'I'm going out with Potts after he finishes work at Mrs Wickes, and then we're going fishing in his boat. Lucy says she'll be waiting for us when we get back, so probably go back to Potts' after that.'

'That's good. I was hoping you were going out. But I have to tell you something first.' She took another drink of her tea and drew on her cigarette. Callum sensed something big. 'I wanted to tell you before Jim got back.' Another drag on the cigarette, her hand visibly shaking, 'I am going to divorce Jim.'

'What!' They had spoken about it; Callum had told her that she should leave Jim, she should divorce him, but he never believed she would do it.

'I saw a solicitor the other day, and he's going to do all the legal stuff.' Callum didn't know what to say, he was pleased, but there were so many questions. 'Is that okay? Do you think I am doing the right thing?' Callum looked his mum in the eye seeing she still needed reassurance.

'Oh yeah - Yes, mum, it's the best thing you can do.'

'So, it's probably best you're not here.'

'No way, I'm going to be here; you're not going to be alone when you tell him.'

'Callum, this is my problem, not yours.'

'You know what he's like, mum. You can't be alone when you tell him; it's too dangerous. He's dangerous, no, mum.'

'Callum, I can't let you do this.'

'One minute,' Callum interrupted her; he thought of Potts across the road. 'Mum, what I'll do is go and speak to Potts and tell him what is going on. And, tell him to listen out for any arguing or shouting, and I'll leave the door open, so if it gets really bad, he'll come in and help out.'

'I'm sure he doesn't want to get involved in our domestic problems.'

'Mum, he's a friend, he won't mind, and have you seen the size of Potts? Jim wouldn't dare do anything if he came in.' Callum realised he was playing a game of bluff here. He knew how Potts was suffering, and it would be unfair on him, but he could not leave his mum alone.

'Okay, but check he is all right with that. And, then afterwards, you go out fishing and meet up with Lucy.' He finished his toast and went to see Potts opposite.

From the bay window at the front of the house, Rachel watched him cross the road and approach Potts. A big smile came on Potts' face as Callum approached. She watched intently, trying to read his mind and thoughts from his facial expressions and the twitch of every muscle movement in his face. The smile dropped from his face to a look of concern before Callum turned and left. Neither of them was smiling anymore.

'What'd he say?' She asked as soon as Callum entered the front room.

'He's fine, nothing to worry about,' he said, convincing nobody.

24

Orange, purple and red bustling with joy, recompense and remorse, Jim returned armed with flowers. The radio in the van fired out Thin Lizzy's Cowboy Song vocally accompanied by Jim, windows open, as he drove along the seafront just a few minutes from home. This time it would be different. He looked out to the grass banks that overlooked the frothing waves, couples walking hand in hand on a sun-soaked October morning.

***

Potts looked around warily, nervous about what was on its way. Trying hard to control the fear already crawling over him, gripping from within, snake-like sneaking up on its prey. This was for Callum he told himself, his friend. And, Woody, the thought of the life lost tormented still. Guilt and shame had been the dagger that lodged deep for all these years. An animal tearing away at his soul, his body shook. All his strength escaped like a punctured tire deflating. He sat on the grass. Never could he repair what he had done, but maybe this was his chance for atonement. From Callum's open bedroom window, he heard the music start. The volume amplified with The Clash's Tommy Gun sending warnings down the road. The lyrics resonating and tormenting Potts:

You'll be dead when your war is won
Tommy gun

But did you have to gun down everyone?
I can see it's kill or be killed

He closed his eyes, wanting to be somewhere else, but he knew he wanted nowhere else. The music ended, a short burst, one song, and then the sound of a diesel engine in the distance grew closer. A V2 bomber honing its direction for the defined end. Potts opened his eyes. The white van crawled up the road, snarling its way onto the drive.

Callum, in his bedroom, heard the front door close. He looked out the window at the van on the drive. Potts opposite sat head down; Callum worried he was on his own in protecting his mum. Inhaling deeply, hoping to find strength from somewhere, he turned and left the safety of his room and made his way downstairs. He opened the front door wide and entered the living room. The wind routed itself from the open front bay windows blowing the net curtains inwards, passing through Callum's body transfixed in the living room doorway, out the front door behind him, a ghost fleeing the scene.

'Thank you, Jim, they're lovely.' Over Jim's shoulder, his mum's eyes met Callum's as he entered the dining room.

'Do you like them?' Jim asked.

'They're lovely,' She said, a look of guilt carried across her face as her gaze dropped to the bouquet of flowers in her hand. 'Let me put them in some water.' She fumbled around in the cupboard for a vase. Near the back of the cupboard, she found a tall vase and pulled it out clumsily, knocking over the other pots and pans stacked to the front. 'How was work?' Small talk, Callum recognised, avoiding the moment, evading the subject. Callum moved in further and sat at the dining room table, opening the Melody Maker, trying to be invisible but watching every move. Jim moved into the kitchen and flicked the switch on the kettle.

'Tea, Rachel,' Jim turned to Callum and forced a smile, 'Callum, d'ya wanna cuppa?'

'No, thank you, I'm all right,' Callum replied, wanting nothing from that man. He feared the old routine. Would his mum fall for it again? Not now; she had gone so far. His mum cut the stems, filled the vase with water, arranged the flowers, walked out of the kitchen, and placed them on the dining room table. The flowers in front of Callum gave off the vial stench of Jim.

'Jim, we need to talk.' He ignored her and instead started to clear the plates and cups by the sink. He never did that. Opening cupboards, placing cup next to cup, 'Jim, did you hear what I said.'

'About what?' Knives and forks next, his breathing deepened. Preparing for something, he did not know what but knew nothing good was coming.

'I want a divorce.'

'No, you don't,' Jim replied as if it were a question he heard daily, dismissing it as a trivial request with the subject now closed. He picked up the carving knife from the draining boards and wiped the droplets of water from it with a tea towel.

'Jim!' Rachel tried again to get him to listen.

'What's for dinner?' His eyes narrowed, daring her to repeat herself. Knife in hand. A threat, A game of chess, he waited her next move. Callum surveyed the tension filling the room and looked at his mum, willing her not to back down.

'Jim, I'm sorry, I can't do this anymore. I need a divorce.' He stabbed the carving knife hard down into the wooden chopping board on the counter and screamed.

'You are not listening. I said – No, you do not.' Callum and his mum looked at the carving knife, still twanging and swaying from the force he had used to thrust it into the wood. Callum looked to the window in the front room. The breeze blew an invitation for rescue or escape against the net curtains. The front door within reach if need be. He thought about standing up but worried Jim might see it as a threat and make things worse. 'Now, get on and make the dinner, you ungrateful bitch,' still, his voice at a scream, he walked into the dining room area from the kitchen and picked up the vase, removed the flowers and threw it against the wall. She ducked and screamed in shock as it smashed behind her. Jim moved fast, slamming Rachel against the wall, wrapping his hand around her throat and gripping tight, lifting her off her feet, he pinned her against the wall and with the other hand, thrust the flowers with force and aggression into her face and mouth.

'No,' her muffled cry choked out from his grip around her throat and the flowers in her mouth.

'These were for you, you fuckin' bitch,' he sobbed. And repeated the words, his voice reduced to a whimper, his understanding of what went wrong evading him, 'These were for you.'

Outside across the road, Potts had heard the vase smash against the wall and Rachel's scream. The moment he feared, the confrontation he had managed to avoid all these years, here now waiting for him. He knew he had to help but looked at his hands, uncontrollably shaking. Repeating to himself over and over in the hope of overcoming his fear, 'Help him, get control – face it'. Hesitantly he crossed the road and was now outside the house where he could hear everything clearer. Maybe things would now calm down, he told himself, he hoped. The complete uselessness of himself haunted him.

Callum stood up from the chair. Jim turned, stared him straight in the eye and smiled, inviting him to try his luck. Callum held Jim's stare.

'Leave her alone,' fear quivered in his voice.

'Come on then, come and save your mum.' Jim threw

the remaining flowers at Callum, who ducked. Jim laughed, 'scared of a bunch of flowers.' His gripped hand eased from Rachel, who wriggled and managed to break free.

'That's enough,' Rachel's voice raised trying to get control of the situation. 'We can't go on like this, Jim. We're killing each other.'

'Killing each other!' he scoffed, evil present in his eyes, 'Oh, you don't know what I am capable of.'

'Let's just calm down,' her voice lowered, and she eased herself away, putting distance between her and him.

'Rachel, you don't understand. I love you, I can't live without you,' his face now soft and loving, emotions ping-ponged.

'You say that, but then you start hitting me. I'm leaving you, Jim.' Callum moved to stand by his mum. Together they were stronger. Jim ignored him as insignificant as he brushed past.

'I have done so much for you.' Tears again rolled down Jim's face. The tears Callum thought to be genuine. He looked at his mum, worried and concerned, hoping she would not weaken. 'Everything I have done, you can't just walk away.'

'Jim, it was good in the early days, and I know you have brought in money to support us, but things have changed. We are not the same people we were when we met.'

'So what, that's it, as simple as that, you're just gonna leave?' Jim leaned against the countertop and stroked his index finger against the handle of the carving knife that was offering itself to him. From sadness to madness, he bounced back and forth. His stare fixed on Rachel, all the time daring her to continue. A stalemate had ensued. Callum looked through to the lounge; the net curtain flapped about in the breeze. Outside he saw Potts; relief came over him with the secure thought Potts was nearby. 'Where you gonna go anyway?'

'Jim, Callum and me aren't going anywhere. It's you who has to go. This is the family home. I have spoken to a solicitor, and he says that as this is the family home, we should stay in it.' Jim's face contorted, trying to understand what he had heard. It made no sense. Everything he had done was for her. How could she now throw it in his face?

'You've seen a solicitor?'

'Yes.'

'Without talking to me,' he screamed and slapped her hard and fast with the open palm of his hand. The echo around the room so loud shocked Callum as he watched his mum fall to the ground from the impact. Jim followed in and kicked her in the stomach with the work boots he still had on. Callum reacted without thought and grabbed hold of Jim from the back and tried to pull him away. He was too strong, too big and threw Callum aside with a jerk of his arm backwards. Callum came again; Jim turned and punched Callum in the face.

Rachel screamed aloud, 'Get off him, you - get off him, you bastard.' Jim ignored her and continued hitting Callum like he was a punch-bag in a boxing gym. Callum went to the floor, blood streaming from his mouth. Jim reached over to the counter and pulled the knife from the wooden chopping board. Rachel backed away but trapped herself against the wall as Jim approached.

He smiled.

'Game over, darling.'

Holding her back with his left hand, he pushed the blade against her throat.

'Leave her alone,' Callum said, lifting himself from the floor back onto his feet.

'Stay back, Callum, or she's dead, and you'll be next.' Callum stopped, terrified of what he believed Jim was capable of and the safety of his mum.

Outside Potts heard the screams. He had to help. The front door wide open beckoned. Gripping his fists, why was it so hard? Why did his mind have no control over his body? Every muscle and every tendon fought against his will. Frozen to the spot, the net curtains blew outwards, grabbing Potts' attention. He saw the silhouette of a man's profile in the window that turned and looked at Potts. The sunlight crossed the man's face that was cracked down the middle, where congealed blood held the two parts of the skull together, and then the man in the window called out to Potts in a blood-gargled voice.

'Shoot the bastard.' Potts recognised the face. It was Woody's. Potts fell to the floor, crumpled and about to break down, but a sudden, power from within surged, lifting him. He rose to his feet and entered the house by the front door, through the living room, and there framed in the arch to the dining room, he saw the three of them. Jim, with the knife to Rachel's throat, Potts stopped still. A voice behind repeated, 'Shoot the bastard.'

Jim looked at Potts in disbelief, 'Oh, you're having a laugh, aren't you. Look, Callum, it's the cavalry.'

Nobody said anything as Jim laughed. Maniacal, he continued to laugh louder and louder. Nobody got the joke but Jim. He pulled Rachel out from against the wall and held her in front of him, dragging her into a stranglehold with the knife against her throat. He stood up and stared hard at Potts. 'It's the old war hero come to save you all.' There were now three to one, but it did not seem to bother Jim. It seemed to have the opposite effect, and he revelled in it.

'Put the knife down,' Potts said.

'I think you're gonna have to take it off me, soldier boy.'

'No one needs to get hurt.'

'That's true, but it's not me that gonna get hurt. You can watch her die if you like Potts. Would you like to watch me slit her throat? Tell you what - Why don't you just leave, like you did in the war. Leave your friends to die, ain't that right? Isn't that you?' Callum behind Jim watched, unsure if Potts had a plan, uncertain if he could take Jim out without risk to his mum. Maybe he could attack him from the back. Callum looked around for something sharp or heavy to hit him on the head and bring him down.

'Go on then, Jim,' Rachel spoke, 'go on do it, you're the big man here, so if you're gonna do it, stop all this talk and do it.'

'Shut it, Rachel,' Jim said, aggravated by her interruption.

'You ain't got the balls.'

Potts looked Jim in the eye, trying to determine if he did. It took a lot to kill another person, he knew, but there was a wild look in Jim's eyes that told Potts there was a credible risk.

'You really don't know what I am capable of, Rachel, so I would hold that mouth of yours shut if I were you.'

'Oh yeah, what's that, big man? Tell us what you're capable of then,' she continued to test him, 'we'd all really love to hear it.'

'Well, as we're all here, and before you say goodbye to this world, let me tell you about a rainy night in December.'

'What?' Rachel said, confused by the change of subject.

'There was a big poker game going on, of course, I was not playing, too big a stakes for me, I was just there keeping everybody topped up with drinks. There was this one guy, Michael, his name, but he wasn't drinking, just coca-cola. Now, this Michael had a wife. Hot stuff she was. I had a hunch she liked me, but of course, nothing was ever gonna happen whilst he was around.' Rachel listened in fear and disbelief at what she was hearing. Still unsure what the point was, an enormous tsunami of emotions washed through her with every word Jim spoke. 'Anyway, this Michael, I knew he was driving home later. Nice new E-type Jaguar. Fast those cars. You need to be careful. Very dangerous if you're not focused on your driving. So I topped his coca-cola.'

'You what?' Rachel shocked, understanding but not believing. It could not be true. This was madness. It was not possible.

'LSD. Acid - makes you see things, crazy things. And here's the spoiler. You should never get in a car and drive; you could end up wrapping it around a telephone box and killing yourself.' The room fell silent; it took moments for the truth of what was said to filter its evil paws through the disbelief before acceptance permitted. Callum reacted first and ran and punched Jim hard around the left temple with a right-hook. Rachel elbowed backwards, with anger triggering her strength; the knife Jim held to her throat flew out of his hand and fell to the floor. With a free hand, she grabbed Jim's face and pierced his skin with her nails that broke from the pressure. He yelled in pain and at the same time let her go from his grip. Callum saw the knife on the floor behind Jim, picked it up, and ran towards him.

'No,' Potts shouted, stretching forward to stop Callum and take the knife from him. Jim and Rachel turned to look.

25

It was Gilly's first day for real after completing her two weeks of intensive training. Excited but nervous yet bristling with enthusiasm to get on with the job. She wasn't a big smoker but lit her second cigarette of the day to calm her nerves. Settled at her desk, she put her headphones on, straightened them up against her recently styled feather-cut hair and took a deep breath. Janet stood beside, as was customary for new recruits and assured Gilly if there were any problems, she was at hand to help. Gilly liked Janet. She had been her supervisor and mentor since joining. Although older and they had little in common, she was kind and experienced. The phones rang out around.

'Don't forget, stay calm, and remember you're training,' Janet's soft calm voice reassured. 'Select a call when you're ready.'

Gilly braced herself and pressed down the button in front of her to receive her first call. 'Emergency Services, how can I help you?'

The voice at the end of the phone was calm and clear.

'I have just killed a man.' Gilly's mouth dropped open.

***

Three police cars parked outside; in the back of each car, they sat separated, Rachel, Potts, and Callum in the one parked directly outside his house. Callum looked out from the backseat, dazed in disbelief at what had happened.

Neighbours stood on their driveways, looking and chatting, speculating on what had happened. The police car parked on the opposite side of the road to the house started its engine. The sound jerked Callum out of a trance, and he looked towards it. In the back, Potts sat still, staring forward. Callum wanted him to turn and look over, to give him reassurance everything would be alright, or to wake up and find that it was just a bad dream. Potts did not turn but kept facing forward. The car drove off; Callum watched it taking Potts away; it reached the end of the road, turned left and disappeared. From the opposite direction, another car turned into the road, passed the police barricade, and parked their car in the spot where Potts had just been. Two men got out. The driver wore a suit and tie, young and smartly dressed and the passenger older, slightly balding, with no tie and his jacket slung over his shoulder. The older of the two, Callum suspected to be the boss. Whatever he was, Callum was sure they were CID, and the seriousness of the situation was driven home, pulling him out of the daze he had been in since the moment he watched Jim fall with blood soaking the dining room floor. Two uniformed officers who had been standing outside the car he was in got in, with one in the back next to Callum and the other in the driver's seat.

'We're going to take you to the station now to answer some questions and make a statement,' the officer said to Callum after he had settled himself in next to him. The officer in the driver's seat started the car. As they pulled away, Callum turned his head to watch the two plain-clothed officers walk towards the house that had blue and white striped tape across the front door that was still open. The older, scruffier one turned and looked at Callum with direct eye contact until the police car had driven out of range.

***

WPC Willis lifted the tape across the front door upwards; they both still needed to duck under to enter the house. A breeze ran through the house from the front windows that were wide open.

'So what we got?' Coombes asked PC York who was keeping watch. He referred to his notebook, making sure he missed nothing out.

'Myself and WPC Willis arrived at twelve-thirty following a call to emergency services where a man had confessed to stabbing and killing another man. The victim was dead on arrival.' DCI Coombes looked at the body on the floor face down in the archway between the lounge and dining room. On the countertop was the knife with blood on the blade.

'Was the knife there when you arrived,' Coombes asked the PC as he walked to the counter. Wet blood still shone on the blade.

'Yes, Sir, nothing has been moved.' Coombes looked at Hurst, both with the same thought. It was unusual to remove the knife from a body and place it far away. If it was an accident or a moment of lost control, the knife would either have been left in the victim or dropped nearby. Somebody had deliberately removed the knife and calmly placed it on the countertop.

'Where's forensics?'

'Here,' came a voice from a man entering the living room door with his colleague carrying a camera.

'About time. Where you been? Bit early for the pub, in't it?'

'Good to see you too, Clive,' DCI Clive Coombes and Harry Carter went back a long way. Both had joined the force in the early sixties, and both were due to retire in five years. And both enjoyed a drink at the Rose and Bloom on a Friday night. Harry took various samples of blood from the area surrounding the body and then turned the body over onto his back. 'Looks like he was stabbed twice,' Coombes knelt beside

Harry and fumbled in his jacket pocket for his glasses to inspect the stab wounds. 'We'll take him back to the lab and do a full autopsy. I'll be able to give you more information then, but looks like multiple stab wounds. Two from what I can see here.'

'Thanks, Harry. It sounds straightforward, but let me know what you come up with?' Coombes stood up with a groan from the effort. His knees had ached a lot over the last few years; he was not getting any younger. Each day he counted the days down to his retirement; he had seen enough death, violence and misery and now just wanted to get out of it. And today, he wanted to go home, put his feet up with a can of beer and watch the wrestling on Grandstand. But it was going to be another late one.

'Nothing up there, guv,' Hurst said as he returned from his search of upstairs, 'looks like all the action took place down here.' Coombes looked at the dead body. They already had a confession, and it had the smell of domestic argument getting out of hand. They returned to the station to interview the three who had been taken in earlier.

Potts was the first to arrive at the station. Three police officers escorted him with hands cuffed in front of him. The Sergeant waiting at the front desk on their arrival was already prepared. He placed the charge sheet on the desk for Potts to read, 'Can you confirm your name, please?'

'Arthur Norman Potts.'

'You are being charged with the murder of James Thorne.' Potts said nothing but looked lost, a million miles away. 'You'll be taken to a cell and later questioned in relation to the incident. You are entitled to a phone call, where you can contact a solicitor if you have one. If you do not have your own solicitor, we can contact the duty solicitor who will act on your behalf.' the Sergeant waited for Potts to respond, 'Mr Potts, do you understand?'

'I don't have a solicitor,' Potts responded. The Station

Sergeant indicated to the officers to take Potts to the cell. The weather had been hot, but as Potts walked down the corridor escorted by the police officers, it felt very cold. As they reached the cell, one of the officers took the keys he had taken from the front desk and unlocked the cell door. Potts sat on the bench with his back to the wall and watched the cell door close. And with the clank of the metal lock, Potts knew there was no way out. He had reached the end of the road.

Nineteen-Forty-Two

Potts had not walked far before being picked up, and two days later, he sat in the back of a truck with his head down, listening to his two guardians talk about him like dirt.

'You're a piece of shit, you are. Leaving other men to fight your battles as you run away. Scum,' said one and spat on the floor where Potts' eyes were focused. Maybe they were right. He failed his friend and let him die. Confusion ran wild, and he could not understand why he had not pulled the trigger. It didn't matter; whatever the reason, it changed nothing - Woody was dead. The friend he no longer had.

They travelled for several hours and were heading to Alexandria in Egypt. 'Wait till you get to Mustafa barracks; you'll wish you were back at the front. That was a picnic compared to where you're going,' the guardian's voice droned on. Potts learned to tune out from the continuous insults and provocation that started from the moment the truck picked him up that morning. It made no difference to Potts. None of it made any sense. Men killing men over and over again, and now because he could kill no more, they will lock him up. Regret preyed on him, leaving him with an empty sadness. The one and only time in his life he had found a friend. Someone he shared dreams with and spoke about things they would do in the future after the war, all of that erased by a moment of madness.

The truck stopped outside the perimeter gates and waited for them to open. Potts lifted his head to look out. The truck crawled through the opened gates. Armed guards closed them after the truck moved inside.

'Get out,' the guard instructed Potts. For once he was pleased to hear his voice in the hope they would be parting company soon. Potts rose up and made his way to the back of the truck to climb down. A sudden sharp pain smashed into the small of his back. Potts had been in the army long enough to know it was the guard's rifle saying his farewell. The intense pain shot through his body, forcing Potts to fall from the truck to the floor. With his eyes closed, the pain moved to his fingers. He opened his eyes and saw the heel of a boot crushing into the back of his hand as if stubbing out a cigarette.

'Get up, man,' came the voice above him from the Sergeant who was there to greet him at Mustafa barracks. Potts staggered to his feet. 'Stand up straight, man,' spittle hitting Potts in the face from the effort of the Sergeant's scream. 'You may be a deserter, but you are still in the army. I would not call you a soldier, as you are a disgrace to the uniform.' Potts looked the Sergeant in the eyes.

Who was this man to question him? Had he seen the things Potts had seen or experienced? Potts doubted it, and the situation made him lose, if it were possible, any lasting faith in humanity.

'Whilst you are here,' the Sergeant continued, 'you will learn you are inferior, a lesser man than your fellow soldiers.' Whatever the Sergeant said had little effect on Potts, believing he could not get lower than he already was at that moment. The Sergeant read Potts the rules and told him his life was from that day forth to be hell before leading him across the sandy forecourt to the block behind him by two other soldiers. One of the soldiers unlocked the door, opened it and locked it behind them after they had entered. The corridor they walked down smelt of urine and excrement, and Potts heard the whines of the men behind each cell door. Ten doors down on the left, they stopped. The same soldier who had opened the entrance door opened the cell door and said nothing but nodded his head to indicate to Potts this was where he was to stay. Potts entered and sat on the bed. He watched the door slam closed. Alone at last, he thought and would be content if that door was never opened again.

26

Callum remembered nothing about the trip to the police station but the detective's eyes staring directly at him. Seeing through him, reading his mind, tearing away strip by strip, each layer leaving him fully exposed. A cold chill crept through him whilst he sat alone in the interview room at the wooden table. The radiator on the wall, forbidden to provide heat or comfort, cranked and gurgled its omniscient awareness. The clock on the wall, its second hand, signified the end was near. Callum had forgotten to check the time when he entered the room. Time had deserted him; he didn't know how long he had been there waiting. But he now noted it was three-thirty in the afternoon. He thought of Lucy. She would have been waiting for him and Potts on Tankerton slopes. What would have gone through her mind? Had word spread, and would she have already heard. Whitstable was a small town; news travelled fast. Desperately he wanted to get word to her and let her know what had happened. Mostly he just wanted to see her and hold her.

He felt alone. The three of them were separated when the police arrived at their home, and he had not seen his mum or Potts since then. He worried for his mum and Potts in the other room, waiting to be interviewed. He blamed himself. Potts should never have been arrested; he was not to blame; he should never have asked Potts to come and help. It was his battle and it was his responsibility to deal with it. He looked at his leg under the table, shaking, his fingers tapping on the desk. Fear, anxiety, and guilt all returned with force. He sat back on the plastic chair and tried to calm himself, drawing in deep breaths as he had done in the past. Surprisingly it worked; he rested his hands, placing one over the other, and his leg slowed its rhythmic synchronisation.

The door opened. A WPC he had not seen before stood by the door and let the two detectives he had seen outside his house enter and sit on the chairs opposite. They brought the smell of stale tobacco and a reality Callum could still not believe.

'Hello Callum, I'm DCI Coombes, and this is DI Hurst,' DCI Coombes, the one with the eyes, the one with the power to see right through him. He spoke slowly and softly, 'Callum, you have been through a traumatic event. So try not to worry if you can't remember everything, but it is good to get a few facts recorded whilst it is fresh in your mind.'

Again he paused, letting each word sink in, which was complicated with so many thoughts bombarding for dominance, he was forgetting what had happened as each second passed. A hole in his head appeared, letting escape memories he'd rather not have. 'Are you okay to continue, Callum? Just let us know if you want to stop at any time.'

The roof of Callum's mouth was sandpaper dry; he ahem'd his throat quietly, not wanting anyone to notice he was there but was unable to speak without doing so, 'I'm okay.'

Coombes continued, 'Callum, can you tell us what happened at your house today? You can tell us in any order, whatever feels right to you.'

Callum averted his stare from his leg, confident it was still and showing no signs of stress and looked at the DCI and then the DI, who both smiled but still with their eyes fixed on his every movement for any signal his body gave away as a tell. They were trained in this, he knew, he had read how they interrogate prisoners. His focus was to remain calm and as still as he could. 'There was a fight. Jim had hit me after he had attacked mum. He hit me so hard he knocked me to the floor,' Callum touched his face where the pain remained from Jim's fist. So strong he was, yet now he was nothing. 'Jim then grabbed the knife and put it to my mum's throat. That was when Potts came in. He heard the screams, so he knew something was wrong.'

'So where was Potts when he heard the screams?' Hurst intervened, 'He was doing gardening at Mrs Wickes' house, we understand, a neighbour. That's quite a distance for him to hear the screams.'

'No, I think he was outside, in our front garden,' Callum started to get flustered, 'I think, I don't know, but he came in.'

'That's okay, Callum,' DCI Coombes said. 'Why would Potts have been in the front garden?'

'Because I was worried for my mum and I'd told him to keep a check on us, he's my friend. He came to help. It weren't his fault.' Callum started to get confused and worried.

Again Coombes spoke calmly, 'That's okay, carry on. You're doing well. Now, what happened when Potts came in?'

Callum looked at the two officers, then at the WPC who was at the door to the interview room. It was closed, escape was not an option, but with sweat clamming up the palms of his hands, he desperately wanted to get out. 'Jim had my mum around the neck with the knife, and he started talking. Horrible things, he started talking about,' he could not help himself; the tears started to come as he revisited those words. Anger returned from the pain inflicted by Jim's words, the theft of his life and his father's.

'Callum, shall we take a break? WPC Grimes will get you a drink.' The two detectives left the room, and Callum lost control unable to hold back the tears that came streaming. WPC Grimes told Callum she would get him a drink of water and when she returned, told him the detectives were going to speak to his mum before they came back, so he had a little time to recover.

Rachel was in the other interview room. The set up the same as the one Callum currently sat in at the other end of the corridor. DCI Coombes kept a soft tone but was sterner and pushed harder for answers than he had with Callum. Rachel had grown tired of the endless questions and wanted to take a break. 'Tell me in as much detail as you can, what happened after Jim had told you he had drugged your ex-husband?'

'I've told you.' It was only four-thirty in the afternoon, but she felt she had not slept for days. Questions from all angles torpedoed, desperately she tried to articulate as best she could what she had to say, 'I went mad. The bastard had just told me he had killed my ex-husband. Living with a man for six years and you find out that,' she spat the words. 'I would think it was pretty damn normal. There was a struggle, and I managed to elbow him, and he dropped the knife.'

'You're doing well, Rachel; sorry we have to put you through this, but please continue,' DI Hurst spoke in a more friendly tone to the DCI. Good cop, bad cop routine; Rachel had seen it on television but never thought she would actually be living it. And like on the television, she felt removed, as if she was not really there but viewing safely from the fictional world. Floating around, tuning in, unsure if it was from the tiredness of the day or the never ending questions they kept asking over and over. Nauseating bile travelled up from her stomach that she forced back down when it approached her throat, reminding her that it was not fiction, but reality.

'The knife fell, and Callum picked it up. He started to run at Jim with it, and Potts managed to grab him and got the knife off him. Jim then turned on Potts and started hitting out at him.' She paused and picked up the glass of water from the table. Her heart palpitated, her breathing desperate and her hands trembled as she drank. She returned the glass to the table. 'It's difficult. It all happened too fast, but somehow in the struggle, Potts stabbed Jim, and then he fell to the floor.' She breathed deeply, deep, deep breaths, trying to get oxygen into her lungs, circulating throughout her body, and ease her brain which was a furnace of fire. 'It was an accident,' she added. The room went quiet, and Rachel sensed the detective waiting and willing her to continue, but she remained silent. Pacing her breathing, slowly and deeply, trying her best to get her heartbeat back to a resting beat, but it did not work.

'You say he stabbed him. When we checked the body, there appeared to be multiple stab wounds. Was it just the once? Twice or more, can you tell us, Rachel?' DI Hurst now took over most of the questioning.

'It might have been a couple of times; I'm not sure. It all happened so fast.' She started to cry. DCI Coombes had seen it before the constant interruption from questioning where the witnesses broke down. He was unsure if it was an ageing factor, but recently, he became more intolerant and frustrated with the scene. They left the interview room.

There were no comforts in the cell; he looked around, a bench, a bed with a blanket and a toilet. Concrete walls surrounded him where graffiti remained from half-hearted attempts to remove it.

God Save The Queen

Once A PIG Always A PIG

The one that resonated with Potts:

I Am Going To Die Here

The steel armoured door a few yards from where he sat was glued shut. He wanted to be back at his hut in the woods with Marilyn, Lizzie, Sophia and Doris, harvesting his vegetable patch once more. He knew he would never see any of it again. He wanted his simple life back. Thoughts turned to Callum and concern for what he must have been going through. The boy who changed his world for the better, he reflected, and although doubt crept in as he processed the chain of thoughts, he had no regrets. Thanking Callum, knowing as he always had, life came with complications, but now he was prepared to accept them. He could hide away as he had for twenty plus years, but nothing could replace the fulfilment he had received from knowing Callum. Finding common ground, a purpose, an altruistic love and looking out and caring for another. The laughter and tears made it worthwhile. He knew they would be questioning Callum hard. The boy had only just started to get himself back on track and now this. Life was cruel. He knew from experience, but he wanted to believe Callum had the strength to get through this. Face up to what had been. A lesson he wished he had learnt earlier himself.

The clank of the cell unlocking fired his eyes to the door. The WPC opened the door, and a man entered. Dressed in jeans and a white polo shirt, Potts was initially confused, thinking he was about to share the cell with the man. 'Good afternoon, Mr Potts. I'm Stephen McDonald,' said the man in a well-spoken and educated voice.

'Hello,' Potts replied.

'Apologies for the casual clothes; I'd normally wear a suit, but I was on call and was actually watching my son playing football when my pager went off. I've been appointed as your solicitor' He turned and looked at the WPC. 'Is there a room we can use? It's a bit uncivilised to talk to my client in a cell,' Stephen McDonald spoke with confidence and was clearly a man who got what he wanted. Potts took an instant liking to him, but he knew, however confident he was, he was not going to get what Potts wanted.

'Yes, sir, I'll get one organised.'

They moved to one of the interview rooms in the station. McDonald arranged a cup of tea for them both as he talked non-stop. 'They were losing six-nil. And they hadn't even made it to half-time. Don't think my son or any of his teammates for that matter are going to be playing in the FA Cup final soon,' he continued making small talk as he unloaded papers from his briefcase onto the desk. 'Okay, Mr Potts, you can call me Stephen or McDonald, Mac or Mr

McDonald, whatever you are most comfortable with. But best use Mr McDonald when we are speaking with the detectives, a little formality. Don't like it myself, don't get it, but that's the way it is.'

'Stephen,' Potts replied as his preference, 'Most people just call me Potts.'

'Great, Potts it is then,' Stephen agreed. 'We have serious charges here, so let's go through everything so I have all the facts before they formally start the interview.'

Callum was told his mum was already outside when he came out to the police reception area. He opened the main entrance doors into Bexley Street and stepped down the few concrete steps from the station to the path. It was still light, although he felt so tired he thought he had been there all night. The fresh air he breathed in was something he did not think he would taste again. He looked to his left and saw his mum with cigarette smoke shooting out in front of her and pacing in circles. As she turned, she saw him, threw her cigarette to the ground, and ran to meet him. They hugged both in tears from exhaustion and relief.

'Callum, are you okay?' she asked, and although he was in shock, he thought the worst was over, for them at least. 'We need to find somewhere to stay for a few days? They said we can't go back to the house for maybe three or four days.'

Callum searched his pockets for a set of keys he had almost forgotten he had from all the traumas of the day, 'I have the keys to Potts' place, mum. We could stay there. I know he wouldn't mind.'

Too exhausted to argue or consider anything else. 'Okay, but let's get something to eat first,' Callum told his mum about the black and white fish and chip shop, the best in Whitstable.

'According to Lucy, that is - And they were great. I'm not so sure they're gonna taste so good tonight,' he said solemnly. 'I need to call her.'

They had decided to eat on the seafront on the grass bank at Tankerton Slopes before heading off to Potts' hut. The fish and chips tasted dry in his mouth, but the sea air felt good. It made him feel alive, which at the same time riddled him with guilt as he thought of Potts stuck in a cell.

They got the bus and got off at the Radfall Hill stop, and Callum said he needed to make the call to Lucy. They walked to the telephone box, both saying nothing but knowing that this was where his dad had crashed. He pulled the door open; cobwebs straddled inside the box from its infrequent usage. He dialled the number he knew off by heart and waited for someone to answer.

'Hello,' there was urgency in Lucy's voice. Callum sighed upon hearing her again. The pips sounded, and he pushed the two pence into the slot.

'Lucy,' he said, excited to make contact.

'Callum, what the hell has happened? I've been so worried,' he heard her start to cry in relief. 'I came to your house when you didn't turn up on the seafront, and a neighbour said someone had been murdered.' She worsened into a state it was now hard to understand the words she spoke.

'It's okay, Lucy, I'm okay, but …' he continued to tell her the cut-down version of events knowing he had only a few minutes before his money ran out. They arranged to meet in the morning. She would come to Potts', and he would then tell her the details. The pips on the phone interrupted. 'I love you,' he squeezed in before Lucy's sobbing voice was gone.

He worried his mum would not be happy with Lucy coming first thing; he thought she might not want to talk to anyone. But when he told her, she said that was fine. She knew how much Lucy meant to him; he needed her as much as she needed him. They walked up the beaten-up old track towards

Potts' hut. The trees rustled and the birds sang. It seemed wrong to be in a place so peaceful where there appeared to be no problems in the world, as if the woods were lying, covering and veiling the truth.

27

Stephen McDonald looked at his watch, an Omega, his wife had bought him for his fortieth birthday last year, then at the WPC at the door and grunted in disgust. They had been moved into the interview room fifteen minutes ago after being told DCI Coombes and DI Hurst were ready to start the interview.

'Can you pass the message on? I don't know what games they're playing, but if they're not here within the next fifteen minutes I will be gone, and they will then have to wait until tomorrow to interview my client.' He knew exactly what games they were playing, the games they always played to try and unnerve the suspect. Leave him hanging on; the more time left to think, was more time left to worry. But this was different; Potts willingly confessed and had already accepted his fate from what McDonald could see. WPC Grimes shuffled on her feet, looking uneasy. She knew McDonald was not a man that joked about things like that, but she also knew DCI Coombes, and if she told him, she would get an ear-bashing and more. The door opened, WPC Grimes exhaled, and a smile she tried to hold back, faint but for sure, appeared at the corner of her mouth in relief that DCI Coombes and DI Hurst had entered with them a fresh trail of nicotine supplying evidence of where they had been and without apology sat at the table opposite Potts and McDonald.

DI Hurst placed his A4 notepad and pen on the table in front of him and eased himself into a relaxed position on his chair. DCI Coombes dropped his notepad and pen on the table in front of him, leant back twisted and stretched and screwed up his face, grunting as he did, as if in pain, then leant forward with elbows on the table and right hand clamping left, looking at Potts who had his head down. 'Mr Potts, you called the emergency services and told them you had just killed a man; when our police officers arrived on the scene, you confirmed the situation. You are charged with murder. We would like to confirm that this is still the case that you admit to stabbing and killing Mr Thorne.'

Before Potts had a chance to speak McDonald jumped in, 'My client has not admitted to murder. DCI Coombes, I would ask you to be careful what words you try to put across as this may influence the direction of the investigation.'

'Okay, but you do not deny killing Mr Thorne?'

Potts leant forward, lifted his stare from the table and looked Coombes in the eye, 'I killed him, whether that's murder or manslaughter; the fact is I killed him. A scuffle broke out, and Callum grabbed the knife that Jim had dropped on the floor. I managed to get it from Callum, and Jim then came at me, and I stabbed him.' The story they had heard from Callum and his mum. Almost verbatim as if it had been rehearsed, DCI Coombes thought.

'How many times Mr Potts?' DCI Coombes continued.

'What?'

'How many times, Mr Potts, once, twice, how many times did you stab him?'

'Twice, I think.' DCI Coombes kept his eyes focused on Potts, who had now dropped his gaze back to the tabletop in front.

'You're a trained soldier, I understand. Infantry, trained in hand-to-hand combat, trained to use a knife. Is that right? I would think someone trained to use a knife would know clearly how many times he stabbed a man.'

'It was a long time ago.' Potts focused on an inkblot on the wooden tabletop as he spoke.

'Okay, so two times, you say.' Coombes waited for a further reaction from Potts but knew he would get none. 'When did you know he was dead?' Potts remained focused on the inkblot on the table. His mind concentrated on the blue lines inside one another, with thick blue at the inner part and fading to a lighter shade on the outer parts. Coombes' voice echoed, fading in the distance, like in a tunnel, but Potts knew he was there. The detectives across the table continued to fire their questions; he was trapped. The ink became darker and denser, expanding outward, and Potts felt himself sucked towards it. Then it disappeared, and the room went black. There was nothing, which was followed by a thud; Potts' head hit the desk. Light flashed back into the room; his vision blurred and went out of focus. He groaned in pain and confusion.

'Quick, get a doctor,' Potts recognised the voice; it was Stephen McDonald's, 'get some water.' There was movement and commotion, and Potts instinctively knew he was lying on the floor. He looked up to see Stephen's face blurred above him. There was movement behind, and through the blur, he recognised it to be the WPC leaning forward with a glass of water feeding it towards him. She gave him a sip; his vision slowly returned to see the concerned look on Stephen's and the WPC's faces. Behind them, standing were DCI Coombes and DI Hurst, who looked less concerned. 'A doctor's on his way. You fainted,' Stephen informed him.

By the time the doctor arrived, Potts had returned to his cell. Stephen remained in the cell when the doctor checked him over, confirmed his heart rate and body temperature were normal and diagnosed it to the day's stress.

'Are you feeling better now?' Stephen asked after the doctor had left.

'Yeah, I'm okay, thanks,' Potts said.

'They have decided not to continue the interview today but will start again tomorrow,' Potts knew he had to face them at some time, and the sooner he got it out the way, the better he considered. 'One important fact you should know is they have set a date next Tuesday for the court appearance at the magistrates.'

Although Potts knew it was inevitable, hearing a date somehow hit home. Tuesday, his freedom was to be removed, Tuesday he would be sent to prison until the Crown Court, and there the full hearing would occur as Stephen had explained earlier.

'There is something else I need to tell you.' Potts said just as Stephen was about to leave.

Stephen McDonald was experienced enough to recognise that Potts needed to reveal from his tone. Something he was not telling, but now it looked like he had to do so.

***

She had slept on the settee, and it was early when Rachel awoke. All night she had tossed and turned, the blanket on top of her itched, and it was cold. But mostly, her mind could not stop thinking about Jim, Potts and Callum. Light boomed through the curtains, and birds sang outside. She stood up and opened the door. There was damp morning dew on the ground, and the air greeted her with fresh innocence. Behind her, a noise made her turn to see Callum emerging from Potts' bedroom, where he had slept. 'Couldn't sleep?' she asked the obvious.

'Not a wink, couldn't help but think of Potts all night, locked up in that police station.' No Good Morning, No How Are You? His world had fallen apart. Callum walked towards the door where his mum stood, 'I'll make some coffee.' She followed Callum outside to the kitchen outbuilding; silent and scared, she looked out to dense woodland wishing she could get lost in there and hide from all the problems that lay ahead.

Coffee was drunk and forgotten, and Rachel found a packet of cereal in the cupboard above the stove that they ate without registering.

'They need feeding, mum. It's the least I can do.' Robotically Callum threw the feed into the chicken coop. Although Callum spoke, he was only semi-conscious of his mum standing next to him, with arms crossed and painful thoughts of worry. 'It's not fair, mum,' he said, looking at her, still lost in her own world. 'He shouldn't be locked up. He's not guilty of anything.'

She turned and looked at him with horror, 'Stop it, Callum, we've already spoke about it. I don't want to go through it all again,' her tongue sharp and Callum felt a pang of guilt for bringing it up again. Already there had been enough pain, and he did not want his mum to suffer any more than she already had. 'Sorry,' she said in a softer voice realising they were both worried and suffering. 'Potts did it for you,' after some thought, she added. 'For us, he knew what he was doing. Remember that when Lucy gets here. Let's not complicate it any more than it already is.' Marilyn clucked at Callum, wanting more. He had no more to give.

The clunk of the metal bolt escaping through the woodland got his attention. Outside in front of the hut, Callum had sat waiting for nearly two hours. There was nothing else he could do but sit with his mind swimming. The gate opened, and there was Lucy, no smile this time, just a look of concern; she saw Callum and ran to him and held him. Her warm body against his triggered the release of all the emotions he had pent up since yesterday. Whatever was to happen, Lucy was there; he cried, sobbing into her shoulder. 'Oh, Callum, what the hell has happened?' She heard rumours but knew little. It was a small town and word spread like wildfire, and normally, that word was exaggerated to make a better story. Never spoil a good story with the facts, Potts had told her once, and no place was that more true than Whitstable. Desperately she wanted to find out, but Callum was in no state to talk, so she just held him, and as she did, she worried that the rumours might be true.

When Callum and Potts had not turned up at the seafront, she knew something was wrong. She knew they would not let her down without good reason, so she walked to Callum's house. Horrified to see the house with police tape stretched out across the front door and a policeman standing at the top of the drive.

'Sorry, miss, you can't go in there,' he said with an outstretched arm to block her from entering the driveway offering no further information. Lucy pushed for more, explaining she was Callum's girlfriend, but the police officer refused to say anything more than *it was a crime scene*. She almost screamed out loud, assuming the worse; her heart dropped upon hearing those words. Jim had killed Callum or his mum. They had spoken of how dangerous he was, a ticking time bomb, Callum had told her.

'You've gotta let me in or tell me what happened. I know them,' she raised her voice and was now shouting at the officer.

'Miss, you must calm down. I can tell you no more information than I already have,' he repeated.

'At least tell me they are okay,' she insisted, but he kept tight-lipped. Fury and anger gripped her and she wanted to hit him, but the look in his eyes warned her off the idea. She returned home and ran into her house in a sweat and fluster. Her mum and dad were in the front room waiting for her. Lined up as if they had something to say, she stopped dead in her tracks.

'Where have you been?' The concerned look on her mum's face as she asked tore fear into her.

'I've been to Callum's, but the police were there, and they wouldn't let me in,' she looked at both her mum and then her dad, both with the same expression. 'What is it?'

'There are rumours all over there has been a murder. Callum's step-dad was murdered, and they have arrested the gardener, your friends Potts we believe.' She questioned them, but they knew little more to offer other than all three of them had been taken to the police station. Those hours before Callum called seemed so long, her mind playing games and imagination running wild down a dark street.

She held Callum shaking against her and tears perforating her jumper onto her shoulder. A movement by the hut distracted her attention. Callum's mum tried to give Lucy a reassuring smile, but she was not buying it.

A few minutes passed, and Callum calmed down. Later, they were going back to the police station he told her to continue the interview.

'I'm coming with you,' Lucy immediately bounced back. Although Callum said she didn't have to, he really needed her there. She gave him the strength he needed at that time.

28

It had turned bitterly cold and Lucy, wearing her jumper was shivering for the first time that year. Desperate not to miss them, she had been waiting outside the police station for thirty minutes before Callum and Rachel arrived. They both looked drawn and tired, living a nightmare Lucy could only imagine. She knew they would not allow her to go inside, but she wanted to kiss Callum before he did. For what good it would do, she was unsure, but it made her feel better. There were half-smiles when they greeted. Rachel was polite but distracted.

'Hello, Lucy, how are you?' she asked but was deaf to Lucy's reply. Callum hugged her without letting go. 'Come on, Callum, we have to go,' Rachel spoke softly. Reluctantly he released his grip from around Lucy and let his hand trail through hers as he and his mum made their way up the steps towards the station entrance.

'Callum,' Lucy called, and on her voice, he turned and looked at her as he stood in the opening of the door. Without sound leaving her lips, she mouthed the words, 'I love you.'

Outside, Lucy paced up and down Bexley Street and then around the block three times before hovering outside the entrance where they had entered. With only an hour passed, she did not expect them out so soon but, at the same time, wanted to be there when they did. Deciding now, she would stay in Bexley Street with the station doorway in view. Within a few minutes, the door opened, and to her relief and surprise, Callum exited first, followed by Rachel. Lucy ran and hugged him as they had just over an hour ago, but it felt more like a year.

'They set a date for the magistrates' court for this Tuesday,' Callum said, eager to update Lucy with everything they had learnt. 'We have to go, but they think it's unlikely we'll have to speak as Potts is pleading guilty. They say he will be sentenced, so he will go to prison, and because it is such a serious offence it will be passed to the Crown Court.'

'I'll come with you,' Lucy said without hesitation and eager to offer her support.

***

The wicket opened, and through the small hole in the door, Potts could see the bright blue eyes of WPC Grimes. Potts had been waiting for hours. It had been impossible to sleep with the light on all night, but WPC Grimes had been kind to him. He greeted her with a good morning as she opened the cell door accompanied by PC Willis, whom he had spoken to on several occasions.

'Breakfast,' she said as she placed it on the bench beside Potts. 'We will be leaving in one hour as your hearing time is scheduled for midday.'

'Thank you,' he said as he looked at the sausage, bacon and beans on the plate and plastic forks beside. Breakfast tasted and looked better than he had expected. He was ready to face the music when the door opened again to escort him to the police van outside. Standing to attention as if on parade at the first days of army training a lifetime back, it seemed like only yesterday. He had to believe he was doing the right thing. And, he remembered that was what he had believed on that day too.

'Ready?' WPC Grimes asked with an unofficial smile

that gave Potts faith there was good in the world and that his actions had released the years of pain Callum and his mum would have suffered. A small sacrifice, he concluded.

'I'm ready,' he said, returning a smile. Around his wrist, she clamped the handcuffs, and two police officers escorted him out to the van that waited with the engine running and the driver in place. The van bumped and jolted, and the engine breathed anger from all its previous occupants. Potts felt different, he did not consider himself a martyr, but at the same time knew he had done no wrong and would live out the rest of his life with that thought to comfort him. No words were spoken other than those of WPC Grimes advising him of the procedure and protocol of what was to follow.

***

The cheese and tomato sandwich that Stephen McDonald had got Potts was dry. With each bite, he struggled to chew and swallow. One o'clock had passed, and Potts chewed on the sandwich in sync with the clock's second hand on the wall that ticked slowly, revolving itself around the face purposefully with intent but going nowhere. Ten minutes passed, the door opened, and the court's usher appeared. In a black gown hung over his dark suit and plain tie, smart and official, he referred to the clipboard he held in front of him.

'Mr Potts, the court is ready for you now. Constable, if you would like to escort Mr Potts to the dock.' Potts stood, muscles spasm vibrating throughout his body; unable to control them, his whole body shook. WPC Grimes rested her hand on his back in reassurance. For a brief second, it distracted him and helped until, all too soon, he remembered where he was going. Be strong, he told himself as he followed Stephen into the court. Potts went to the dock and sat. Trying to take in every moment, every movement as if it was the last civilised place he would ever step. To Potts' right,

Stephen McDonald had taken his seat. Potts looked around the courtroom. Opposite, he saw Rachel sitting next to Callum and then Lucy. Callum's eyes bulged in fear. Potts wanted to speak to him, to reassure him everything would be alright, but he knew it was forbidden. Lucy's hand moved over and took Callum's hand, and Potts' body eased with the sight of the two of them together. The tension and worries he had earlier when he first entered the courtroom evaporated and released themselves, leaving him convinced he had done the right thing. Seeing them together supported the reason he was here. From across the room, Callum's eyes glistened, and Potts worried tears were not far away. But he knew it would be okay. We all need tears at times to release the hurt and pain we suffer, and then once they are gone, we can get on with our lives. He so hoped it was true.

'All stand,' announced the usher holding the door to the courtroom open. Three magistrates entered and took their seats at the top of the court to Potts' right. The magistrate sat and the rest of the court followed. All the magistrates were as old if not older than Potts, he thought, and the trio of bespectacled, grey-haired men eventually nodded to the clerk, who stood up and looked at Potts. 'Will the defendant rise,' the usher called over to Potts who had already stood in anticipation of the command.

The clerk adjusted his tie and opened the file on the desk, 'Would the defendant please state his full name for the court,' a stronger voice than Potts had expected for such a diminutive man.

'Arthur Norman Potts,' although Potts tried keeping his focus on the clerk every so often he looked towards Callum and Lucy for the strength he needed.

The clerk continued, his voice booming around the acoustically aesthetic room that Potts found oddly euphonious. 'You are charged with the murder of James Duncan Thorne on the morning of Saturday the seventh of October, nineteen-seventy-eight. How do you plead?'

Just one word was all he had to say, Stephen had told him; after that he would take over and do the talking. One word, but it was so hard to find. He knew what it would mean. Locked up, his freedom removed, the freedom he'd had all those years. But he realised then it was not years he had had freedom, but merely months. In those few months, since he had met Callum, he had been free.

'Guilty,' he spoke with belief. He heard a gasp from Callum that sucked away his strength with rampant force. He looked to see Lucy move her left hand to hold his arm.

'Thank you, Mr Potts,' the clerk said and returned his attention to the folder where he turned page after page before finding what he had seemingly lost. 'Mr McDonald, I believe there are some points you wish to make the court aware of.' The clerk sat, and McDonald stood.

Potts tried not to look over at Callum. He didn't want eye contact, this was the part he had wanted to tell himself, but it had been impossible to get word to him.

'Thank you, sir,' Stephen McDonald started. 'There are a few points I would like to be taken into consideration in respect of the sentence to be passed.' Potts saw Callum turn to Lucy, trying to speak to her without disrupting the court, trying to get an answer from his confusion about what else needed to be taken into consideration. 'Firstly, my client has never been in any trouble with the police before or been convicted of any crime. And, although I had advised my client there was a possible case for manslaughter that would serve a lesser sentence, he has decided to enter a plea of guilty.' McDonald looked towards the magistrate and paused. Potts was unsure if this was for effect or not; he had grown to like Stephen's flamboyance even in the current situation. The magistrates seemed less impressed with their three straight emotionless faces staring back at him. 'The reason for his plea is based on two reasons that my client has provided. One to save the court time and the costs of an extended trial that would be drawn out in the higher courts and,' Potts looked at Callum, whose eyes focused back hard on Potts. He didn't know how, but in Callum's face, Potts recognised he had worked out what was to come. A sixth sense perhaps, whatever it was, Potts knew he had read the signal correctly; Callum's mouth opened in disbelief, willing it not to be true. McDonald continued, 'my client is terminally ill and would not be able to cope with the stresses of a crown court trial. The doctor's report I have here confirms my client has lung cancer that has now spread throughout the body and they put his life expectancy into weeks and not months.' The magistrates grunted and started to confer between themselves.

'No,' Callum screamed, silencing their murmurs, 'no,' hysterically again, he cried out. Lucy wrapped herself around him.

'I'm sorry, but you will need to leave the courtroom if you can't control yourself,' the magistrate in the middle of the other two spoke directly to Callum, who by now had broken down completely. The usher of the court came over and helped Callum with Lucy and Rachel out of the court. His cries still audible as he went and continued outside until the door was shut again.

Order was restored and the magistrates and the clerk spoke between themselves. Stephen looked over to Potts and nodded an acknowledgement and conveyance that life's a shit.

Outside in the reception area, the three of them waited. Although Callum had regained control of himself, they had not been allowed to re-enter the courtroom whilst the case was in progress. They waited eagerly for Stephen McDonald to exit the court to get the news they did not want. The noise of movement from inside the court indicated the case was over; Callum's heart sank, and for a moment, he thought it would give way. In desperation, he prayed when the door opened Potts would come through it and greet them, saying they had released him due to his health condition. He knew that would not happen in reality, and even if he did,

Potts already had a death sentence.

The door opened and Callum was right. There was no Potts. He had been taken out the rear exit, escorted into the back of the van and taken to prison. Stephen McDonald was one of the last to exit, and as he did, he looked around and, spotting the three of them made a direct approach towards them and sat down with them.

'Not good news, I'm afraid, but it was as we expected,' he said with a genuine look of concern. 'He has been taken to Canterbury prison until a date is arranged for an appearance at the crown court for sentencing.'

'When will that be?' Callum asked eagerly. He wanted to but dared not ask the question the three of them needed to know.

'Callum,' Stephen McDonald continued, his facial expressions dropped, looking sorrowful, 'it is probably never going to happen. Potts' cancer is spreading fast, and at some point he will be transferred to a hospital when he is too weak to be a risk to anyone.'

'He's not a risk to anybody now,' Callum added.

'I know, Callum, but for a guilty verdict of murder, there were no other options.'

'Can we visit?' Lucy asked as she sat next to Callum, holding his hand that she could feel shake with grief. McDonald gave them the prison telephone number and said it would typically be a week after he first arrived at the prison before he could receive visitors.

Callum walked Lucy home before getting the bus back to Potts' hut, where his mum had gone off to earlier. 'I wanna call the prison now, see if we can arrange to see him,' Callum said to Lucy when they reached her house.

'It's too early. You need to leave it a few days, Callum,'

Lucy said, worried for him. 'Are you sure you'll be okay getting home?'

'I'll be alright; it's Potts that's not going to be.' She kissed him goodbye and watched him walk away.

29

Every day for the last two weeks, Callum phoned, and every day he received the same response.

'Sorry, Arthur Potts has not been processed yet to see visitors. Please try again tomorrow.' Two weeks of hell and still no indication when they would be able to visit. Callum needed to see Potts; he needed to know he was doing all right. It was tearing him apart. Those words from that day in court formed a dark cloud that hung over him, with no conclusion, left on the edge of a cliff waiting to fall. Terminally ill, what did they mean by that? Nobody would give him any further information, and whilst unable to see Potts, he wanted hope to exist. Until he heard the words from him directly he refused to accept it.

A signed note from the doctor had given Callum two weeks off school. Compassionate leave they called it. A joke. The compassionate leave was for the death of his stepfather. It was Potts he cared about, not Jim. Never seeing Jim again gave him a sense of relief. He just wished it had been in some other way. Why could he not have just left and run off with another woman? Why couldn't the bastard do something like that? Even in death, he left behind mess and misery. They had moved back into the house the following weekend. In the second week after Jim's death, his mum had picked up a bit. She had spent all Monday and Tuesday cleaning; Callum had sat on the settee, staring at the television. Programmes rolled by, of which he saw and heard none. When not in front of the television he would sit in his room looking out of his window, watching the grass grow in Mrs Wickes' garden and weeds that were never there before appeared.

'I'm thinking we could buy some wallpaper. Redecorate, a fresh start, what do you think?' His mum would ask over dinner, potato fritters and fried spam, his favourite dinner that had lost its taste alongside everything else in this world.

'Maybe,' he replied, non-committal, not wanting to upset his mum, knowing it was hard for her too. But at the end of the day, and he hated himself for thinking it, she would be in a better place. Next week he was meant to return to school. He had agreed with his mum he needed another week. They informed the school, who understood and said to take as long as it took. He would return the following week regardless of whether he had seen Potts. He had been doing well at school, and Rachel worried he might rebel or drop down the class. She wanted him to have the things she never had.

Monday came; he called the prison, and again the answer was the same. He slammed the phone back down on its receiver.

Lucy, every night after school, turned up like clockwork. Four-thirty, she would ring the bell. The routine was Callum would see her from his bedroom window approaching the house. The doorbell rang, his mum answered the door, and the conversation was the same every day. 'How's Callum today?' Lucy would ask.

'Not much better, but I know he's always better for seeing you,' his mum would reply, 'he's upstairs.' Lucy would gently tap on his bedroom door, ease it open, and then enter and kiss Callum. The kisses that used to taste so good now felt sour. The world around him had been destroyed. Lucy gave him space, she gave him time, and he knew that, but it did not expel his anger. She updated him on what had happened at school each day.

'Ray Blackman set fire to the chemistry lab stock room; they had to call the fire brigade and the police. They say he's gonna get expelled,' Lucy said with controlled excitement, which Callum was appreciative of knowing she had calmed her enthusiasm for his sake. So what, who cares, was all he could think. There was only one care he had. From her bag, she would get her school books, tell Callum of the topics they had covered in class, and leave him notes she had made the night before so he could read through them during the day. He never did. Most of the time the conversation was about Potts, and when it was not, it would always return to him. It was not just Callum who was suffering, it was Lucy too. She had grown fond of Potts and missed him dearly, and when they spoke about him, the barriers seemed to drop. They would hold one another and sometimes cry; it helped to know they each had someone who cared for them.

That weekend the clock went back an hour, and with it, the sun fell out of the sky, leaving only the clouds and dark skies surviving. Tuesday morning, he left it later than usual to call the prison. Maybe to give them more time to process Arthur Potts, his reasoning, but the real reason he knew he could not cope with another rejection.

'I'm going to ring the prison,' he called to his mum, who was in the kitchen.

'Okay, darling, let's hope it's good news. I'm just making a cake for when Lucy comes over later. Coffee cake, she tells me, is her favourite,' his mum replied. He was lucky to have his mum and Lucy; he knew he had been a pain the last few weeks and had to change. It was unfair to them. He had lectured himself and demanded that whatever the response, the response he already knew, he would start to help his mum more. And would be more open with Lucy, let her in, she too was suffering. She had been there for him and now it was his turn to look out for her. But it was so damn hard and far easier said than done. Yet losing Lucy would be something he could not let happen, and he feared she would back away if he continued as he was. If she were to drift out of his life, it would be his fault.

'HMP Canterbury,' the rough voice at the end of the phone yawned. The same woman answered yesterday and every day last week; surely she must know his voice by now, but she goes through all the security questions, rattling them off waiting for Callum to provide a wrong answer so she could cut him down.

'Can you tell me if Arthur Potts can receive visitors yet?' Callum bit his lip; surely they had processed whatever they needed to process by now. At the other end of the phone, he could hear her ruffling through papers. Then her muffled voice through her hand covering the phone called out to someone else. Callum could not make out what she said but hoped it was positive news. Never had he got this far before. Normally it was two seconds followed by a rejection.

'Yes, Arthur Potts can receive visitors, and I can confirm you are on the list as an authorised visitor,' she said.

'When can I see him? When is the next day and time,' Callum rushed the words out in excitement. 'And I will be with Lucy Curtis,' he added. To see Potts again was something he was beginning to believe would never happen.

'Tomorrow at eleven o'clock is the next visiting time.'

'Thank you, thank you so much.' The woman who he had despised a few minutes earlier he now wanted to add to his Christmas card list.

He met Lucy on the bus as they had planned the previous night. Callum had been bursting with the news when she called around after school. Excited to see Potts but nervous to enter the prison. They had queued with about thirty others before being allowed into the open area of the prison. Those waiting were mostly women, some having small children beside them. They all stood in an orderly line with Lucy's arm wrapped inside Callum's to keep warm and for protective comfort. The tarmac path where they stood had a grass-bare field area to their right, which Callum assumed was from where the prisoners exercised. There were no prisoners around, just several guards eyeing them suspiciously as if one of them were about to smuggle a prisoner out. It was clear that for some it was a regular Wednesday as they chatted with each other as if they were outside the school gates waiting to collect their little loved ones. The door to the prison opened and they filed in. Once inside, the door they entered through was locked behind them, where they then queued again for the woman behind a glass-screened office who was issuing visitor cards and lanyards.

Callum and Lucy stood five back and waited. It didn't take long before they were at the screen where an uninterested woman in uniform sat. In her late fifties, Callum thought she must be, looking beaten by life.

'Name?' abrupt and hoarse, Callum wondered if everyone who worked there was as miserable as the people he had encountered. The Christmas party would be a whale of fun, and then decided that on leaving school he would not be pursuing a career in the prison service.

'Arthur Potts,' and unsure if the question referred to who they were visiting or their name added. 'And my name's Callum McNab, and this is Lucy Curtis.' Callum caught Lucy's smile, and for the first time in two weeks, the joy that filled his body as the normal reaction came with it.

'Wear these and take this card to the guard at the end of the corridor,' she said, sliding the lanyards and visitors' cards through the slot beneath the glass screen. They moved out of the way and followed the others ahead of them down the corridor, where three further guards waited. Two males and one female, where they searched the visitors. The flaw to the system, as Callum could see, was that most visitors were women, and that was the job of the female guard to search them; it slowed the process down. Callum waited until Lucy was searched and passed inspection.

The last door Callum thought and hoped, and with that, his heart started to pound with the excitement of seeing Potts again. They handed their visitors' cards to the guard who said nothing but eyed them, as every other guard had with suspicion, before unlocking the door where they entered a hall. Twenty or more tables were spread across the hall, and prison officers patrolled, keeping an eye on each. Callum scanned the room for Potts.

'There he is,' Lucy jumped with excitement. Across the room, Callum followed Lucy's arm to where she was pointing and saw Potts sitting there smiling over at them.

'Callum, Lucy, how are you?' Potts said as they sat themselves down opposite him. His voice was tired but his words expressed emotion and warmth. Callum tried not to stare at Potts but could not help himself. Dressed in the prison uniform, a blue and white striped shirt under his cotton jacket with HQ stitched onto the lapel. He looked around at all the men in the room dressed the same. All criminals but Potts, Callum thought, and he wanted to shout out telling everyone of the injustice of it.

'Callum, are you okay?' Potts repeated.

Callum looked back and realised that Lucy had already responded, and he had drifted off into another world. 'I'm all right,' Callum replied.

'Oh, it's so good to see you,' Potts went on.

'Callum's been calling every day,' Lucy responded and nudged Callum to jolt him into the here and now.

'I thought they were never gonna let us see you,' Callum added.

'They don't rush here; you get what they decide when they decide,' Potts conceded to himself. 'Have you been to the hut? Have you checked up on my girls?' He questioned with concern.

'Yeah, we've been there pretty much every day. Hope

you don't mind but me and mum stayed there a few nights as the police wouldn't let us back in the house.'

Potts waved his hand to indicate it was no problem, 'But how about my Marilyn and Lizzie and co?' It seemed the most significant thing on Potts' mind was the chickens. The biggest concern in his life. Maybe it was something he needed for a focus to take his thoughts away from greater problems.

'They're fine, Potts,' Callum confirmed, 'Sophia has been laying loads of eggs last week.' Potts smiled, and from his face, Callum realised he had formed a picture in his mind. Callum wanted to bring an egg with him when they next visited, but he knew it would not be permitted. In case it was injected with some drug or a concealed weapon, the thought saddened him knowing how much it would have meant to Potts. But there were other things he had to ask, things he was uncomfortable with, the question he did not want answered. Callum held on to the hope. Hope that what had been said in court was some elaborate plan Stephen McDonald had concocted to get Potts a reduced sentence. Please let it not be true, he told himself. But he had to know, 'What your solicitor said in court?' Callum lowered his voice and hesitated, unable at first to get the words out, 'Was it true? About you being ill, that you are dying,' Callum bit his lower lip to control himself. Lucy rested her hand on his thigh.

There was no smile on Potts' face as he looked directly into Callum's eyes, 'It is true, I'm afraid to say.'

'Why didn't you tell us?' Without meaning to but the anger displayed in Callum's voice.

'I'm sorry, I only found out on the Friday before.' Potts rubbed his face nervously with his hand, covering his mouth. 'I was going to tell you that afternoon.' He paused and let the words sink in, 'But there was no time with all the confusion from the situation.'

Callum breathed in deeply, accepting the inevitable, 'How long do they say you have?'

'They don't know for sure, but it is weeks, maybe a month. The cancer has spread, and there is nothing they can do.'

30

Imagination was all he had left. Potts closed his eyes and listened to the birds singing, the cold chill grabbing for attention, and then a few droplets of rain splattered his cheeks and sprung life into his world. The specks of rain fell unexpectedly, as the sky looked clear when they had walked outside from their prison cells, but he knew if he had focused hard enough, they were predictable. It was just he had missed it. Men at varying distances chatted and murmured, and the occasional chorus of laughter diverted his attention away from an otherwise peaceful and perfect moment. Keep them tightly closed, he commanded, blocking out the light where now the world was tranquil and satisfying. To his left, he heard the inhale and exhale of the man next to him in a non-rhythmic pattern Potts knew would continue after his time had been. The exhale had more force and passion devoted than the inhale that was more relaxed, and an intense smell of Old Holborn rolled sparingly in his cellmate's green Rizla Papers followed. The smoke was violent and shocking at first, but it had become comforting with the familiarity after a few days.

Each day at eleven, they exited through the east wing after breakfast and morning chores to the exercise area to walk and stretch, but mostly Potts just wanted to sit and count every minute and second, he could experience. Darren knew those fifteen minutes of peace meant a lot to Potts, so he would sit next to him quietly and allow him that grace. And why not? They had enough time, locked up, together within those four walls to talk. Now was the time to escape the hell for that short moment.

Darren had been placed in Potts' cell the day after he arrived. It was his first stretch in prison and the two of them had got on well. A second offence for grievous bodily harm had left the judge with no choice but to give him a short sentence in the hope the shock would scare him from committing the same offence again. Darren seemed a good lad but had been dealt a bum hand and surrounded by those who were always in and often instigating trouble. He needed a break, and Potts wished he could help but knew his time was too limited to make a difference. He saw Callum in Darren. Both were completely different in how they reacted to their environments, and Callum had his mum, whereas Darren had no one who cared for him. But Potts could not help but believe that if Darren had the right chances and opportunities, life would be completely different. It saddened Potts to think about how many Darrens there were out there.

The whistle's shriek broke the bliss; he kept his eyes closed, wanting just one more moment of nothingness whilst absorbing everything. 'Potts, you ready, mate? Don't want Adams screaming at us.' Darren tapped Potts on the shoulder but he had travelled so deep into another world he struggled to prize his eyes open. The blinding rays from the sun of the cloudless day made Potts feel dizzy as he went to stand up and Darren held out a hand to help him to his feet. 'You okay?' Darren checked.

'Yeah, I'm good,' Potts confirmed as they began to walk towards the entrance. Being late could mean the penalty of missing the next break, which neither of them wanted. They picked up the pace when a rush of blood exploded inside. The world started whirling, his vision kaleidoscopic, voices fading in and out. Potts stopped still; he could feel his legs no more and then the urgent grip under his arm of what he presumed to be Darren from stopping him from hitting the floor.

'Mr Adams,' Darren called. Potts heard chaos around

him, 'Mr Adams, quick, we need help. Potts has collapsed.' Beneath Potts' back, he felt the uneven ground, damp but relaxing, like getting into bed after a long tiring day. Footsteps in an urgent rhythm approached. On his face, he felt Adams' breath, sweet and minty as if he had just brushed his teeth. Maybe to hide the alcohol he had already drunk that morning. The well-known fact within the prison was Adams liked a drink with his cornflakes. Well, who wouldn't? Potts thought in a place like this and wondered if he was visibly smiling. And reflected, it could be one of his last thoughts as he grew weaker and drifting further away.

'Call a bloody ambulance,' Adams shouted to another guard. Potts knew his time was limited. He was content. Potts would like to see Callum and Lucy again, but it was beyond his control. The hubbub around him continued, 'Hurry, just get a bloody ambulance.' Potts thought Adams was probably more concerned about the heaps of paperwork he would have to complete if a prisoner died on his watch than his actual health. That didn't matter to Potts.

31

He had been on a journey, but Potts was unsure of the destination of where he had arrived. He had moved from the prison grounds. No longer did he feel the uneven ground beneath but softness and warmth. Fresh air removed, usurped with a clean clinical smell, inducing unwanted claustrophobia. The pure white light rebounding off the white walls and ceiling strained his eyes as he eased them open cautiously. He eased his head gently to one side to see a monitor beside him beeping, with wires and cables outstretched and attached to his arm. He was alone in the room, he tried to sit up but strength failed him. The vertical blinds on the window to the room were angled to allow him to see only an unfinished jigsaw of the outside world. To the other side, on his right through the glass panel in the door was a corridor with white painted walls, which was briefly interrupted by an occasional glimpse of a person and sometimes two of them in white laboratory coats passing by that told Potts he was still alive. Five minutes passed before the door opened and a doctor entered. A young man with dark hair and sporting bags pulling heavily laden beneath his eyes smiled in what he presumed to be the relief that Potts had woken up.

'Mr Potts,' he said, and he moved the plastic chair from against the wall to beside the bed, sat down, crossed his legs and continued, 'I'm Doctor Chivers.'

'Hello,' Potts' voice was hoarse as he spoke.

'You've been transferred to the hospital as you collapsed in the prison grounds. We have your medical records, and it looks like your condition has worsened,' he paused a moment to let Potts reflect on what he had said. There was no need; Potts had already accepted he would not get any better. 'We are going to do some further tests, but I am recommending that you are not in a sufficient condition of health to return to the prison and will need to stay here.' It was a matter of days Potts had left; they would only transfer him if he was not going to return. Maybe there was one last chance to see Callum and Lucy.

'Would I be allowed visitors?' Potts asked, his voice clearer and determined.

'Don't see why not. I don't think you are going to be running off anywhere too soon,' Potts laughed at the doctor's comments. 'Do you have the names and phone numbers of who you want to visit you? I'll get someone to give them a call.' Potts told the doctor the name and phone number. 'After we have done the test, I'll get that sorted for you.'

'Thank you, doctor,' Potts said and closed his eyes, bringing the vision of Callum and Lucy into his mind.

32

A week had passed since Callum returned home from school and his mum told him the news that Potts had collapsed and been transferred to the hospital. He worried he might have the same problem arranging to see Potts as he had had at the prison. Fortunately, the hospital was more accommodating, and a day later, he and Lucy visited, and every day since.

Callum returned to school and spent all his time with Lucy during breaks. At the end of the school day, they would take the bus directly to Canterbury hospital, stay for an hour, longer on the first few visits, and then return home for something to eat. His mum helped out by feeding the chickens and taking care of them each day. Getting out of the house made her realise she had been a prisoner in her own home for the last six years. She would cycle there. Lucy had suggested it. Her mum had recently got a new bike, and the old one would have gone to the tip, so she gave it to Rachel.

Jim's funeral was next week. Callum and Lucy had both said they would go with her if she wanted. After all those years together, her inner voice nagged and argued she should be committed to showing her respects. But her thoughts conflicted, jumping back and forth before she decided. No – he had controlled her for too many years and ruined her life in so many ways he deserved nothing from her. It was time to move on. She would cycle to the seafront during the day whilst Callum was at school. Time to herself, which was a funny thing; there had been many times she had been by herself and alone, but now it was different. Before, she was enslaved

THE BOY WHO CHANGED HIS WORLD

under Jim's control. Sitting on the slopes of Tankerton looking out to sea, she felt the shackles break. The world smelt and tasted different - better. She stood up and walked along the front. The waves crashed against the breakwaters allowing her imagination to dare to think of the future. It would be a long journey, and nothing was resolved overnight, but her spirit was alive with optimism. She had started formulating a plan and decided she would start looking for work in a few weeks. Maybe working behind the bar as she had before, a shop or something, anything would do, she didn't mind. She was undecided but knew that she had a life, and she was going to live it. Callum was to be a big part of it. At times she was saddened when she thought she had let him down in the past. It had never been her intention, and he had always been the most important thing in her life, her reason for being and ballast to hold on to her sanity. But with all the problems with Jim, it was easy to forget, and sometimes she felt she had neglected Callum. Through it all, he had come out strong, and she was elevated with pride in him.

Her thoughts turned to Potts, whom she realised she had so much to thank for and wished he could be part of their lives, especially for Callum. That was one thing she could not change, but she was determined that he would remain alive in Callum's heart.

With time to play with, she remembered the Polaroid camera Michael had bought just before they had moved into their house. When she returned home, she hunted everywhere. A whole morning passed, searching under beds and backs of cupboards before venturing up into the loft, and there it was, behind a pile of old curled-up Town and Country magazines that Michael loved to read. Dust floated in the air when Rachel blew on the camera that captured memories of good times.

***

Saturday 11th November at ten o'clock in the morning, Callum and Lucy boarded the bus as they had last week. It was a mild autumn, and Callum had his blue windcheater jacket on and bag over his shoulder, with Lucy wearing a ripped jean jacket with safety pins strategically positioned. She looked good and cool, Callum thought, but then she always did to him.

It was nearly eleven when they had walked through the hospital grounds and made their way to the final corridor. Potts had his own room due to being a prisoner, so it was easier to keep a check on him. But there were no police or guards in or near his room. It was a meaningless policy for everybody knew Potts was going nowhere. After he had been admitted to the hospital, he had perked up a little. He was sitting up on his bed when they visited on the third day, but nobody was under any illusion. They had spoken to Doctor Chivers on each visit. He would always put his head around the corner to say hello and see how they were doing. It made Callum feel good to know Potts was being looked after by someone kind and caring. The private room made it easier to visit. Doctor Chivers had told them they should be flexible with visiting times at reception. A lot of the time Potts would sleep and one day he didn't wake up throughout the whole visit. It didn't matter for Callum; it was the fact that he was there. He wrote a note and left it on the cabinet beside the bed to let him know he and Lucy had been there. Holding hands, they broke off for Callum to put his hand to pull down on the handle to open the door to Potts' room.

'Callum,' the voice of Doctor Chivers called out with urgency, 'can I speak to you first before you go in?' They went to another room and sat down. Callum had seen people go to this room before, and he had seen them leave in tears. No good news was ever spoken within those four walls. 'I'm glad I caught you before you saw Potts today.'

'Why's that? Is anything wrong?' Lucy eagerly worried. Callum sat, waited, and put his hand over Lucy's that rested on her knee.

'Overnight Potts' health deteriorated, I'm afraid I have to tell you.' He gave a sympathetic smile but knew it helped little. 'You must prepare yourselves.' Callum felt Lucy's hand grip his tight as if the news had only just reached her and registered.

'How long do you think he has, Doctor?' Callum spoke with control and confidence, and he felt Lucy's grip loosen.

Doctor Chivers paused; there was a limit to how much he could say as an opinion over his medical diagnosis. 'It could be any time. Potts is fully aware.' He looked at Callum and then Lucy, 'Each visit could be the last one.'

'Thank you, Doctor,' Callum couldn't think of any other words to say, and now the only thing on his mind was he wanted to see Potts. Grateful it was Saturday, knowing they could stay longer than their weekday evening visits. Lucy leant into Callum and cried, 'Come, Lucy, dry your tears for now; let's spend these last moments with Potts whilst we can.'

Although Potts was flat on his bed, his head was tilted toward the door with eyes open when they entered. Callum wondered how long he had been waiting like that.

'Callum, Lucy sit down, come tell me the news.' there was a chirp in his voice as if everything still mattered.

'Well, we do have something for you, actually,' Callum said and delved into the bag dropped on the floor by his feet. Lucy leant over and reached out placing her hand on Potts' whilst Callum searched his bag. 'Oh, where is it? It's here somewhere,' Callum mumbled to himself. Potts looked at Lucy. It was a deep look, identifying every detailed feature of her face, and she looked back at him, remorseful that this could be the last time they would see each other making her want to cry again. She tried desperately to hold back the tears, but one betrayed, beyond her control, and it rolled down her face. Potts smiled reassuringly. It will be alright, his face said.

'Here it is,' Callum spoke with the excitement of his find. 'Mum found an old Polaroid camera and took these pictures when she was at your place. She thought you'd like them.'

'Show me,' Potts took them from Callum, releasing Lucy's hand as she did. She wiped the tear, and Potts gave her a nod before looking at the photographs. 'Oh look, it's Marilyn; what is she doing to Sophia, so bossy,' Potts chuckled to himself at seeing his girls again. There were five photographs, three of the chickens, one of his hut and the other of a panoramic view from further back showing the outbuildings. Potts studied them all, taking in every detail. On the panoramic photo, he run his finger over each building. 'Callum, look,' he pointed to the washroom. 'You remember that place, the place that saved you from the attack of the ants.' The memory came back vivid, 'The day we first met.'

'I remember, Potts,' he said, and as he spoke, Potts' eyes glistened, 'the best day of my life.'

'Don't say that in front of Lucy,' he joked.

'It's okay, Potts,' Lucy joined in, 'meeting you has changed everything. Without you, me and Callum would never have got together. I'm sure of that.'

'I'm sure that's not the case, and I think the best days of your lives are still to come, Callum, and that goes for you too, Lucy. And there will be many of them.' It was a thought that both of them hoped to be true, yet wished they could share a few more of them with Potts. 'On the cabinet,' Potts pointed to the cabinet at his bedside, 'Callum, there's a sealed envelope there.'

'This one?' Callum held up an A4 brown envelope.

'Yes, that's the one,' Potts nodded, 'I want you to take it home with you and open it after I have gone.' Callum's body tightened at those words. 'Promise me you won't read it until then.'

'Promise,' Callum put the envelope into his bag, 'anything else?'

'Look after my girls,' Potts said. 'This week, I've been lying here thinking about the both of you a lot. Lucy, I was going to ask you to look after Callum,' Lucy was about to speak but Potts held his hand up to indicate he had more to add. 'But the more I thought about it, the more I realised how much he has grown and how strong he now is. He is a changed man.' Running short of breath, he tried to recover himself; both Callum and Lucy remained quiet and allowed Potts time for what they both knew were words he had been thinking of for some time. 'But we all need somebody at times, so my wish is that you both look out for each other. Just remember, sometimes there are things best left unsaid; we all have our secrets. Look out for each other. Promise me that.'

'We will, don't you worry.' They replied. Potts seemed to be drifting away.

'What day is it?' Potts asked.

'It's Saturday,' Callum replied.

'No, I mean the date; what date is it?'

'It's 11th November.'

Potts smiled, 'Remembrance day,' he said pensively. Callum and Lucy watched him drift away somewhere. 'We all make mistakes,' Potts rambled. Callum thought of what Potts had said. He hoped Potts forgave himself for any mistakes he had made in his life, for Callum knew he had made up for them now, whatever they may have been.

They held hands and spoke little on the bus going home, knowing they would never see Potts again. At ten-thirty the following morning, Doctor Chivers called Callum. Before his emotions unravelled he called Lucy to tell her the news. They agreed to meet up in the afternoon to comfort each other.

33

The evenings had drawn in and it was dark outside, but the sky was clear and the air was crisp to greet the first weekend of December. Callum had been stripping the wallpaper all day in the spare room, then his mum's room, and at four o'clock, he satisfyingly pulled the last strip from the wall. He returned to his bedroom and sat on the bed, partly from exhaustion but mainly to imagine what it would be like with the new look. 'A new start,' that was what his mum had suggested, and she had been downstairs clearing the walls there. Callum had thought about Potts every day. He cried himself to sleep for the first two weeks, with the pain at times unbearable. The sealed letter Potts had left him he had not opened for a week. He feared of what was inside, but realised the worst had already happened. That morning at breakfast, he had sat with his mum and they opened it together.

11th November 1978

Dear Callum,

As I lie in this bed I know I have only a few hours left in this world. It's important to me that you know how you changed my life. I didn't know, but until you came along, I was hiding. I thought I had it all worked out. But it took you for me to see there was more to the world than shutting myself away in the woods. You made me realise how important friendship was. In my life there have only been two special friends. One of them, I felt I had let down badly and never forgave myself for what happened. You made me realise some things are outside of our control. True friends accept our failures and weaknesses and would never want them to live the rest of their lives suffering for those flaws. The length of a person's life is not the important thing. If I lived to a hundred and two and had not met you, my life would not have been complete and fulfilled. That is why the second real and special friend I had was you. I want you to always remember that.

The sealed envelope you found when you opened this one is my will. I have left The Hut and land to you. I know you will look after it and my girls. Tell them I miss them but will always be looking over them as I will with you and Lucy.

Potts

Between them, they had been to The Hut every day. On school days when Callum and Lucy had a lot of homework, his mum cycled there instead. His mum had got her old job back at The Pearson's Arms. Four nights a week and five weekday lunchtimes. There had been a noticeable change in her since taking the job. A purpose to life and interactions with other people had restored her confidence and self-belief. Together, they had bought the wallpaper and tomorrow, Lucy was coming over to help. When he went downstairs, his mum was nearing the last part of the dining room area where she had been working.

'You look shattered, mum,' Callum said.

'I feel it, but I'm done now, so gonna rest up. You off to see Lucy?'

Lucy would have come over to help but had been to the hospital with her mum and dad for one of his check-ups, so they had decided for Callum to go over there after he had finished. He took his usual route and cycled along Tankerton Road; today, he cycled straight across the roundabout, with the ice cream parlour to the right and then onto Lucy's.

The front door opened before he rang the bell with her excited to see him. They walked down to the town, queued at the Black and White fish and chip shop and ordered two portions of chips, a sausage in batter for Callum and a small cod for Lucy. 'Can we eat on the slopes by the canons?' Lucy asked.

'Sure,' Callum agreed, and they took the ten-minute walk to Tankerton Slopes. They sat astride the canons. Lucy looked out to sea with Callum sat at the end facing Lucy and the road, with fish, chips and battered sausage spread out between them.

'Isn't that beautiful?' Callum swivelled around to look out to the sea where Lucy pointed. The moon reflected off the sea while the tide ebbed. It was beautiful but awkward for Callum to eat his chips in that position, so he twisted back to face Lucy, taking in the view and her smile.

'Unquestionably beautiful,' he replied. She leaned forward, kissed Callum, screwed up the empty newspapers they had been eating from and gave them to Callum.

'Your job to clean up,' Callum dismounted from the canon, walked to the rubbish bin and dropped the empty wrappers inside. Lucy continued to gaze out to the sea until he returned and sat back down to face her. 'You know this was the place I waited to meet you and Potts that day. I sat on here looking out and I sensed something was wrong.'

'He was a special man, Lucy, he gave me a lot, and I learnt many things from him. That last day we were in the hospital, I got the feeling he accepted what was about to happen and that he had left his demons behind.'

'Me too,' she said thoughtfully, 'I learnt a lot from him too. He was very wise, but there was one thing he was wrong about.' Lucy paused and looked at Callum, 'There should never be any secrets between us, and as long as there are stars above us, we should tell each other everything.' Lucy leaned forward, her nose touching Callum's and continued, 'Or how else could we love each other.' Those words shocked Callum, surprised him, he recognised it as a statement rather than a question. A fact that left no doubt. He wrapped his arms around her tight. It was the most incredible feeling in the world, he thought to himself, sharing the heat from their bodies that passed between them. 'I'm glad,' Lucy said, 'there are no secrets between us.'

'Look up there, Lucy,' he rested his head against hers, and they both looked up to the clear night sky with stars glistening brightly, 'until there are no stars above us.' Nobody ever really dies, Callum thought. Those that matter are always there. And, he hoped he was right in believing Potts was there looking out for the two of them.

***

A gentle breeze blew the sands of Africa in a spiral upwards before they came down to the ground, where they rested until there was no movement, just stillness, and in the desert there was calm.

Robert Whanslaw

Robert Whanslaw writes with a deep passion for narratives that intricately weave into the fabric of human experience and the complexities of real life. A fascination with everyday individuals who could find themselves in wholly different circumstances had the unpredictable twists of life taken an alternative route with a focus on the thin line that separates us all, resonating with readers through the shared essence of the human journey.

The Boy Who Changed His World marks his debut novel whilst working on another book due for publication later this year.

Twitter @robertwhanslaw
www.robertwhanslaw.com

ACKNOWLEDGEMENT

I am deeply grateful to the individuals who made this journey of creating my novel an enriching experience.

First and foremost, my darling wife, Olga, deserves a medal for her unwavering support and invaluable input. She patiently read and re-read countless chapters, guiding me through the labyrinth of this story.

Lisa, your reviews and insights were instrumental in perfecting the final manuscript of this book. You made the writing process infinitely smoother.

To my exceptional team of beta readers, your feedback was pure gold. Your dedication and constructive criticism pushed me to refine this work into its best form.

To all those who endured my incessant chatter about this book over the past 18 months, your patience has been a gift. I'm excited to announce that I've already embarked on my next project, which you'll hear about soon.

Last but not least, I extend my heartfelt gratitude to you, the reader. Your presence in these pages validates my purpose as a writer. Thank you for being the reason behind my words.

ONE FINAL THING

Promise I will let you go and get a cup of tea or a refreshment of your choice, but I had one favour to ask.

As an indie author we rely on word of mouth and reviews, so if you can add a quick review on Amazon it would be really appreciated. If you don't have time for a written review just hitting the star rating is also a great help, and don't forget to tell your friends and random people as you are walking down the street.

Thank you!

Robert Whanslaw

Printed in Great Britain
by Amazon